STEWART FOSTER

SIMON & SCHUSTER

LR1

First published in Great Britain in 2021 by Simon & Schuster UK Ltd

1 3 5 7 9 10 8 6 4 2

Simon & Schuster UK Ltd
1st Floor, 222 Gray's Inn Road
London
WC1X 8HB

www.simonandschuster.co.uk
www.simonandschuster.com.au
www.simonandschuster.co.in

Simon & Schuster Australia, Sydney
Simon & Schuster India, New Delhi

A CIP catalogue record for this book is available from the British Library.

PB ISBN 978-1-4711-9126-8
eBook ISBN 978-1-4711-9125-1
eAudio ISBN 978-1-4711-9636-2

Printed and bound by CPI Group (UK) Ltd, Croydon, CR0 4YY

ME AND ERIC

You might walk past me every day, when you're on your way to school, or going to town shopping with your mum. You've probably stood just down the road from me, talking to your friends, but I bet you've never even looked in my direction. Next time you're out, just stop for a second and look down the alley that runs along the back of the shops. The alley you never go down because it's dark and damp, with bags of rubbish strewn at the sides. The one full of silver bins and a big yellow recycling skip with a ladder leaning against it.

Can you see them?

If you creep down the alley, just a little, you'll see the skip has lots of writing on the side, such as:

CLEAN ME

DO NOT PUT HOT ASHES IN HERE

CITY RULE

ERC

I call the skip Eric and for the moment I want you to ignore all the things written on it and keep walking, just like I did the first time I came here, four months ago.

Oops, sorry, I forgot to tell you to duck under the line of Coke cans I've tied across the top of the skip. Now you've rattled them. This is my early warning system; it's how I can tell when people are coming, my alarm for when the bin collectors from the council arrive in their truck to empty the skip. Or sometimes it's just the wind blowing and the cans tinkling. But today, right now, it's not the wind, and it's not the workers from the council. It's you.

And I'm on full alert because you're past the cans and you've seen the ladder leaning against the skip. You're not sure you should climb it, but it's okay, you can. Just put two hands on the sixth rung and start to climb. That's it. Then, when you're on the tenth rung, peer over the yellow metal, into the skip. Inside, can you see the rope I use to lower myself in, and the pieces of cardboard propped up in the corner? The Samsung sixty-five-inch TV box lying across the top?

These are my walls and my roof that stop the sun baking me in summer, and the rain soaking me in winter.

Can you see me?

No?

Wait, I've just got to push myself up because the boxes have crumpled.

Ha, there I go.

'Hi! I'm Sam, little c, big C McCann. This is my home, and I'm pleased to meet you.'

CHAPTER 2

PLANES AND DREAMS

You might think it's weird that I call a skip my home, and not the house where I sleep and eat. But you see, a house and a home aren't the same thing. A house is the place you live in, made of bricks and cement with double-glazed windows and doors, with pipes and radiators inside. A home is only made by the things you put in the house, like sofas and chairs, beds and paintings, and pictures of you and your family at Santa's grotto or on your holidays. I live in a house with all those things, except the pictures are of Christmases I never had and holidays I didn't get to go on and the family isn't mine at all.

I've lived in nine houses over the last five years and they're all the same, with foster-parents who tell me I'm part of the family and that they'll treat me as if I was one of their own children. But they don't leave their own children out of a trip to the cinema, nor at a respite home in Keynsham while they all go away to Spain on holiday. It's like they think I won't notice, but it's obvious when they come back because I'm maggot-white and the family are tanned-brown. At the moment I live with Reilly and his mum, who gets paid for looking after me. I've been here for four months and twenty-two days, which is the fourth longest I've ever stayed anywhere. They haven't been on holiday without me yet, but they will.

I stay in Eric to escape from all that. It makes me feel better when I can lie back on the cardboard and look between the grey buildings at the sky. Yesterday when I was here, I saw a plane and imagined I was on it, flying to Disneyland. I pictured a big hotel, with Mickey Mouse and Donald Duck welcoming everyone in the foyer and saying, 'Have a great day!' every morning when I went out to ride on the roller coasters. I dream of going to Disneyland a lot, but today there are no planes in the sky to take me, just stacks of pigeons flying over the alley as the traffic rumbles by on the high street.

Reilly will be in his house, in his room, playing Ace Pilot on the Xbox he got for Christmas. I'd only been here for two weeks, so all I got was clothes, as usual. I sat on the sofa and watched Reilly open his box. I knew what it was before he even ripped off the paper. 'It's an Xbox One,' I said out loud when he stared at the box. He asked me how I knew. I just shrugged. I didn't tell him I'd watched James open one on his birthday, in the house I'd stayed in before. James had loads of friends who came for sleepovers and they'd eat pizza in his room and play Star Trooper until midnight. Reilly doesn't have many friends, and he doesn't have loads of sleepovers. I'm glad because it means I don't get left out when everyone else is shooting aliens on multiplayer.

I stare at the sky and wonder what it must be like to have just one family and live with them all your life. Well, not *all* your life, because you'd have to leave sometime, after you finished school and had to go to university or get a job. But if I had a family of my own, I don't think I'd ever want to leave them. Why would I want to leave the people I love? I'm not sure I loved Brad and Angie, my fourth foster-parents, but I did like them so much I didn't want to leave. They lived in a bungalow in Felton. It had a massive garden with a football net at the bottom. Brad used to go in goal, and I'd whack the ball at him while Angie watched from the patio. That was my record stay: nine months – three quarters of a whole year. So long that Brad even bought me a second-hand bike from eBay and we cycled together to town whenever he wanted to go to Forbidden Planet for comics. I thought I was going to make it until Christmas. I even started thinking about what presents I would like – not computer games or DVDs, just clothes and stuff. I really liked Brad and Angie, and I think they really liked me, but I could feel the end coming. I always can. The end is when people go quiet, and start having whispered conversations about me in the kitchen. That's what Brad and Angie did – whisper, whisper, whisper – every evening after they got home from work, every night when I was in bed. It was like listening to mice under the floorboards. I noticed Angie's belly was getting bigger. She started eating whole tubes of Pringles, while she showed Brad pictures of baby clothes and prams that she had searched on her laptop. And then she'd ask Brad if it was bad luck to paint the spare room before the baby came.

Yes. It was bad luck. It was bad luck for me.

'You can still visit, Sam,' they said. 'Still play football in the garden.'

But visiting isn't the same, I thought to myself. Even if they did let me keep the bike.

CHAPTER 3

MY TOP TEN THINGS FOR PERFECT PARENTS

Brad and Angie fitted four of the things that are on my list of top ten things I'd like from my adoptive parents. My best friend Leah says I spend too much time writing lists, but I still write one every day. Sometimes the same things are on the list, sometimes they change, but the list is always to do with my perfect parents. I showed my list to my social worker, Rock Star Steve. He said it was okay to hope, that it was no different to people going to church and saying prayers. They don't give up after just one Sunday if the thing they pray for doesn't happen. That's why churches are full of people. I think they'd be empty if God answered their prayers first time. I'm not sure if Rock Star Steve even goes to church or believes in God. I've not seen many grown-up men with spikey blond hair walk into church wearing snakeskin shoes like his.

I reach over a vacuum cleaner box and pull my pen and writing pad out of my school bag. I should be getting back to Reilly's house soon, but I've still got time to add to the list I started in geography this afternoon.

Top Ten Things I'd Like From My Adoptive Parents

1. A massive garden where I could ride a petrol go-kart.
2. A garage wall with a basketball hoop.
3. Holidays to Disneyland. (Doesn't have to be Florida. Happy with Paris. ◡)
4. They should have brown hair like mine so people think I'm their real kid when I walk down the street, or at parents' evening at school.
5. They've got a daughter, slightly older and she helps me with my homework.
6. They haven't got a dog (because I don't like them).
7. They've got a nice car and the dad taps the steering wheel to music, like the man in the Citroën advert, when he drops me off at school every day.
8. The car MUST BE A BMW M5!
9. They will have a massive flat-screen TV in the lounge so we can all sit on the sofa and watch *Guardians of the Galaxy* together over and over.
10. They've got to have a fridge with an ice dispenser built into the door so on hot days I can run into the kitchen with my friends and we get to choose crushed ice or cubes.

I stop writing. The tins are clinking on my early warning system. But why? It's Wednesday. Eric gets emptied every Thursday.

I push myself up and peer over the top.

Nothing, just people walking by the end of the alley.

Must be the wind.

The tins clink again, like a fish pulling on a hook at the end of a line.

Someone giggles as the line wobbles again.

I shake my head and smile.

'Leah,' I shout. 'I know it's you!'

Leah steps out into the alley, laughing. 'Sam, one day it'll be the bin collectors.'

'I'd hear the engine,' I say. 'And you're the only one who knows I'm here.'

'True,' she says, walking towards me. 'So, what are you up to anyway?'

I raise my list.

'Oh, should have known,' she smiles. 'What's on this one? A house in Hollywood with an Olympic-sized pool?'

'Nearly.' I laugh. 'You want to come up?'

'No thanks, it stinks in there.'

'Hey.' I tap the edge of the skip. 'That's no way to talk about Eric.'

'Only saying the truth,' says Leah, reaching up. 'So come on, let me see what you've written.'

I hand my list down to her. I don't mind Leah seeing it. She's my best friend. Leah's got long brown hair and brown eyes and some people say we look like brother and sister, which really annoys her. She was the first person to speak to me four months ago, when I got to Dunham High. I was doing what I usually do when I start a new school – walking around the quad at break, keeping my head down, trying to be invisible, until Leah stepped in my way. She said I'd been at her primary school when she was seven. Didn't I remember her? She used to wear her hair in bunches. I shrugged. I'd been to lots of schools; I'd seen loads of girls with hair in bunches. Then she pushed me on the arm and said, 'You must remember me – I'm the one who turned up at school in a tiger suit when I thought it was Pyjama Day.' I smiled because I did remember that.

Her mum met my foster-parents at the last parents' evening, and they exchanged telephone numbers. You might think it's because they are friends, but it's because my foster-parents want to check up on where I am. But the good bit is that my foster-parents like Leah, so I get to spend lots of time with her.

'Ha.' Leah's chuckle jolts me back to the present.

'What is it?' I ask.

'Nothing,' she says. 'It's just . . . you think families are like the ones you see on TV adverts, or films on Netflix.'

'Aren't they?'

'No. Well, at least mine isn't. My mum's always arguing with her new boyfriend and going on at me to clean my room or help with the washing up.'

'But at least you're together,' I say. 'And you all go to sleep and wake up in the same house.'

Leah looks back at my list. 'Then maybe you should just say that . . . Hey, do you want to come to the shops with me? Mum gave me five pounds.'

'Why?'

'Don't know.' Leah shrugs. 'Just did. So, are you coming?'

I'm tempted to stay in Eric but Leah gives me a look that tells me I shouldn't.

'It's okay,' she says. 'You can come back after.'

I grab my bag and swing my legs over the top.

As we walk side by side out of the alley, I think that my list might never come true, but at least I get to share my dreams with Leah. It's hard locking all my secrets in my head. Sometimes I can be at a school for months and leave without anyone knowing I'm a foster-kid, but I'd told Leah at the beginning of the second term at Dunham High after I found her crying outside the girls' toilets. Her dad had left during the summer holidays, and she hadn't told anyone. Once she'd told me her secret, I told her mine, but I think she'd guessed something was up anyway because I never invited her back to my house for tea. She told me she missed her dad and asked what mine was like, and I said I didn't know.

I don't even know my dad's name. I do know my mum's name is Vicky. I last saw her when I was eight, but that was only for ten minutes at the council offices, and even then she hardly looked at me because she was crying most of the time. I've got a picture of her in my memory box – the box that social workers help me put my memories in. I don't have many memories, at least not many I want to remember. Rock Star Steve says it might help if I did, that remembering the past might help me settle down at school and with my foster-parents. I do try, but something always happens that means I get moved on.

'Sausage roll?'

‘What?’ I shake my thoughts out of my head.

Leah is waving the five-pound note in the air as we stop outside Smiths Bakery.

‘Pizza.’ I grin. ‘A whole one.’

‘So it takes longer to eat?’

‘Exactly,’ I say.

It’s good to have a friend. They make you feel like you belong, and they understand how you feel. I just wish there was someone who made me feel like that in Reilly’s house.

CHAPTER 4

THE HUG REILLY JUST HAD AND A FRONT DOOR KEY

The hallway smells of lemon and chocolate when I open the front door. Reilly's mum bakes cakes for people's weddings and birthdays. She's always baking. That's why she always seems tired when I get home.

'Sam, we're in here.'

I hang my bag at the bottom of the stairs and walk into the dining room.

Reilly's got his back to me, leaning over the table, scooping baked beans. His mum looks up from her dinner plate. She still has bits of flour in her hair. 'Where have you been?' she asks.

'Drama club,' I say. 'I told you.'

'Sam.' She frowns. 'I really don't think school would allow it three times a week.'

'Yeah, but . . .' I scramble for a lie. 'We had an extra one . . . We're doing a new play.'

'You never said. Reilly's been waiting for you.'

Reilly spins to face me, tomato sauce around his mouth. 'Hey, Sam.'

'Hey, Reilly,' I mumble.

His mum sighs as she stands up. 'Your tea will be ruined,' she says. 'Another ten minutes and I was going to call the agency.' She walks past me into the kitchen. I glance at Reilly. He usually smiles but this time he just keeps eating, like he knows I'm in big trouble. I always am when I go to Eric after school but his mum keeps on, even when I haven't done anything wrong. 'Where have you been?' 'Who were you with?' 'What were you doing?' It's every evening when I get back. I'm her first foster-kid and I think she's scared the agency won't place another one with her if she doesn't do a good job with me.

I turn back into the hallway.

'Now where do you think you're going?' Reilly's mum is back with a plate of fish fingers, chips and beans.

'Upstairs,' I say. 'I thought that's what you wanted.'

'No, Sam,' she says. 'That's not what I want at all. I just want you home on time. Now come and eat.'

I follow her back to the table and sit down.

Reilly's mum picks up her knife and fork. Reilly picks up his glass of water. I look at my plate.

'Come on, Sam,' says Reilly's mum. 'You know I don't like to keep on at you. I'm only doing it for your own sake. What would the agency think if I didn't keep you safe?'

I cut a fish finger in half.

'It's fine for you to make plans,' she continues, 'but you have to tell me, and not just go missing all the time. Okay?'

I nod and start to eat. I've been here four months, but Reilly's mum still seems like a new teacher at school.

Real parents smile and hug their children when they leave for school in the morning. They hug them when they come home, and they hug them before they go to bed.

Hug.

Hug.

Hug.

Sometimes it's just for a few seconds. Sometimes it feels like minutes and they hug them so tight that the children look like they will burst. Reilly's mum is hugging him now, on the landing after he's showered. I'm standing at the top of the stairs in my pyjamas, waiting to get by.

'Have you cleaned your teeth?' Reilly's mum asks, smoothing his hair. Reilly nods. 'Good,' she says. 'I'll tell Dad when I call him. Or did you want to?'

'No,' says Reilly. 'I want to play Ace Pilot with Sam.'

Reilly's mum smiles, then she pulls Reilly towards her, hugging him tight again.

'I need to go, Mum,' Reilly says, pushing away.

'Too old for a hug, are we?'

'No, I just want to play.' He turns and runs into his room and I grab my chance to get away, follow him.

'And what about you, Sam?' says his mum.

'What about me?' I stop dead. For a moment I think she's about to try to hug me too.

'Have you packed your bags for school?'

'Yes,' I mumble.

'Good,' she says. 'Your sandwiches are in the fridge. Don't forget them . . . again!'

'I won't,' I say.

Reilly's mum smiles. I don't know what I'm supposed to do next, but luckily Reilly yells, 'Come on, Sam! Help me get to level three.'

'Just for half an hour,' Reilly's mum says, 'and keep the sound down.' She nods at the computer in her office. 'I've got to do some invoices.' As I walk past her she suddenly says, 'Sam, you won't forget to do your diary, will you? It's always good for you to have something to bring to our chat at the weekend.'

'No,' I sigh. 'I won't forget.' She uses the word 'chat' but she means 'family meeting'. It's when we all sit around the dining table – her, me and Reilly, and Reilly's dad (if he's back) – and we 'chat' about what we've done in the week and any problems we might have with each other. But mostly it's just a chance for Reilly's mum to complain about me being late home.

I walk into Reilly's bedroom. It's where I sleep, but it's his room. It's his old spaceman duvet on my bed. It's his posters of Transformers on the walls and his model tanks and aeroplanes on the windowsill. And it's his Xbox that flashes as we sit down on the bottom bunk and wait for the game to load.

Out of the corner of my eye, I see Reilly looking at me.

'Where do you go after school?' he whispers.

'Drama club, I told you.'

'But she was sooo mad.'

'I know,' I say. I press X. 'Are you still stuck on this bit?'

'Yes.' Reilly shuffles closer to me. 'I can pick up the gold okay, but I keep crashing in the sea.'

I smile. Reilly wants to go in the air force like his dad, but he can't get past level three on Ace Pilot.

'Come on,' I say. 'Just watch and I'll show you.'

I press the triangle and the plane soars into the sky. I press O and stall the engine and get ready to send it into a dive. Reilly is a good kid. I like that he lets me play on his Xbox even when he's not here. And I like that he lets me share his room. I like most things about Reilly, but most of all I'd like a hug like the one he just had.

But it's not his fault. It's written in the *Foster-Parent Handbook*. I read it once. It's got all the things that foster-parents are and aren't allowed to do, including no proper hugs. It's okay to give hugs standing side by side, with one arm. But that's not a proper hug where people wrap their arms and squeeze you tight, like the one Reilly just got. Like the one I've never had. The *Foster-Parent Handbook* has loads of rules about how to behave when you are the only adult left with a foster-child alone in the same room, and how both foster-parent and foster-kid should keep a diary.

Reilly's mum shouts out that it's his bedtime.

'Can we play again tomorrow, Sam?' he asks.

'Okay,' I say.

He puts his controller down and I watch him climb the bunk ladder in his dinosaur pyjamas.

I reach over to the bedside table and take my diary out of the drawer. I'm supposed to write down what I've done and how I am feeling every night.

I open it to today's date and start writing.

Got up.

Went to school.

Went home.

Ate tea.

Went to bed.

Reilly's mattress pings. I wait for his head to appear like an upside-down jellyfish over the side of his bed.

'Hi, Reilly,' I say.

'Hi, Sam,' he whispers. 'Can you come back from wherever you go earlier tomorrow? So we can play longer?'

'I might,' I say, even though I know I won't, which makes me feel bad.

'Cool,' says Reilly. 'Shall I turn the light off now?'

'Yes, Reilly,' I say. 'You can turn the light off now.'

The light switch clicks and the room goes black.

I roll over on my side and face the wall. The plastic sheet rustles underneath me. It's like Reilly's mum thinks I'm four, or maybe she just left it on when Reilly moved to the top bunk.

I run my hand over the wall, picking at the lumps of Blu Tack where Reilly's posters used to be. When I arrived, his mum told me I could put up my own, but I haven't because I don't know how long I'm going to be here. Sometimes it can be a week, sometimes months, but I still don't put my posters up. The last time I did, at Jean and Ralph's, Rock Star Steve turned up the next day and I had to pack my bags and go somewhere else.

One day, I'd love to live in a house I called home. I'd love to be given my own front door key and not have to ask permission to get Coke from the fridge or a biscuit from the tin. Reilly says his mum wouldn't mind and that I should just do it, but I don't.

REASONS WHY . . .

'It was partly my fault too,' Leah says as we walk to school the next morning. 'It was my idea to go to WHSmith.'

'I know,' I say. 'But I bet your mum didn't go on at you like Reilly's mum did. The only reason she asks if I want a lift when she drops Reilly off at school is so she can keep her eye on me longer. I always say no, but every foster-parent I've had does it. It's like they're scared they're going to lose me or something. The only way it will stop is if I get adopted and it doesn't seem as if that'll happen any time soon.'

'If it makes you feel any better, my mum said she'd adopt you if we had enough space.'

'That's nice,' I say, forcing a smile.

Leah knows that I want to be adopted. She said she'd guessed I wanted to be by the way she'd seen me looking at parents playing with their children in the park. It isn't that I look at them strangely, she says, just that I look at them for too long. But everyone looks at things they want, imagining riding a new bike in a shop window, or eating a McDonald's triple-cheese burger on the menu. That's all I'm doing when I stare at people – imagining what it'd be like to be a part of their family.

The traffic stops. As we cross the road, I can feel Leah looking at me, like she wants to say something else. Some kids from Year Eight overtake us.

'What?' I say, checking no one is close behind. 'Why are you looking at me? Have I got a zit?'

'No.' She shakes her head.

'Toothpaste around my mouth?'

'No.' She stops walking. 'I was just thinking, maybe you should go back to Reilly's on time, at least for a while, so his mum doesn't get mad at you again.'

'Are you on her side?'

'No, of course not. But you know they always bring it up at your PET meetings.'

'It's PEP,' I say. 'And it's fine. All they do is talk and write stuff in their files.'

'Still,' says Leah. 'I think you should, and maybe don't skip any more lessons either. Mr Clunes has given you loads of chances already. You might not have many left.'

I shrug as we walk alongside the school railings. The cans on Eric aren't my only early warning system – Leah is one too. Only her alarm doesn't rattle or screech like a security alarm, it just comes out in her soft voice. She's right, I shouldn't miss lessons. It's not that I miss many, but if Mr Clunes, the head of year, catches me, it always gets brought up at our PEP meetings. That means Personal Education Plan. It's a bit like the weekly 'chats' at Reilly's house, except it's at school, with Mr Clunes, Rock Star Steve, Mrs Sorrell (the school pastoral care person) and Reilly's mum. Everyone talks and asks me questions: 'Are you okay, Sam?' 'Are you happy?' 'Is there anything you'd like to talk about?' Usually I just shrug and look at the floor. If I do speak, I listen to the scratch of their pens as they write stuff to go in my file. I have lots of notes in lots of files. That's because I've had lots of PEP meetings in every school I've been to. The best thing about them at Dunham High is that I get to miss home economics. I don't tell anyone in my class where I go though, otherwise they'd find out I'm a foster-kid. They think I'm having extra maths lessons with Mrs Khatri.

Me and Leah turn and walk through the school gates. Other kids join us as we walk into the main reception then head down the east corridor. Leah asks what lessons I've got this morning. I tell her double science, then English.

She nods.

'It's okay,' I say. 'I said I'll go.'

'Good.'

We walk towards our form class.

Leah suddenly stops.

'Hey.' She nods at the noticeboard. 'Have you seen this?'

Kids brush past as I look at the notice.

SCHOOL PLAY

Cast wanted for the end-of-year school production

of *Bugsy Malone.*

Open to all years.

Put your name on the attached list or contact Mr Powell or Miss Dowsett before Easter break.

Auditions will start the week we return.

You don't have to be a great actor, singer or dancer.

We just want you there!

'Oh that,' I say, turning around. 'It's been up a week.'

'And you never said!'

'What's the point?' I shrug.

'But you love drama club,' says Leah.

'I know, but only because we do a play a week so I know I can finish them.'

'So?'

'So *Bugsy Malone*'s at the end of next term. I won't be here.'

'Sam, you've got to stop thinking like that. Maybe that's why you haven't been . . .' Leah checks over her shoulder to make sure no one is listening. Apart from the teachers, no one in school knows that I'm a foster-child. 'Maybe that's why you haven't been adopted, because people can see you're nervous about leaving.'

'That's because I *am* nervous.'

Leah takes a deep breath. 'I know and I don't want to be mean, but maybe you should stop feeling sorry for yourself. Just put your name down. Amala and Lewis have and I bet they're nowhere near as good as you.'

'But it's happened before,' I say. 'When I was in *The Pirates of Penzance*. I went to every rehearsal for two months, then got moved a week before the first performance.'

‘Then do something about it. If you really like it somewhere you should do something to help you stay, and stop running away.’ Leah goes to say something else, but the rest of the kids are piling through the corridor, pulling us apart. I want to say something too, ask her why she suddenly came out with that, but I’m still trying to understand exactly what she meant.

‘I’m sorry if I’ve upset you Sam, but you’ve got to do something as you look a little miserable.’

‘Do I?’

‘Yeah, just a bit.’

I turn away and walk down the corridor. Leah doesn’t know what it’s like to be a foster-kid, to get moved all the time. It’s hard hiding it from my class. I don’t want to stand out or be different. I just want to be Sam. Not Sam the foster-kid. But maybe I should do something to help myself, like she said. *Stop running away. Do something. Do something* . . . Leah is half the length of the corridor behind me, but her words are still echoing through my head.

CHAPTER 6

A TALK WITH MYSELF

Mr Grosicki always smiles when he reads out my name during the register in maths. Mrs Stevens always smiles at me when I walk into English. Miss Yallop always smiles and says 'Hi, Sam!' when I walk into history. All the teachers smile at me (except for Mr Marsh in science, who is always grumpy). And I sort of smile back, then walk to my seat, wondering if they are smiling because they are pleased to see me, or because they feel sorry for me because I'm a foster-kid. Leah says it's in my head, that the teachers smile at the other kids too, it's just that I don't see. But I notice Miss Wilkins smile at me when I walk into geography, even though I'm late and she's already pointing at a picture of the sea and a white cliff on the whiteboard.

'Pebbles are formed from the sea bashing rocks against the cliff,' she says, switching to a picture of pebbles on a beach. 'Can you see that? Maybe it's shown better on this diagram.' She shows a drawing of a cliff and the sea with arrows pointing along the coastline. But

I can't concentrate on what she's saying because of Leah's words. Does she really think I'm feeling sorry for myself? Is that what everyone thinks?

'So the rocks smash against the cliff, shattering them into tiny pieces, and the currents deposit them on a beach.'

Do I look miserable? I don't think so, because Rock Star Steve says I've got a cheeky grin, and Mr Marsh is always telling me off because he thinks my grin is me laughing at him.

I pick up my pen and tap it on my book. I don't feel sorry for myself. I don't.

'And the waves crash onto the beach, making the pebbles even smaller and sometimes turning them to sand. What's this process called?'

Darek's hand shoots into the air next to me.

'Abrasion, miss.'

'Yes, well done, Darek, but what's the *whole* process called?' Miss Wilkins looks around the class.

Maybe Leah just thinks I'm feeling sorry for myself because she knows how much I want to find a family of my own. Perhaps I *should* stop thinking about it so much and do something about it. Because I love drama, and I want to be in *Bugsy Malone*, but most of all I want to stay around here because of Leah.

I open my notepad. *Yeah, Sam*, I think to myself. *Do something about it – don't sit around waiting to get dumped, like Leah's mum.*

'Sam, what's this whole process called?' Miss Wilkins is standing right in front of me.

'Umm . . . S-s-s-sorry.'

Someone giggles behind me. Miss Wilkins darts a look that says, ‘Stop it,’ then turns back at me and smiles. Please don’t smile.

‘The whole process, Sam,’ she says. ‘What’s it called?’

‘L-l-longshore drift, miss.’

‘Yes,’ she says. ‘I’m amazed, Sam. You looked like you were miles away.’

I *was* miles away, but I’m not any more. Because I didn’t just know the answer to the question, I’ve also figured out what I need to do. I turn my notebook towards the window and make a barrier with my arm so Darek can’t see it. I start to write:

Wanted

Two adults (or one) prepared to look after and love an 11-year-old boy. And he promises to do the same for them.

No dogs.

Or cats.

Or hamsters.

Interviews by the bandstand, The Downs,

Saturday 4th April, from 10 a.m.

If there are loads of people, please wait.

Email: Don't have one yet

‘It’s brilliant.’ Leah beams as I show her my notebook in the canteen. ‘What made you think of it?’

‘What you said.’

‘About being in the school play?’

'Yes,' I say, 'and because ... because ... I don't know. Lots of things.'

'Well, it's great.' Leah smiles, reading it again. 'No hamsters. Ha. What's wrong with hamsters?'

'They wriggle too much,' I say, 'and they've got cold feet.'

'No, they're cute.' Leah puts her hand over her mouth to stop herself laughing.

Kids are walking by with plates full of food while I stare at my notebook, feeling as happy with my poster as Leah seems to be.

'I thought we could make loads of copies,' I say. 'And post them through people's doors.'

'Yeah.' Leah's eyes open wide. 'And maybe we could stick them to lamp posts and telegraph poles.'

'I'm not a missing cat!' I laugh.

'Okay, maybe not then, but you can't send it like this, with your scruffy writing. We need to do it on a computer.'

'I know,' I say. 'But Reilly's mum goes nuts if anyone uses up all the paper.'

'It's all right,' says Leah. 'We can do it at mine after school.'

'I've got drama club.'

'Then come to mine after that. We'll use my mum's ex's printer – he hasn't taken it back yet. What are you going to call it?'

'Call it?'

Leah checks behind to make sure no one is listening. 'Yes,' she whispers. 'We have to give it a name, like a campaign. Like when my mum's friend's friend set up a fund to save donkeys in Spain.'

'What was that called?'

'Save Donkeys in Spain.' Leah laughs. 'But you could have Get Sam Adopted, or GSA. Everyone shortens the name.'

I bite into my sandwich, but I don't have time to swallow before the lunch bell rings. I've been so excited about my poster that I've had no time to eat.

Leah snaps the lid on her lunchbox and stands up.

'How about Adopt Sam – little c, big C – McCann?'

'That's quite hard to say.'

'Yeah.' Leah shakes her head as we walk out of the canteen. Suddenly my strides feel longer and I feel taller. I have a plan and for once it's to stick around, not run away.

'Sam's Sticking Around Plan?' I say out loud.

'No,' says Leah. 'That makes you sound like a Post-it Note or a fridge magnet.'

We laugh as we head down the corridor.

My plan is all I can think about during English.

As I look around the class, everyone has their heads down, either writing or reading the next question. Me wanting perfect parents is probably the same as them desperately wanting new football boots or a bike for Christmas and feeling mega-disappointed when they don't get them. Actually, wanting real parents and being rejected is a million times worse than that. You don't just feel disappointed, you feel an ache in your stomach that spreads to your heart and all the other parts of your body and it hurts so much that you have to pretend it's not there.

I spot Mrs Stevens looking right at me. She smiles then mouths, 'Sam, write!' and points at my book.

I put my head down and try to write, but all I can think about is that I'm going to find my perfect parents, something I have wanted for as long as I can remember. They will never be my real parents, my mum will always be my mum, but I'm going to find someone who will love and care for me, and I'll do the same for them, for the rest of my life.

CHAPTER 7

THE PEE SCENE

'Okay,' says Mr Powell in drama club, 'let's see what we have then. Remember, sometimes it's the things we don't say that mean the most.'

Me, Lewis and Amala walk out onto the stage. We start rehearsing the scene where Lewis and Amala are arguing in a school corridor and I'm desperately trying to get past them to go to the toilet. But all the time I can't stop thinking about the things I'm going to put on my poster, like how people can contact me, and whether I should say that you shouldn't bother replying if you haven't got a BMW M5. I don't want to sound like a spoilt brat though, so perhaps I should leave that off. But no gerbils. I want to add that.

Amala stops suddenly in the middle of the stage.

'You said you'd call me,' she shouts.

'I tried, but my phone was dead,' Lewis argues.

'Oh yeah, and what about the other ten times?'

'I don't know, but ... Sam.' Lewis looks at me. 'You were with me. Tell her.'

'I would,' I say, looking past them to an imaginary toilet. 'But I'm ... I'm ...'

'You're what?' says Amala.

'Well.' I put my knees together and squirm. 'To be honest, I just want to go to the loo.' I squirm again. 'Can you ... can you just let me past?'

Everyone in drama club laughs.

'No,' says Lewis. 'This is serious.'

'So is me going to the loo, to be honest.' I try to keep my drama face straight as everybody laughs again.

Amala shakes her head. 'Boys,' she says. 'Who needs them?'

Lewis puts his hand on her shoulder. 'Look,' he says. 'I am sorry but I was ...'

I look at Mr Powell and the rest of the class as they listen to Lewis and Amala talking. As usual, I don't get many lines when I get put with them, but I don't mind because I always get the most laughs. I love drama club – all of us that go do. Lewis says it's because we're allowed to muck about and we're not told off for it. Amala says it gives her a chance to show off, like when she put on drama performances for her mum when she was little. I love it because it helps me escape for a while.

I squirm again.

'Sorry to interrupt, but could I ... possibly ... just get by?'

'No,' says Lewis. 'Can't you see we're making up?'

'Yeah,' I say. 'I'm pleased for you ... But I am ... desperate.'

‘Wait!’ Mr Powell holds up his hand. ‘Sam,’ he says, looking at me. ‘Can I just check you really don’t want to go to the toilet?’

Everyone laughs.

‘No, sir.’ I smile. ‘I’m fine.’

Mr Powell grins. ‘Then that’s very well done.’ He glances at his watch. ‘In fact, that’s all of us done for this week.’

‘But we’ve not finished,’ says Amala.

‘We’ll pick up from there next week.’

‘What?’ I say. ‘I have to hold this in for a whole week!’

The room erupts into laughter.

I relax from my squirming position and jump down off the stage. As some of the group head towards their bags, Mr Powell shouts, ‘Oh, before you go, you haven’t all put your names down for *Bugsy Malone*. Anybody would think you don’t want to be in it. I’m depending on all of you to get involved.’

Everyone looks at each other, like they’re trying to work out who hasn’t, but I checked the list at morning break and I know the only name missing is mine. Everyone else from drama club has signed up.

I head to the back of the room as the others talk about their scenes, what went wrong and how they can improve them next week. I only speak to the kids in drama club because most of us are from different year groups and this is the only time we get to meet. Except sometimes they go to each other’s houses to practise after school. But I never do.

I bend down and pick up my bag.

‘And don’t forget to tell your friends,’ says Mr Powell. ‘It’s a big cast, so we need as many as we can get.’

‘Well done, Sam.’ Lewis pats me on the back. ‘You were hilarious.’

'Yeah,' says Amala. 'For a minute I thought you really wanted to pee.'

'Thanks.' I smile as I sling my bag over my shoulder. 'I thought you were both good too.'

'We'll be in the same group next week, Sam, yeah?' Lewis says. 'And we'll get ready for *Bugsy Malone* – custard pies and splurge guns!'

'That's all you want to be in it for,' says Amala.

'Of course.' Lewis grins. 'Isn't that right, Sam?'

'Oh yeah,' I say, rushing away. 'I've got to go, but I'll see you next—'

'Sam!'

I stop and turn around. I knew it. Mr Powell *is* going to say something.

'Come here a minute.' He beckons me.

'We'll wait for you,' says Lewis. 'Me, Darrius and a couple of others are going back to Amala's, if you want to come?'

'It's okay,' I say. 'I need to be somewhere else.'

'Maybe next week,' says Amala.

'Yeah,' I say. 'Maybe.'

I walk towards Mr Powell, who's stacking chairs.

Even if I wasn't rushing to get to Leah's, I wouldn't go to Amala's, because next week it will be Lewis's, then Darrius's, until eventually it would be their turn to come to mine. I never invite friends back. They'd only wonder why there were no pictures of me on the walls. I could tell them it was because I hated having my picture taken, or that I wasn't at the beach with my family when *that* picture was taken.

Even if they believed me, it would be obvious when a foster-parent came back, and they would see that they looked nothing like me, that they couldn't be my parent. I would have to act like they were. Maybe that's why I'm quite good at drama, because I have to be ready to act all the time. Or maybe it's because, apart from going to Eric, it's the only way I can escape.

'Everything all right, Sam?' Mr Powell drags a pile of chairs across the floor.

'Yes,' I say. 'Why?'

'I think you know,' he says. 'You're the only one from the group who hasn't put their name down for the play.'

'I was going to,' I say, 'it was just that I had to do something first.'

'Good.' He smiles. 'I was hoping you'd say that. You're a talented actor, and an asset to the class.'

'Okay,' I say. 'I'll do it in the morning. But I really have to go now.'

'No rush,' says Mr Powell. 'Just as long as you do.'

'I will.' As I head for the door I reach for my phone.

Leah, I type. I'm on my way ☺

CHAPTER 8

ME, LEAH, AND THE . . .

'The Perfect Parent Project!' says Leah. 'Yes, Sam! I'd gone off GSA because it sounds like a disease. But how did you think of that?'

'Don't know,' I say. 'Just popped into my head as we sat here.'

'It's brilliant. PPP. It's like code. Now we can talk about it at school and no one will know what it means.'

I smile and look at Leah's laptop screen.

'What do you think?' she says. 'Do you think we should have bold lettering?'

'Yes. It needs to stand out, otherwise people will just throw it out like they do with pizza leaflets and stuff.'

'And what about a picture of you? No, wait, that'll definitely make them throw it out!'

'Oi!' I push her on the arm and she rocks back on the sofa.

She laughs. 'Aww, I didn't mean it.'

'Can't use a picture anyway,' I say. 'In case someone reports it to the foster agency. And I was thinking that I shouldn't use my real name either. Rock Star Steve and the agency wouldn't be very happy if they found out I haven't gone through the proper channels.'

'But the proper channels haven't worked for you,' says Leah. 'Besides, there must be loads of boys called Sam.'

'What are you two up to?'

Me and Leah spin round. Her big sister Mollie is standing in the doorway, crunching on an apple. She's five years older than us and looks just like Leah, only taller and with longer blonde hair.

As she walks in Leah tries to click off my poster but Mollie is already reading the screen over our shoulders.

'Wanted, two people or . . .' Mollie reads then looks at me. 'That's sweet, Sam.'

'Yeah.' I feel my face burn.

'It's cool, but I'm not sure about the no hamsters rule.'

'See,' says Leah.

Mollie takes a bite of her apple. 'And don't post them in Gordon Road,' she says as she munches.

'Why not?' I ask.

'That's where our dad lives, and you don't want to get him. Even if he said ten times he'd meet you at the bandstand, he wouldn't turn up.'

They both laugh.

I want to stick up for Leah's dad, but she's told me about him not turning up to her netball games so many times that I know it's true.

'I'm going to the shop for bread,' says Mollie through a mouthful of apple. 'Do you two want anything?'

'No thanks,' me and Leah say together.

Mollie goes to turn, then stops and smiles. 'Good luck with your project, Sam. And don't worry about using up all the paper. Mum's ex was a twit.'

'Thanks,' I say.

Mollie walks out. On my list I put that I'd like an older adoptive sister, and if I was lucky enough to get one, I wouldn't mind if she turned out to be like Mollie.

'Maybe we could put some memes across the top,' I say, turning back to the screen. 'Things that describe me, like a smiley face, and one of a boy on a bike and popcorn to show I like cycling and going to the cinema.'

'Yeah, I like that.' Leah's face lights up as she clicks on three memes and pastes them across the top of my poster.

'That's good,' I say.

'Are you sure about no cats and dogs?' She turns to me. 'You're limiting your chances. Loads of people have them.'

'All right,' I say. 'Put dogs are okay, as long as they aren't spaniels. One of the houses I stayed in had one, and it made my clothes stink.'

'Okay. No spaniels.'

'And no Jack Russells . . . They yap and bite. And no hamsters or gerbils. Some of them have long hair and you can't see their eyes and tell what they are thinking.'

'Sam.' Leah raises her eyebrows. 'You're being pretty fussy. For all we know, your perfect parent might have a cat, a hamster *and* a Jack Russell, but you'll never find out.'

'Then they wouldn't be perfect, would they?' I say. 'And this is the Perfect Parent Project.'

Leah nods. 'Okay. I'm just saying.'

I stare at the screen. It would be silly to miss out on my perfect parents by being too fussy.

'You're right,' I say. 'Hamsters are okay, so just make it no gerbils.'

Leah deletes 'hamsters', then types in the meeting place and the date.

'That's it,' she says, rapping the keyboard. 'All done. Oh no, wait, I nearly forgot the email for people to reply to – ThePerfectParentProject@gmail.com. I'll set the account up after you've gone. But it looks great, doesn't it?'

'Yep!' I can't stop myself grinning. Six hours ago it was just an idea in my head and now the printer is chugging out two hundred copies. They can't print quickly enough for me. I can't wait to find my perfect parents. I want to grab the posters from the printer and run off down the street.

'Do you think two hundred is enough?' I say excitedly. 'Maybe we should do double, even treble!'

'Treble!' says Leah. 'I don't think we have enough paper! Maybe you can do some more at yours.'

'I'll try. I'll risk Reilly's mum going nuts for this.' I pick up a poster. It looked great on the screen, but it's even better now it's in my hands. 'We can post them after school tomorrow. In those posh houses at the top of Park Street.'

'You mean The Clift?' Leah laughs. 'Because they've got massive gardens and nice cars?'

'And swimming pools,' I say. 'They're all rich. I could live in a huge mansion like famous footballers have.'

'Or a film star, like Brad Pitt. My mum loves him.'

'But he lives in America. Maybe Daniel Radcliffe ... No, how about a pop star? Ed Sheeran! You could come over for sleepovers in the games room. I could send a driver to pick you up in a limousine!'

Leah laughs. 'Sam, I don't want to spoil your dreams, but I don't think Ed Sheeran would adopt you. Besides, The Clift is a long way to go to deliver posters.'

'We've both got bikes – we could ride there along the cycle path,' I say.

Leah nods. 'We could, but I've got a netball match tomorrow. We'll go on Saturday instead. You call for me on the way.'

'Okay,' I say, then notice Leah's giving me one of her serious looks.

'Sam,' she says. 'You do know finding a perfect parent isn't about money.'

'I know that. I was only messing.'

'Good.' Leah looks relieved. 'My mum says happiness isn't about that, it's about family. At least that's what she tells my Uncle Ray when he comes around here, stressing.'

We both smile as the printer spews out more copies. I'm half joking about living in a mansion, because Leah is right, it's about finding the right family, and there's no way I would want to live so far away that I wouldn't be able to see each other when we want to.

'There you go, Sam.' Leah picks up the posters and knocks them on the table so they are in a neat pile. 'Two hundred chances. Two hundred chances for Sam McCann to perform in the school play.'

'Yes.' I smile. 'Two hundred chances to find my perfect parents.'

'Yes.' Leah grins back at me. 'And all we need is one.'

REILLY'S MUM ☹

'Sam, is that you?'

'Yeah.' I close the front door and head up the stairs.

'No, Sam.' Reilly's mum stands in the lounge doorway. 'You can't just go upstairs, not after being out all afternoon. I've been worried about you. Where have you been? I nearly called the police.'

'But you didn't, did you?' I stop dead on the stairs.

'No, I didn't.' Reilly's mum walks into the hall with a towel. 'But you're lucky,' she says, drying her hands furiously like she's stressed. 'Five more minutes and I would have. So, Sam, where have you been?'

'Drama club,' I say.

'Until six o'clock?'

'We had to do extra scenes,' I say.

'Mmm,' she says, shaking her head slowly.

'It‘s true. That's what happened.' I don't like lying, but it makes me mad when someone is watching my every move.

'Okay, fine.' Reilly's mum sighs. 'I believe you.'

'Except you don't,' I snap. 'Why do you always have to know where I am?'

'Sam,' she says softly. 'I'm only asking nicely. What's brought this on?'

I stare at her. I was so happy at Leah's while we made my poster, but my anger builds insides me like lava in a volcano as soon as I'm here.

'Sam?' Reilly's mum raises her eyebrows and that irritates me even more.

I take a step on the stairs.

'I'm going to see Reilly.' My voice cracks.

'See, now you're upset,' she says. 'Come and sit down. Have you eaten?'

'I'm not hungry.'

'Sam, please.'

'No,' I say. 'I'm going upstairs.'

I storm up. I hate it when she interferes. She asks loads of questions, but she doesn't care. She doesn't understand what it's like to never be wanted or loved by anyone. She's got Reilly; she's got Reilly's dad. No one understands.

I've got a lump in my throat and I can hardly breathe by the time I reach Reilly's door. The music from Ace Pilot is playing inside. I take a deep breath, then another. I'm trying to hold the tears in, but I can't stop them escaping and it's even worse when I don't know where they came from. I wipe my tears on my sleeve and take another deep breath.

I push the door open. Reilly spins round from the screen.

‘Hi, Sam,’ he says.

‘Hi, Reilly.’ I put my bag on my bed. ‘What level are you on?’

‘Three,’ he says. ‘I couldn’t even pick the gold up this time.’

‘I’ll help you,’ I say brightly, as I sit on the bottom bunk. ‘Press X, then O.’ I reach across and point at the buttons. ‘See, that makes him jump further.’ I nod at the screen and wait for Reilly to do it, but he’s still looking at me.

‘I think Mum burnt a cake,’ he says. ‘That’s why she’s grumpy.’

‘Yeah.’ Snot trickles down my nose. I can’t stop myself sniffing and wiping it away. I stare at the screen. All the images of the planes are blurred. Everything was all right until I walked through the door. I blink, then reach across for the controller. ‘Okay,’ I say. ‘Let’s get you to level four.’

‘Yes!’ Reilly grins at me.

I take the controller and press the triangle. The plane soars into the sky. ‘You’ve got to hold down the O,’ I say. ‘See, hold it down until the power cuts out, then press the square to make him dive.’

Reilly nods.

The plane dives through the clouds, heading towards the airport where the gold bullion is stored. ‘Then press this front button to drop the scooper down.’

‘Yes!’ Reilly clenches his fist as the plane scoops up the gold bullion and heads to safety. ‘Again, Sam.’

‘No,’ I say. ‘It’s your turn.’

Reilly takes the controller, presses the triangle and sends the plane skywards again.

I close my eyes. The plane’s engine rumbles as I rest my head against the wall. I take a deep breath, then another. I feel like my energy has been zapped right out of me and is draining through the floor.

The engine rumbles louder.

Press O, Reilly. You need to stall the engines. Press O.

Boom!

'Sam . . . I crashed again.'

I take another breath as the phone rings in Reilly's mum's office. It'll be Reilly's dad. He calls every night. He's a pilot in the Royal Air Force. He doesn't talk about it much when he's home, which is usually every three weeks, but sometimes he's away even longer. I hear Reilly's mum walk across the hall into her office. She says, 'Hello, darling. Yes, we're fine. Busy as always . . . Do I? Maybe I just need an early night.'

Her voice grows louder as she walks out onto the landing. I wait for her to knock on the door and ask Reilly if he wants to talk to his dad, even though he hardly ever does. But his mum doesn't knock this time. I just hear her say, 'No, I'm okay. I'm sure you're tired too. I'm just looking forward to you coming back for Easter.' Then her voice fades away as she walks down the stairs. If I were Reilly, I would talk to my dad every night. I'd tell him everything I'd done at school, and plan what we would do together at the weekend. Maybe it's because Reilly thinks talking to his dad will make him miss him even more. Or maybe it's because he knows for certain that he'll be here when his dad comes home.

CHAPTER 10

THE PEP MEETING (AKA LET'S PICK ON SAM)

People here:

Mrs Sorrell, the school pastoral care person.

Reilly's mum (Reilly's dad comes too, when he's not working).

Rock Star Steve (and his snakeskin shoes).

Me.

We're all sitting in a circle in the room next to the medical office.

'Where do you get to then, Sam?' Mrs Sorrell asks. 'Between leaving school and getting home?'

'Nowhere.'

'You must go somewhere, Sam,' Mrs Sorrell presses.

'But I don't. I just walk around.'

'Sam, I know you don't think this is serious, but you can't keep walking the streets after school.' That's Reilly's mum. 'We're all trying to help you, that's all.'

'I'm not walking the streets,' I say. 'I went to drama club.'

'Okay,' says Mrs Sorrell. 'Last night was drama club, but you didn't get home until an hour after it finished, and that doesn't explain the other nights.'

I think of telling them the truth, but everyone here would go mad if they knew I spent my time in a recycling skip.

'I don't know,' I say.

'But you must know,' says Reilly's mum.

'Okay then,' I snap. 'I'm at Leah's.' Which is true . . . sometimes.

'Okay, okay.' Rock Star Steve holds up his hand. His spikey hair looks weird when everyone else in here looks so normal. 'Let's everyone take a step back,' he says, turning to me. 'Sam, rather than think about where you're going, can you tell us why?'

I shrug and look at the floor. This is the PEP meeting. Rock Star Steve has been to them with me for the last three years. Everyone else changes when I get moved, but the meetings are always about the same thing – Sam's Personal Education Plan. We discuss how I'm doing, and what they can do to make things better for everyone. But most of the time it feels like it's about Reilly's mum snitching on me. And she always says something that makes her sound like she's not snitching at all, like, 'Sam, we're all a family and we want to look after you,' or, 'Sam, if we all work together, things would be so much better,' or—

'Sam, would you rather just talk to Steve on your own?' There, she did it again – making herself seem nice and like it's all my fault.

I shrug once more, waiting for someone to say something, but all they do is glance at each other and nod.

'Perhaps it's a good idea if we wait outside,' says Mrs Sorrell. I look up as she and Reilly's mum leave. Rock Star Steve waits for the door to close, then leans forward.

'So what's going on, mate?' he says quietly. 'Do you want to say?'

'Nothing. I just got home late. I've not missed any lessons this week.'

'No, in fairness, you're not missing that many lessons, but as you said, you are getting home late. Last night was gone six. And it's not just last night, is it? It's every night, and sometimes you go missing from school. Is something bothering you? Is everything all right at home? If you bottle it all up, no one can help.'

'I don't know,' I mumble. 'Reilly's mum and dad are okay, I suppose. And I like Reilly. It's just . . .'

I look at the floor, staring at Rock Star Steve's pointy snakeskin shoes on the carpet.

'Just what, Sam?' He leans further forward, his elbows on his knees. I notice his pink cuffs poking out from his jazzy check jacket. Some of the other foster-kids say he does it to try to look cool, and easier to talk to than someone wearing a suit. He's got loads of different jackets – some check, some plain, but all of them are bright colours, like orange, turquoise, even yellow. Angie said he looked like a canary, but I think he looks like a rock star, like he should be on stage with a guitar. That's why I call him Rock Star Steve, but not to his face.

'Sam.' He nudges me with his elbow. 'Come on, mate, you can tell me.'

'Okay,' I sigh. 'Are you moving me again?'

'What?'

I lift my head. 'Are you moving me again?'

'No.' Rock Star Steve shakes his rock star head, swooshing his blond rock star hair. 'No. No, not at all, Sam. Where did you get that idea from?'

'Because that's what you always do. I've been here four months so you must be moving me soon.'

'Is that what this is all about? You're scared you're going to get moved again?'

'It's usually about this time.' We've had this conversation before, sitting in Rock Star Steve's car, outside Jean and Ralph's.

'Why doesn't anyone want me?' I asked him back then. 'Why don't I get picked when people visit from the adoption agency? What have I done wrong?'

'Nothing, Sam,' he said. 'You've done nothing wrong.'

'But it must be something. Do I smell? Have I got greasy hair?'

'No.' Rock Star Steve laughed. 'None of those things. You've got to be positive, Sam. Think of the good things about yourself.'

'Like what?'

'Like that you're bright and smart and you've got a cheeky grin.'

'Have I?'

'Yep, that's it, right there!' He ruffled my hair.

I looked down into the footwell.

Rock Star Steve stared ahead, then reached out and turned the ignition. I looked back at the house. Rock Star Steve said my move was only temporary, but I never saw Jean and Ralph again.

'Sam ... Sam ...' Rock Star Steve taps my arm. 'Tell me what you're thinking.'

I look up. I think of telling him that I'm tired of being moved, tired of being turned down for adoption, but none of that matters now, because I've got the Perfect Parent Project. I'm going to find my perfect family without the agency's help.

'Sam.' Rock Star Steve smiles. 'You do know Tom and Sarah like you.'

'It doesn't feel that way,' I sigh.

'Maybe not, but what about Reilly? You must know Reilly likes you. They tell me you are all he talks about. Well, you and his computer games.'

'Yeah.' I smile as I picture Reilly crashing his planes. 'I do like Reilly. But why does his mum have to keep on at me all the time. Where have I been? Who have I been with? Have I done my diary?'

'Because she cares,' says Rock Star Steve. 'And the more you play up with this feeling that you'll be leaving, the more difficult you'll make it for Sarah and Tom, who just want to look after you. Do you get that, Sam?'

'Suppose so,' I mumble.

'Come on, let's do better than that.'

'Okay,' I say, looking up. 'I understand.'

'Good lad.' Rock Star Steve ruffles my hair. 'So stop worrying about leaving, because it's not happening now, or any time soon. All right?'

Someone knocks on the door. It's like Rock Star Steve has pressed an invisible buzzer to let people know we've finished.

Mrs Sorrell peers around the door. 'All good?'

'Yep,' says Rock Star Steve. 'We've had a chat, haven't we, Sam?'

I nod. Mrs Sorrell walks in. Behind her Reilly's mum smiles at me from the doorway.

'Everything okay?' she asks.

'Yes.' But it's not okay really, because even though Rock Star Steve says I'm not moving, I know it's only a matter of time before he comes and picks me up in his red car. But that's all right, because the Perfect Parent Project is going to start tomorrow when me and Leah post the leaflets, then next weekend I'll interview people at the bandstand. I'll meet the perfect couple or person, and by the time Rock Star Steve arrives to get me, I'll already be with them.

CHAPTER 11

I HATE TELLING LIES

I'm lying on the bottom bunk, making another list. This one's called: Things I'd Like to Do With My Perfect Parents. Number one is go to Disneyland, of course, and number two is to have the best seats at Wembley and watch England play Brazil. But it's hard to concentrate because Reilly's mum was irritable this evening. She'd been baking cakes all day, then went to print an invoice and found out all the paper had gone. I was playing Ace Pilot with Reilly, but I could hear her in the office searching through the drawers, muttering, 'I can't have used it all,' and, 'I'm sure we had another packet somewhere.' Then she came into Reilly's room and asked, 'Have you been using my paper to make paper planes?'

'No.' Reilly shook his head. 'It wasn't me.'

'Are you sure? You know you should always tell the truth.'

'Always.' Reilly nodded.

I was pressing buttons on the controller, staring at the TV, but I could tell that Reilly's mum was now looking at me. Foster-parents always blame the foster-kid when something goes missing, like food or money. I liked Brad and Angie, but I knew they thought it was me who ate all the chocolates off the Christmas tree, even though it wasn't. It must have been Rufus, their smelly spaniel. They gave me the same look that Reilly's mum was giving me.

'It wasn't me,' I said before she even opened her mouth.

'I didn't say it was, Sam.'

'But it wasn't,' I said. 'I might have used a few pieces for homework, but that's all.'

I could feel Reilly looking at me and my face started to burn, because I hate telling lies. I had used the paper to print another two hundred posters, while she was outside talking to Mrs Hodgson from next door for ages. What Reilly's mum didn't know was that the black ink had started to run out too.

I really wanted to tell her it was me, but I couldn't explain it was for two hundred Perfect Parent Project posters. Leah had just messaged to arrange to meet tomorrow and told me the ones we'd printed at hers were neatly packed into a Save the Rainforest reusable bag. Mine were in my rucksack at the end of my bed. They were right next to Reilly's mum's feet all the time she was talking. Eventually she said maybe she'd got it wrong, perhaps there hadn't been as much paper as she'd thought.

That was when she walked out of the room.

That was when the house went quiet.

That was when Reilly started reading *Charlie Changes into a Chicken* out loud and I started making the list. On Friday nights we often play Ace Pilot until eight, but I wanted to start my Things I'd Like to Do With My Perfect Parent or Parents list. (I don't mind having just one parent, but two might be better in case one annoys me.)

I push Reilly's mum out of my mind and focus on the list.

1. Go to Disneyland.
2. Watch England play at Wembley.
3. Drive to Scotland in a BMW M5 (*doesn't* have to be Scotland, but it *does* have to be a long journey and in a BMW M5).
4. Do a McDonald's drive-through in a BMW M5.
5. Get dropped off at school in a BMW M5.
6.

I stop writing as I hear footsteps on the stairs, then Reilly's mum talking quietly. She's almost whispering, saying things like, 'Yes, I know . . . I will . . . I'll try.' I hold my breath, thinking she might be talking about me. Her voice fades as she goes into her office. For a moment I think she's going to tell him about the missing paper, but then she says, 'Yes, you left it behind. Shall I send it up to you?'

I breathe with relief.

Reilly's mum says, 'Okay. Miss you. Looking forward to you coming home.' And I feel sorry for her when she says that, because it must be horrible if you love someone so much that when you are apart you miss each other loads. Reilly has been quiet for ages. I wonder if he's asleep or listening too.

The bunk knocks against the wall.

Oh. Here he comes.

'Hi, Sam!'

Reilly's head is hanging over the side of his bed.

'Hi, Reilly.'

'What you doing?'

'Nothing,' I say, holding my list against my chest.

'Are you coming to watch *Toy Story 4* at the weekend?'

I smile. His mum has planned a special treat because his dad is away and she thinks Reilly must be missing him too.

'We can get sweets,' he says. 'And sit in the big seats and you can share my Coke. And Mum's going to buy me new shoes. She might get you some too, so you've got to come.'

'Thanks, Reilly,' I say.

'So will you come?'

'I can't,' I say. 'I've got something I need to do.'

'Can I come with you then?'

I reach up and pick at the slats with my fingers. 'No. But I won't be long.'

'Okay,' he says. 'Play Ace Pilot when you get back?'

I can't think about what I'll do when I get back. All I can think about is delivering the posters for the Perfect Parent Project on my bike ... *Ah, my bike! I've forgotten to get my bike out of the shed.* I could go down now, but Reilly's mum will hear and have a thousand questions about what I'm doing. I'll just have to sneak it out in the morning.

Reilly leans over further. 'Play Ace Pilot when I get back?'

'Yes.' I smile.

'What are you laughing at?'

'You,' I say. 'You look like a jellyfish.'

'What do they look like?'

'Like this.' I draw a jellyfish with big eyes on the back of my pad, then show Reilly.

'Cool,' he says, then flips back onto his bed.

I shake my head. Sometimes I wish I was Reilly, when all you have to worry about is watching the new *Toy Story* movie. But then I wouldn't want to be six again. I don't want to be stuck in the flat with Mum. I don't want to hear her shouting and crying. I don't even want to think about it now.

I look back at my list. It's a list of places I want to go with my perfect parents, but that doesn't mean I can't write:

6. Get Ace Pilot so Reilly can come over.

I put my pen down. I hate lying to him, and I wish I could tell him the truth. I'm so excited about tomorrow that I want to share it with him. I want to jump out of bed right now and shout it out in the room. 'Hey, Reilly, I'm meeting Leah in the morning and we're going to post leaflets to try to find my perfect family! Wanna come?'

And I'd love him to say yes, because we'll be quicker posting them with him, and he'd love to go up on the Downs afterwards and play Frisbee or football with us. I know he'd rather be out with me than walking around town looking at shoes.

I roll over on my side and close my eyes, but my head is racing with thoughts about tomorrow, wondering what will happen and who I'll meet. We're delivering four hundred posters. All I need is a reply from one of them. I roll over onto my back, staring up at the slats. Just one reply and I could have parents of my own. I want to tell the world, I want to tell Reilly, but I think he'd get upset because I'm also saying, 'Hey, Reilly, I don't want to live with you.'

CHAPTER 12

THE PERFECT PARENT PROJECT STAGE ONE

'Oh no. Ha, Sam!' Leah's got her hand over her mouth, trying not to laugh as I push my bike to the corner of her street.

'What?' I say.

'It's a bit small.'

'I know.' I look down at my bike. 'I think I must have grown a bit.'

'A bit?' Leah giggles. 'Are you sure you didn't take Reilly's by mistake?'

'It's okay,' I say, slightly hurt. 'I've just got to put the seat up a bit higher. I couldn't do it at Reilly's because I didn't want his mum to stop me going.' I reach down and pull a lever under the seat.

'There,' I say. 'That better?'

'Maybe we can swap,' says Leah. 'My mum's is way too big for me.'

'But it's yellow!'

‘Don’t worry about it.’ She slides the carrier bag off her handlebars and onto mine. ‘The most important thing is we get there.’

‘Yeah.’ I blow out my cheeks. ‘You’re right.’

As we swap bikes, I take another deep breath. This is it. This is the day I get to deliver the posters. I was so nervous and excited that I didn’t sleep all night. When I got up this morning my stomach felt like it was full of bees and my hands were shaking so much I could hardly fit the key in the shed’s padlock. Reilly’s mum saw me and asked why I needed it. I told her I was taking it to Leah’s to jump over ramps in her garden. I’m not sure if she believed me, but I was already out of the gate before she replied.

‘You okay?’ Leah looks across at me.

‘Yeah,’ I say, trying to sound braver than I feel. ‘I think so.’

‘It’s okay to be nervous. I would be too, if I was looking for my perfect parents.’

‘I can’t help it,’ I say. ‘Look at my hands. I’m shaking like it’s Christmas.’

‘Then there’s only one thing for it,’ says Leah.

‘What’s that?’

‘Get it over with! Come on!’

She jumps on my bike and heads off down the road.

‘What about Tanya Billings, do you remember her?’

‘No.’

‘You must do. She wet herself in assembly and Mrs Shore lent her some clothes from lost property so she didn’t have to go home.’

‘No.’ I laugh. ‘I think I must have left by then.’

Leah leans back in the sun. We've stopped by a bridge because the bike saddle was hurting Leah's bum. She's been trying to remember exactly when we were together at primary school. I've not been much help – I've been to so many schools that I get all the teachers and pupils jumbled up.

'I can't think of anyone else you might remember,' says Leah, sitting up. 'But I can remember the day after you left.'

'Can you?'

'Yes, it was horrible. I was sitting there waiting for you while Miss Knight took the register. I thought you were just late. But you never turned up. I spent all day looking at your empty chair next to me.'

'Did you miss me?' I ask. 'You did, didn't you?'

'A little bit.'

I smile.

'But only for a day.' Leah smirks. 'Because Miss Knight moved Sofia Long next to me, and she was way better at maths than you.'

'Anyone is better at maths than me!'

We both laugh, then Leah says quietly, 'Sam, you didn't even tell me you were leaving.'

'That's because I didn't know. Rock Star Steve picked me up from school. I didn't even go back to the house I was staying in to pick my things up. At least I don't think I did. I don't really remember.'

'Well,' says Leah. 'As long as you don't go off again. Especially when you're in your posh new house with your perfect parents, diving in the pool or driving your quad bike around the garden while I'm stuck at home on my own with Mum.'

'I won't.' I turn and look at her. 'I promise.'

‘No, don’t say promise. That’s what my dad said, but then he never came back.’

I wait for her to repeat something funny that her mum said, but instead she reaches down by her side and picks at the grass.

I haven’t spoken to Leah much about her dad since he left. Apart from the day I found her crying outside the girls’ toilets, she never seems to want to. Or maybe it’s just that I never ask.

‘Do you want to talk about him?’ I say.

Leah shrugs. ‘No. Nothing much to say really. They argued. He left. And I miss him.’

‘But you still see him.’

‘Yeah.’ Leah looks up. ‘If you can call going to TGI Fridays and the cinema seeing each other. He never takes me back to his flat. It’s like he’s hiding something. I told Mum I think he might have a new girlfriend, but she thinks it’s because Dad’s embarrassed that I’ll think his place is a mess. Which it probably is.’

‘Would you like him to have a new girlfriend?’

‘What I’d like is for them to have never split up. Then I wouldn’t have to worry about either him or Mum being on their own.’

‘But what about you?’

‘Oh, I’m okay.’ But I’m not sure she is.

‘You can tell me,’ I say. ‘You’ve helped me lots.’

Leah smiles. I wait for her to say something about her dad, but all she does is stand up and announce, ‘My bum’s stopped hurting now.’ Then she picks up her bike.

I grab mine and we walk side by side along the cycle path.

I glance across at her.

'What?' she says.

'Nothing.'

'Then why are you looking at me weird.'

'I'm not,' I say. 'But . . .'

'But what?'

'Nothing.'

I don't tell her I'm thinking she's the best friend I've ever had.

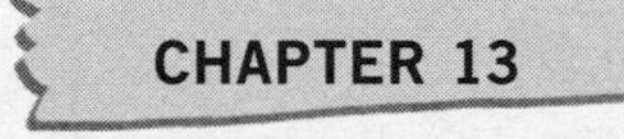

CHAPTER 13

THREE HUNDRED AND NINETY-EIGHT CHANCES

'I've got new trainers!' Reilly shoots his feet over the side of his bunk. 'I'm too old for lights, but they've got stripes!'

'Cool,' I say.

'Thanks.' Reilly grins. 'Mum says I can wear them to bed because I've not worn them outside yet. And *Toy Story 4* was great. It's about a girl and her friend Forky. You should have come. I saved you some jelly beans.' Reilly hands me a striped pink bag.

I peer inside.

'They got a bit stuck together. Look.' He holds out his hands and grins. 'I've still got bits on my fingers.'

'Eeew.' I pull away, pretending I'm grossed out.

Reilly kneels up, giggling, like he's coming after me.

'Bean monster!' I shout. 'Bean monster! I give in – I'll have one. I'll have one!'

Reilly sits back on his heels, still giggling as he puts his hand into the bag.

'You can have the black ones,' he says. 'And the green. I don't like them.'

I hold out my palm and Reilly drops sticky jelly beans into my hand, then some into his mouth. 'Don't tell Mum,' he says. 'Or she'll make me clean my teeth again.'

'I won't,' I say.

'So where have you been?' he garbles through a mouthful of spit and sweets.

'Studying.'

'With your friend Leah?'

'Yes.' I sit down on my bunk.

'Is she your girlfriend?'

'No, Reilly. She's not my girlfriend.'

'But I heard Mum tell Dad. She said you're still coming home late, but she feels better because you made such a good friend.'

'I never heard her say that.'

'She called him after *Toy Story*.'

'Get to sleep, you two!' Reilly's mum shouts from the other side of the door. I hear her pull the light cord in the bathroom. The bed creaks as Reilly rolls back onto his mattress.

I roll over on my side. I'm so tired and my feet are throbbing. Delivering four hundred posters in three hours was hard work, especially when the houses at The Clift were so big it felt like there were miles between each door. Some of them had long gravel paths with posh cars parked in front of the house – Audis, BMWs, Mercedes.

Two of them had Porsches and some were so grand they had huge iron gates with an intercom. We missed those houses out when we couldn't find the letter boxes, but I wouldn't have delivered to them anyway – if I made a mistake and chose the wrong parents, I'd need a ladder to climb out of the front garden! At one of the houses a man came out and pointed at a NO JUNK MAIL sign by his letter box. 'Can't you read?' he asked. I told him I could, and that my poster wasn't junk mail. He told me to get off his land, but by that time I'd decided he was so grumpy there was no way he would be my perfect parent anyway.

On the way back, me and Leah stopped and posted the rest of the leaflets in an area called Montville. Leah thought the area was nice and closer to school. The houses weren't as big as those in The Clift but they were all painted different colours – red, light blue, green, even orange – and they bordered a park that was big enough to play football in or throw a Frisbee. If I ever got to live there, every morning would be like waking up to a rainbow. We saw some of the people who lived there. A lot of them were too old to adopt me, and just seemed to want to talk to us about their gardens and their grandchildren. But we still left them a leaflet because it seemed rude if we didn't. Leah also missed out a group of houses because she was pretty sure she saw our cookery teacher Miss Wylie's yellow VW Beetle parked on the road. I'm glad she did – it doesn't matter how nice a person is, having a teacher for your mum would mean no escape! Most of the other people we met took the poster and smiled without even reading it. Some folded it in half and said they'd read it later. Leah said they were busy, but twice I turned around and saw them put it straight in the bin. But I still had three hundred and ninety-eight chances left.

And Leah thinks I should look smart for the interviews, to help my chances. She said first impressions count, so we're going to town tomorrow to buy me something, even though I haven't got any money.

The bunkbed shakes as Reilly rolls over above me. I hope he's not going to be sick after eating too many jelly beans.

'Night, Sam,' he whispers down the crack between the bed and the wall.

'Goodnight, Reilly.' I smile. *Three hundred and ninety-eight chances*, I think to myself. Now all I have to do is wait for loads of them to reply.

CHAPTER 14

NO CHARITY

'Sam, hurry up.'

'I'm doing the belt up.'

'But you've been ages.'

'I know.' I poke my head out from behind the changing room curtain. 'Leah, I don't think this was a good idea. When you said get new clothes, I didn't think you meant from a charity shop.'

'It's our only choice,' she says. 'You said you don't have any money.'

'I don't.' I check the charity shop assistant isn't listening, then whisper, 'But this belonged to a dead person!'

Leah puts her hand over her mouth. 'Just try it,' she says between giggles. 'If the trousers are too long, I'll get my mum to shorten them.'

'Too long?' I say. 'They go down to the ground then halfway up my leg again! And the cuffs—'

Leah bursts out laughing. 'Just show me, Sam.'

'Okay,' I say. 'But promise me you won't laugh any more.'

'Okay,' she says, trying to keep a straight face. 'No more laughing.'

I glance down at the trousers flapping over my trainers. I look stupid but at least coming shopping has taken my mind off the fact it's been nearly twenty-four hours since we delivered the leaflets and we've not had one single reply. Leah thinks I'm panicking, that lots of people won't reply on a Sunday, and they might when they go back to work. I just hope she's right.

I step out just as the assistant asks, 'Is everything all right?' then looks at me and says, 'Oh my. You do look smart – just like one of my grandsons.'

'Really?' I say, looking at Leah. 'I don't look like a penguin?'

'No.' Leah smiles. 'You look cute.'

'That's what you say about meerkats.'

'Well,' says the assistant, 'meerkats are cute too.'

'So you think I look all right?'

'Yes,' they both say at the same time.

Then the assistant says, 'It was brought in by a lady whose son grew a foot in a year.'

'Oh, so it's not from a dead person.'

'No!' The assistant's mouth makes an O shape and she shakes her head quickly. 'No, not dead people. Most of our clothes are just things people outgrow.'

I smile even though I'm not sure I believe her.

'How much is it?' asks Leah.

'Oh.' The assistant looks back into the shop. 'I think everything off that rail is twenty pounds.'

Leah opens her bag. 'I think I've only got ten . . . oh, and two fruit pastilles.'

'Well, I'm afraid we don't take those.' The assistant smiles.

'But he really needs it,' says Leah.

'Oh, I don't know.' The assistant looks at me. 'It's a charity shop, and we do try to get as much money as we can.'

A minute ago, I hated the suit, but now my heart sinks. If Leah and the old lady like it, then maybe it would be perfect for interviewing my future parents.

'You'd better put it back then,' says Leah quietly.

'Okay,' I sigh. As I turn I think maybe I could ask Reilly's mum for the extra ten pounds, but then she'd want to know what it was for. I don't even have anything I could sell. All the things in Reilly's room belong to Reilly and there's no way I could survive without my phone.

The curtain swishes as Leah pulls it across behind me. I take the jacket off and hang it on the hook. As I struggle with the belt, I catch myself in the mirror. *It was a stupid idea*, I think to myself. *I'm too young to wear a suit anyway. Kids my age only wear them if they're posh, or to go to a funeral or wedding. If my perfect parents really like me, they won't care what I'm wearing.* That's what I tell myself, but when I see my old hoody and jeans in the mirror, I know I don't stand a chance of finding them dressed like this.

When I walk back out, Leah is standing by the counter, talking to the assistant.

'Oh, here he is,' says the assistant. 'Why the long face?'

I shrug as I hand the suit to her.

She glances at Leah, then smiles at me.

'We've decided you can have it,' she says.

'Really?' I look up at the assistant then Leah disbelievingly. 'But we haven't got enough money.'

'It's okay,' says the assistant. 'We've worked it out.' She gives Leah a smile, like they've agreed a secret plan.

Leah smiles back. I want to smile too, I want to feel happy, but when people talk behind my back it can only mean one thing. They've been talking about me being a foster-kid. That's why the assistant is looking at me like she feels sorry for me. That's why Leah is now looking at everything in the shop, and out of the window, anywhere so she doesn't make eye contact with me. I hate it when people do things just because they feel sorry for me, like when the dinner ladies at primary school gave me extra chips because I had free meals.

'There you go, my love,' says the assistant, handing me my suit in a plastic bag. 'You two must pop back in and let me know how it went.'

'Thank . . . you,' I say cautiously. 'But how what—'

'We will!' Leah grabs my arm. 'Let's go.' She hurries me towards the door and pulls me out onto the street.

'Wait,' I say, putting on the brakes. 'What did you say to her?'

'Nothing.' Leah grins.

Two people walk between us.

'You did!' I say, squirming. 'Leah, please don't say you told her I was a foster-kid. Please. You know I hate it when people find out.'

'Sam.' Leah puts her hands on my shoulders. 'Calm down. I didn't tell her. I didn't say anything about that.'

'So what did you say?'

'It doesn't matter.'

'It does.'

Leah gives me a guilty look. 'Okay,' she sighs. 'I might have told her we were going on a first date.'

'What!'

Leah smiles. 'Does it matter? At least we got you a suit.'

I look at the bag, think about taking it back, but it's a suit, my suit, one that I'd be proud to wear to meet my perfect parents.

I shake my head slowly.

'See, you know I'm right. Come on.' Leah starts to walk on. 'You'd better get back if you want to keep Reilly's mum happy.'

'Okay,' I say, walking beside her. 'But there's one thing.'

'What's that?'

'We're not actually going on a first date, are we?'

'God, no,' says Leah.

'Because that would be tragic,' I say.

'Yes.' Leah smiles. 'Tragic.'

WAITING FOR MAIL

'So have I got any now?'

'Sam, that's the fifth time you've asked me.'

'Fourth.'

'Okay, fourth, then add on the hundred from yesterday.'

'It's your fault. I tried checking at Reilly's but you didn't give me the email account password. I tried Leah1, 2 and 3. Perfect Parent Project. Adopt Me—'

'Koala,' says Leah as we walk by the school railings.

'Koala? What's that got to do with me finding perfect parents?'

'Nothing,' she says. 'It's just my favourite animal.'

'Okay,' I say. 'Koala, but can we still check them now?'

'All right.' Leah stops in the middle of the pavement. 'I've wanted to look too but I thought I'd wait for you.'

I guide her to the side of the path, out of the way of some Year Nines walking towards us. Down the road, Mr Evans is barking that anyone not through the gates soon will get a detention.

'Hurry up,' I say to Leah. 'Or we'll be late.'

Leah raises her eyebrows as if to say, 'Like that's ever bothered you before,' then she presses the keys on her phone.

'Here we go!' she says excitedly. 'We've got four!'

'Four!' My voice cracks in excitement. 'Show me!'

Leah shows me her phone. My eyes dart around the screen but I'm too excited to take in the information.

'Who are they from?' I ask.

'Oh wait,' says Leah.

'What?'

'Two of the emails are from Google, welcoming us, the third one is a message from something called Groupon and the fourth is from someone called Halle.'

'What does that one say?' I ask eagerly.

Leah clicks on the mail.

'It says her name is Halle from Sierra Leone, and you've won a million pounds. All you have to do is give her your bank account details.'

'Is that it?' I say, peering closer. 'A coupon for a meal in a city I've never been to, and someone wanting to pay a million pounds into a bank account I don't have?'

'Mmm, sorry. But hang on,' she says brightly. 'There's something in the junk folder.'

'I thought that *was* the junk folder!' I say.

Leah laughs. 'It should be. But don't worry, we only posted the leaflets on Saturday. Some people might not even have been home. Or they might have put it on the table thinking they'll read it in the week.'

'Yeah, of course, that'll be it,' I say. 'Or they just aren't bothered with email and a hundred people will turn up and I'll be interviewing people all day.'

'You two! Inside now!'

Me and Leah jump. Mr Evans walks towards us. 'And put that phone away,' he says. 'Or I'll take it from you.'

'We'll try to check again at lunchtime,' Leah says under her breath.

'Can you at least show some urgency?' barks Mr Evans.

'Lunchtime,' says Leah.

I nod. 'Lunchtime.'

We hitch our bags over our shoulders and start to run.

I haven't stopped thinking about the emails all morning.

That's what I tell Leah when we meet at lunchtime and we check them again. There aren't any, and the one in the junk folder is about how to lose two kilos a week by joining Slimberland Slimming Club. Leah agrees that if people responded too quickly, they might not be serious, like when people buy a puppy for Christmas and realize it pees and chews shoes, so they take it to the dogs' home in January.

'But I don't pee or chew shoes,' I say.

'I know,' she laughs, 'but you know what I mean.'

'I suppose,' I say. 'But this is killing me, having to wait five days until I get to meet what could be my perfect parents for the first time.'

We stop talking as Lucy and Sofia from our form class put their trays down beside us. We slide our trays towards the end of the table to give them more room, but really it's so we can keep talking.

'You need to use this time to prepare,' Leah whispers.

'You sound like Rock Star Steve,' I say.

‘I know, but you should. Why don’t you think more about what you want from your perfect parents, and the questions you might ask them? I mean, it’s not like they’re going to be your parents for a few weeks – it’s for the rest of your life.’

I take a bite of my sandwich, and think I could do that in RE this afternoon.

I look across the tables and spot Lewis sitting with Amala, by the window. He waves at me. Amala smiles. I wave back.

Leah looks over her shoulder, then back at me. ‘Have you put your name down, yet? For *Bugsy Malone*?’

‘No,’ I say.

‘But I thought you told Mr Powell you were going to.’

‘I will. But I was going to see what happens on Saturday. I don’t want to put my name down and then have to scratch it off.’

‘Sam.’ Leah leans across the table. ‘You’ve got to put your name down. It’s coming up to the end of term. Mr Powell might think about the cast over the holidays. He’ll think you’re not interested and give all the best roles to other people.’

I nod.

‘Promise me you’ll do it!’ Leah says urgently. ‘You’ve got to give yourself a carrot to aim for.’

‘Okay. I will.’

Leah takes a sip of her drink. She is right, because it has happened to me before. I was away one day before the nativity play at infants. I thought I was going to be Joseph or one of the Three Wise Men, but when I went back all the good parts had gone and I ended up being a sheep.

Top Five Cars I'd Like My Perfect Parents to Have

1. BMW M5.
2. Maserati GranTurismo.
3. Audi R8 V10.
4. BMW Z3.
5. Jaguar F-type Convertible.

'That's not quite what I meant,' Leah says as we sit on the wall outside school.

'I know. They are expensive,' I say, 'but you saw the type of cars in the driveways of those houses at The Clift.'

'No.' Leah shakes her head. 'It's not that. When I said you should prepare, I didn't mean make a list of cars. I meant things like the type of people you'd like them to be, whether you want two parents or if one is okay.'

'I don't mind,' I say. 'One's okay, just as long as he or she loves me.'

'That's sweet.' Leah looks at me and I feel a bit embarrassed because what I just said sounded soppy.

'Anyway,' I say, trying to cover up what I just said, even though it's true. 'Have we got any more replies?'

'I checked before you got here,' says Leah.

'And?'

'Sorry, Sam.' She pushes out her bottom lip. 'None yet.'

'But this is killing me,' I say.

'Just be patient,' says Leah. 'It's only five days, but then you could be sorted for the rest of your life.'

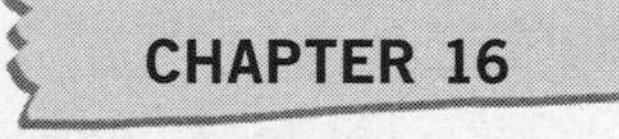

WAITING GAME

I wish it was Saturday already. I wish we were at the bandstand. But the only trouble with wishing for something is that every day feels twice as long in between. The last time I felt like this was . . . well, never. Or maybe the time Brad and Angie said they were going to take me to Thorpe Park. I was excited then, even if I did end up going on most of the rides on my own. I thought it was because they didn't like them, but I knew after it was because Angie was expecting a baby. I've been to every lesson and only to Eric twice so far this week, and both times were after school. I know it's only Thursday, but that's quite good for me. I can't risk getting in trouble and being grounded when the most important weekend of my life is about to happen. At least drama club has come around again, even if Mr Powell is insisting that we mix the groups this week, which makes us all groan.

'Just think about it,' he says, standing on the stage. 'If you ever become really successful and you're in a stage play, or a film, you don't always get to act with your friends. So it's . . .' He points at the class. 'You three. You three. You three and . . . you, Jonah and Rhian.'

Mr Powell steps down off the stage. I look up just as Amala and Lewis walk towards their groups.

'All right?' Lewis asks me as he passes. 'Hope you don't pee yourself this week.'

'I won't,' I laugh. 'At least not if I can help it.'

Amala smiles. 'It was funny,' she says quietly.

I join up with my group. Rhian is in Year Nine and is super confident. Jonah is in another class in Year Seven. He started the week after I did, and doesn't say much, except when he's acting.

Mr Powell walks over. 'Okay, gang,' he says, pulling at his beard. 'Now remember, this week is all about character. The best way to find out about someone's character is to notice all the little details. Why don't you start with yourselves? Maybe hot seat . . .' Mr Powell moves away to another group.

'Right,' says Rhian. 'Who wants to go first?'

Jonah looks at me nervously, like he doesn't want it to be him.

'I don't mind doing it,' I say.

'All right,' says Rhian. 'Let's go over there so we can hear ourselves and not the other groups.'

We walk towards the piano and I sit down on the stool. This will be the hot seat. We do this exercise in drama club sometimes. This will be my fourth time and I like doing it because people ask questions, one after the other, really quickly, and you just have to say the first thing that comes into your head. Sometimes it can be funny and make no sense. Mr Powell says that's fine, because we can always use something as 'material', no matter how rubbish it might seem. It's all made up. I just have to make sure that I don't let any truth slip out. Which might be hard today when the thought of finding perfect parents is rushing through my mind.

'Ready?' asks Rhian.

I nod.

'What's your name?' asks Jonah.

'Harold.'

They both laugh.

'How old are you?' asks Rhian.

'Seventy-four.'

'Are you married?'

'Yes.'

'How many ... ? Sorry ...' Rhian looks at Jonah who's only asked one question. 'Am I taking over?'

'No,' says Jonah. 'It's okay. I can't think of anything at the moment.'

'Okay,' says Rhian, turning back to me. 'Do you have any children?'

'Yes. Nine.'

'Nine!' Rhian tries not to laugh because the secret of the exercise is to keep going. 'Nine,' she repeats. 'Nine.'

I try to keep my drama straight face but the more she repeats it the more I want to grin.

'Okay, that's it, gang.' Mr Powell claps his hands at the end of the session. 'We're done for this term, but don't rush off just yet.'

We all gather around him. I've been so focused on the Perfect Parent Project, I'd totally forgotten the end of term sneaking up.

'*Bugsy Malone*,' Mr Powell says, looking at a piece of paper. 'Nearly *all* of you have put your names down here.' He glances at me. 'And we've got some new names from the rest of the school. This is the last chance to add yours before the Easter break.'

My heart skips and I feel myself burning inside. I wonder if anyone else noticed Mr Powell look at me, because I still haven't done it. I still haven't put my name down even though I've stopped and looked at the list every day. I just want to be certain I'll be here.

'Sam.' Lewis nudges me. 'You have put your name down, haven't you?'

I stare ahead, feeling cold sweat dripping down my back.

'So,' Mr Powell continues, 'have you given the play any thought?'

For a moment I think he means just me, but he's talking to the whole group.

Everyone looks at each other.

'It's a great production,' says Mr Powell, 'and we need to hit the ground running. Can I suggest you all watch the film, over the Easter break? Maybe even get into some groups and chat about it?'

Everyone nods except me.

'Okay then, gang,' says Mr Powell. 'Now clear off home. Have a nice holiday and bring me back an egg … or three.' He pats his belly. The group laugh, but I'm still thinking that I haven't put my name down.

As I walk to my bag I wonder if Mr Powell is going to call me back like he did last week, or maybe he's given up on me.

'Sam.' Lewis catches up with me. 'You didn't answer. You have put your name down, haven't you? I didn't see it on the list before Mr Powell took it down.'

'No,' I say. 'I think I might be going on holiday then.'

'But it's in term time,' says Lewis. 'Parents who take their kids out of school for holidays get fined. Michael Hobbs's parents did last year.'

Out the corner of my eye I spot Mr Powell putting books and a sandwich box into his bag, but glancing up at me at the same time.

'Sam, you gotta do it,' says Lewis. 'You can be Bugsy; I'll be Dandy Dan. That way we'll get to throw pies and shoot splurge guns at the others.'

Mr Powell clips his bag shut and heads towards the door. If I don't put my name down now it's going to be too late.

'We could meet up during the holidays, like Mr Powell said,' Lewis continues. 'You can come to mine if you like. I'll text you the address.'

Mr Powell pushes the door open and disappears out into the corridor.

I've got to give myself a carrot. I've got to be positive, stop running, and look forward, I think to myself. But it's horrible to go forward when you're scared of falling over.

'What's your number so I can text you?' Lewis asks.

'I need to go,' I say. 'I need to . . .'

Mr Powell has left with the list. It's too late. It's too late.

My heart thuds as I race across the drama hall.

'Sam, where are you—?'

The door bangs against the wall as I push it open. Mr Powell is walking away from me towards the staffroom.

'Sir!' I shout. 'Sir.'

Mr Powell spins round.

'Yes, Sam.'

'Sir . . .' I catch my breath. 'Can you put my name down?'

CHAPTER 17

MAGGOTS IN MY BELLY . . .

I'm sitting on the sofa, flicking through one of Reilly's dad's copies of *AirForces Monthly* magazine. Most of it is about boring rules and regulations or about members of the air force who are retiring or have died. But in the middle is a brilliant double-page picture of a Boeing Chinook – a helicopter so big it's got two sets of spinning blades at each end. Reilly's in the kitchen with his mum, making a special cake for when his dad comes home at Easter. He's just told her that I helped him to get to level four on Ace Pilot, which is the best he's ever done. He jumped around his room when he did it. Gave me high fives, spun in a circle, then gave me high tens. He sounds so excited about it, even now, but as I stare at the magazine, I suddenly think that if I do find my perfect parents and go to live with them, getting to level four might be the best Reilly ever gets.

The Let's Pick on Sam meeting wasn't so bad at school today. I've not missed any lessons and Reilly's mum said I'd not been back late too many times this week. Even Mrs Sorrell seemed happy, for once, but that might have been because she was excited about breaking up for the holidays and not having to see students for two weeks. Rock Star Steve was pleased, and said it was good we were all getting along. At the end, when we were on our own, he told me well done, to keep it going, that perhaps the holidays were a good time to do things with Reilly and his mum, like watch TV together, or go to the cinema or out on our bikes. That way, he said, I'd have some nice things to put in my diary. I thought it would be fun to do those things with Reilly – lots of kids from school would be doing things like that. But I couldn't tell Rock Star Steve I had big plans of my own. No one else's holiday plans could be as exciting as mine.

'Sam!' Reilly comes in with his hands covered in blue food colouring. 'Come and see what we've done. Come and see the wings we put on Dad's plane.'

'All right, Reilly,' I say. 'In a minute. I've just got to do something.'

'Okay.' Reilly spins around. 'But hurry, otherwise I'll have licked the bowl.'

I smile. 'I will, Reilly, I promise.'

Reilly runs back out to the kitchen. He's as excited about his dad's cake as I am about tomorrow. I still haven't got any proper emails on the ThePerfectParentProject@gmail.com account, but Leah told me not to worry, that sometimes people are suspicious of sending messages on the internet in case it's a scam, like when her mum's Apple account got hacked at three o'clock in the morning and she ended up paying for an iPad she never had.

I reach into my pocket and look at the list of questions I'm going to ask tomorrow. I need to memorize them, otherwise people will think I don't know what I'm doing if I look down at my notes all the time.

1. Do you have any other children?
2. If the answer is yes, will I have to share a room with them?
3. Do you like Nando's?
4. If yes, what's the hottest sauce you can eat?
5. What job do you have?
6. Sweet or salty popcorn?
7. Have you ever been to Disneyland?
8. If no, would you like to go to Disneyland?
9. If yes, would you take me with you?
10. If no, why not?

Leah told me not to ask the Disneyland questions, because she doesn't think it shows whether a parent is suitable or not. I told her that I've always wanted to go there – that I want to go on Space Mountain and all the other roller coasters. She said if that's all I want then I should just go on the school trip to Thorpe Park. I told her that's not the same, and besides, wouldn't I get to find out what they were like if I had eleven hours with them on the plane? But when I look at the questions now, perhaps four questions on Disneyland might make the applicants think that's all I want from them, and that's not true.

I wonder how many people will turn up? What if there are too many? What if there's none? What will the adoption agency do if they find out? When Kyle Simmonds climbed on a school roof and threw tiles at the police, one of the other foster-kids told me Kyle was made to stay in the children's home and would never be placed with a foster family ever again. I don't know if that's true, but I definitely don't want that to happen. I can't let that happen. I pick up my phone.

Leah, are you there?

Yes.

I think we should cancel it.

Why? What happened to positive Sam?

He disappeared ☹

Don't worry, it'll be okay.

How do you know?

Because I'll be there ☺

'Sam, are you coming?' Reilly's mum's shout makes me jump. I put my phone back in my pocket and walk out into the kitchen. Reilly's standing on a plastic stool with a wooden spoon in his hand. Reilly's mum is leaning against the sink, drinking a cup of coffee.

I look at the cake on the counter. A giant Chinook helicopter flying across a blue sky.

Reilly beams. 'I did the clouds.'

'What do you think?' asks Reilly's mum.

'I think . . .' I grin at them both. 'I think it's brilliant.'

'Maybe you'd like to help us with the rotors, Sam, before we put it in the freezer.' Reilly's mum smiles.

'Yeah,' I say. 'I could do that.'

She makes space on the worktop so I can stand between her and Reilly, then cuts a piece of marzipan. 'All we have to do is make sure they are the same size.'

'Yeah, like this,' says Reilly.

'No, Reilly,' his mum chuckles. 'I really don't think Dad's helicopter will get far with blades that look like sausages.'

We all laugh, and suddenly I feel bad that I want to leave. But I have to, because the cake is brilliant. This moment is brilliant. But brilliant never lasts for ever.

THE INTERVIEW

'Stop fidgeting.'

'I can't help it,' I say, pulling at my trousers. 'It's your mum's fault. She's taken them in so tight I'm getting a wedgie.'

Leah laughs.

'And it's not just that,' I say. 'I'm so nervous I can't stop shaking.'

'You'll be fine,' says Leah, peering over the top of the bush towards the bandstand. 'You look great. Just a shame you're wearing your trainers.'

'I'm lucky I got here at all,' I say. 'Reilly's mum caught me leaving the house in this suit.'

'What did you say?'

'I told her I was going to *Bugsy Malone* rehearsals.'

'Great thinking.' Leah grins. 'And . . .'

'And what?'

'You could say it back.' Leah holds her hands out by her side.

I shake my head, confused.

'My dress, Sam. Have you really not noticed? It's been an hour!'

'Oh, your dress,' I say, checking the bandstand again. Still no one. 'Yes, it's nice.' I turn back to Leah. 'It's very . . . yellow.'

'Is that the best you can do? It's the dress I wore when I was bridesmaid at Auntie Cheryl's wedding, and I had to plead with Mollie to borrow these shoes. You have no idea how hard it was trying to ride the bike.'

'Sorry,' I say quietly. 'It's just so horrible being this nervous. And excited. I got up and went to the loo three times in the night, and—'

'Shush.' Leah holds her hand up like we're robbers on a stake-out. 'Look.'

I look across the Downs. In front of us, some men are kicking a ball around, like they're waiting to play a game, and there's a group of women doing exercises while others run along the paths. But Leah's pointing at a man and a woman who have just got out of a blue car.

'Do you recognize them? Could they be from the agency?'

'I don't know,' I whisper. 'There must be quite a few of them, and some of the ones I do know have left. But I don't think anyone working for the foster agency would bring their dog.'

'Okay,' says Leah. 'What about them?' She points at another couple walking.

'I don't know.' I squirm. 'It's hard to tell. Maybe we should have got people to wear something, as a sign, like a red baseball cap – or carry a football under their left arm.'

Leah sits down and sighs. 'Perhaps we shouldn't have got here so early.'

'But it was your idea,' I say.

'I said *early* – I didn't mean a whole hour before.'

I shrug.

'It's okay.' Leah smiles sympathetically. 'I can see you're as jumpy as a rabbit. But there are only ten minutes left now,' she says, looking at her phone.

'Yeah.' I let out a deep breath and sit down beside Leah. I tell her what happened during the night. How one minute I was looking forward to it, the next I thought it was the worst idea in the world. I kept reminding myself of the list of things I would like to do with my perfect parents – living in a big house, having a new car, the holidays to Disneyland – but as the night went on I realized that even though all those things would be great, what I most looked forward to was just sitting at home on the sofa with them, eating crisps or chocolate while watching a film. I didn't care what flavour the crisps were, or what we were watching, I just wanted to do what normal kids do – sit down and watch TV with their parents.

I stop talking, look at Leah, wait for her to say I'm soppy. But she just says, 'That's lovely, but you know, once you're used to it, you'll probably spend all your time in your room like I do.'

'Yeah. But at least you know your parents will always be there if you change your mind.'

'True.' She nods, then kneels up. 'Come on. It's nearly time.'

I take a big gulp of air as I look across to the bandstand. There's a man pushing a girl round and round on her bike, like she's on a ride at the fair. And there's a woman sitting down on a seat, watching them. One couple? One couple, that's all that turned up.

I glance at Leah. She's got her bottom lip pushed out like she's as disappointed as me. Then she says, 'It only takes one sparrow to make a summer.'

'What does that mean?'

'Don't know, but my mum always says it when something's not as good as she'd hoped.' She starts walking towards the bandstand. Her dress does make her look smart and important, even if her sister's shoes make her wobble a bit.

I look over at the man and woman, at the little girl still cycling in circles.

'Maybe we should wait a bit longer,' I say.

'Sam.' Leah turns to me. 'I know you're nervous, but you can't back out now. If you want to be in *Bugsy*, we need to find your perfect parents before we go back to school.'

I take a deep breath. Leah's right – there'd be no point in going to all this trouble if I didn't go and at least talk to them. But I'd hoped at least ten would turn up so I had a choice. There's no choice if it's just one. It's like when Mr Whippy only serves vanilla ice cream. Then again, I'd rather have one than go without.

I reach into the jacket pocket and get out the notes I made when me and Leah googled 'How to meet people and make a good impression' last night.

1. Smile – to make people think I'm confident, but not too much or I'll look weird, like people in toothpaste adverts. Speak clearly, state name and reason why I'm meeting them, for example, 'I'm Sam – little c, big C – McCann. I'd like you to adopt me.' (Or something like that.)

2. Shake hands – to be polite.
3. Listen to the reply – people like people who listen.
4. Establish rapport – that means find a subject I think the person might be interested in, such as football, or holidays, or BMW M5s or Disneyland ☺
5. Pay the person a compliment – for example, 'I like the colour of your dress.'
6. Always keep eye contact while doing all of the above – it shows I am interested and not bored.

I keep reading as I walk. Without realizing it, I'm almost at the bandstand. I'm looking at the couple and using the last few seconds to decide what I think about them. The man is smiling, the woman is smiling, the little girl is laughing, and I'm still walking towards them with my heart thudding hard on every stride. *Do you have any other children?* I think, rehearsing my questions. *Yes*, I answer myself, *I can see you have one. Will we have to share a bedroom? No, we can't share a bedroom. I'm too old to share a bedroom with a girl.* The bandstand is just a few metres away. I wish I'd written the questions on my hands. *Do you like Nando's? Do you like* . . . The girl keeps cycling; the man and woman turn and look at me. He's smiling. She's smiling. First impressions count; the first thirty seconds count. I smile too. Have to be brave. Have to be . . .

'Have you got a BMW M5?' I blurt.

'Sorry?' the man says.

'No. No . . . I mean, hello.'

'Hello,' the couple say at the same time.

'Did . . . did . . . did you . . . Did you . . .'

The couple's smiles disappear. I've blown it. I've put them off in thirty seconds. I look at Leah for help.

'He wants to know if you've seen his leaflet,' she says.

The man shakes his head slowly. 'Leaflet?' he says, frowning. 'What leaflet?'

'The one about a boy wanting to find his parents,' I explain, finding my voice. 'It said to meet at the bandstand.'

'You've lost your parents?' says the woman. 'Do you want to call them?' She holds out a phone.

'No,' Leah jumps in. 'That's not what he meant. He wants to find perfect parents, like to get adopted.'

'Oh, well, no then.' The woman looks at the man like me and Leah are aliens landed from outer space.

'No.' The man shakes his head quickly. 'We were just . . . We were just bringing our little girl here. We do it every weekend.'

'Sorry,' I say. 'I just thought . . .'

The man and woman walk away. I look at Leah. This was a waste of time.

'It's okay,' she says.

'No, it's not.' My cheeks burn like I've been out in the sun all day. 'I feel stupid. I feel stupid in this suit.'

'You don't look it.' Leah smiles, trying to cheer me up. 'Besides, they wouldn't have been suitable anyway.'

'Why not?'

Leah nods at the man and woman as they walk to their car.

'They've got a Vauxhall Nova.'

'Oh.' I smile. 'Then they are definitely out.'

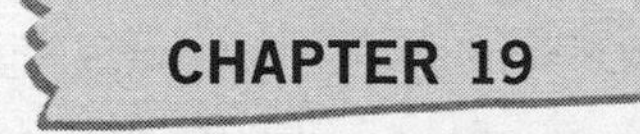

CHAPTER 19

WISH I HADN'T PUT NO GERBILS

The cans are tinkling on Eric, but it's the wind. I felt okay when I was with Leah, but now she's gone home it's hit me that I sent four hundred posters and not one person came. Should I have used my name on the poster? Was it my no-gerbils rule that put people off? Maybe there's just something wrong with me. Are my ears too big? Are my eyes too brown? Is it because I grin too much? People can find that off-putting. But I don't grin all the time, not if things are serious. I know I'm not grinning now.

I shuffle into a corner of Eric and pull a sheet of packing polystyrene and a flattened box over me to keep warm.

I'm never going to get adopted. Why did I even think that I might? I thought Jasmine was going to. She used to take me to watch Rovers with her, even bought us both shirts and hats. I loved that Jasmine liked football, but the thing I liked best was that we went to matches wearing the same clothes. I was eight and she told me she loved me, and wanted to adopt me. She spent loads of evenings on her computer, completing forms. We had to go to interviews together, just to check that everyone understood what was happening. I told them that I did understand, that I was going to be adopted, have a real parent, and she was going to look after me for the rest of my life. On the way home from the last meeting, we stopped off at Nando's for a treat. I thought it was to celebrate that all the paperwork was done. But the next morning I saw Rock Star Steve's car pull up outside, then heard him whispering with Jasmine in the hallway. Whispering isn't good. Whispering is bad. That's what I thought to myself as I heard Rock Star Steve's footsteps on the stairs. I got up off my bed, saw him standing in the doorway. And it was like the world had ended, because as I stood up the world suddenly went dark and Steve grabbed me, held me and I felt his heartbeat through my ear. Then I heard him say, 'I'm sorry, Sam.'

What did I do wrong?

What did I do wrong?

All I remember is seeing Jasmine hugging herself in the back garden as Steve guided me through the hall.

The wind whistles across the cans, jolts me all the way from Jasmine's to the alleyway where I'm sitting in Eric. I sink further down into the cardboard. It's no good. Making the leaflet was a stupid thing to do. What was the point in delivering them when nobody wants me? Maybe I shouldn't have been so fussy with the things I put on my poster. But I can't lie about the things I do and don't like. People take stuff back to the shop if they buy something and it doesn't do what it says on the box. I don't want my perfect parents to take me back, but I am thinking I might have stood a better chance of meeting someone if I hadn't put no gerbils.

CHAPTER 20

THE PERFECT PARENT PROJECT STAGE TWO

I'm in Reilly's bedroom. This evening is supposed to be the family meeting where I sit with Reilly and his mum and dad and we tell each other what has been good and what has been bad. We have them every two weeks, but hopefully it'll be cancelled because Reilly's dad isn't here. I hope so, because after the disappointment at the Downs, all I want to do is message Leah.

Four hundred leaflets, I type, and not one reply, not one person turned up. I feel like stopping already.

What! No! I'll call you.

Don't feel like talking, and Reilly's mum will hear anyway.

Does she suspect anything?

Don't think so. Just asked me lots of questions about Bugsy Malone when I got back. She thinks it's brilliant that I'm interested in doing the play.

It is.

Yeah. Just a shame I won't be around.

You're being pessimistic.

Realistic ☹☹

I sigh. Leah's only trying to help but even my best friend doesn't understand how I feel. Wanting real parents is something I think about all the time: in bed, at school, on the way home, then in bed again. And it's horrible when you build your hopes up and they get trodden on. It's like when I got picked as goalkeeper for the Wilton Primary School football team. I went to practice for three weeks, then I got moved before the first match. Yesterday was like that, only a hundred times worse.

You still there?

Yes.

It's not fair, but if you give up it just means that they win.

Who?

I don't know. The agency? Rock Star Steve?

Rock Star Steve's okay.

'Sam, are you coming down? We're waiting.'

Got to go, Reilly's mum just shouted.

Don't go yet. I haven't told you my plan.

What plan?

Just bring a bucket and sponge and I'll meet you on the corner of my road tomorrow.

What?

Trust me. I'm a genius! We've done the leaflets. This is the Perfect Parent Project Stage Two.

I smile at my phone even though Leah can't see. It's like she wants me to stay as much as I do.

Okay, I type. What do I tell Reilly's mum?

Easy. Just say you're doing a school project with me.

'Sam . . .' Reilly runs into the room with an iPad in his hands and taps me on my shoulder. 'Dad says he'll help us do the Spitfire now.'

I sit up. 'But we've got a family meeting,' I say.

'Don't worry about that, Sam, another time.' Reilly's dad smiles at me from the iPad with his glasses on.

I don't know why the meeting is cancelled, I'm just glad it is.

'So, how are you doing?'

'I'm okay,' I say.

'Bug, the screen's moving a lot. Let Sam hold the iPad.'

'All right,' says Reilly. 'Shall I get the box with the Spitfire?'

'Yeah, Bug.' Reilly's dad grins. 'You go get the box.'

I love that Reilly has a special nickname that only his dad uses. I wish I had one but I need to find a dad first.

Reilly hands me the iPad, then bombs out of the room.

I look back at the screen. Reilly's dad must have just finished work because he's wearing a blue RAF shirt without a tie. I try to think of something to say to him, but he's away so much that whenever I see him it's like meeting him all over again. But luckily he always seems to be able to think of something to say to me.

'So what have you been up to?' he asks.

'Not much,' I say.

'Not much? Hasn't Bug been keeping you busy on computer games?'

'Yeah.' I smile nervously. 'Every day.'

'And what about school? Made any new friends?'

'Not really.'

'It'll come, Sam.' Reilly's dad rubs his hand over his face. 'It's always difficult at first. Even I find it hard whenever I get moved to new places.'

'Yeah,' I say. 'But at least you get to fly real planes, not computer ones.'

Reilly's dad chuckles. He's not as much fun as Brad was, but when he looks at me, he seems interested in what I'm saying.

‘I hear you’ve put your name down for the school play.’

‘Yeah,’ I say. ‘*Bugsy Malone*. I’m not sure I’ll get a part though.’

‘As long as you try, that’s all that counts.’

Reilly bombs back into the room.

‘Found it,’ he says. ‘Mum says we’ve got to put the wrapper in the bin, and make sure we don’t leave any pieces on the floor.’

‘I’m sure we can do that,’ says Reilly’s dad. ‘Got to keep Mum happy.’ He winks at me and I grin. At least he’s not a member of the fun police like Reilly’s mum. ‘So, boys, let’s have a go at making this Spitfire, shall we?’

I kneel down on the floor, resting the iPad against the bedside cabinet, so Reilly’s dad can see what we’re doing.

Reilly picks the tape on the box. I think maybe his dad will tell him to hurry up, but he just smiles patiently. I know Reilly misses his dad, but I never realized how much his dad misses him.

Reilly sits back on his heels, like he’s given up.

‘Maybe let Sam do it, Bug.’

‘Yeah.’ Reilly hands me the box. ‘You do it, Sam.’

‘Just pick it at the end – there’s a tab sticking out, like this.’ Reilly’s dad reaches out of picture, then a box appears.

‘You got the same one!’ says Reilly excitedly.

His dad laughs. ‘Of course, Bug. I thought the three of us could do it together. Just be careful with the glue – you don’t want it all in your hair, like when we did the Harrier Jump Jet. It was everywhere, Sam. He had to have a buzz cut like mine to get it out.’

‘And Mum got mad with you because it was too short,’ says Reilly.

I smile as I take the cellophane off the box. I like hearing stories about Reilly – they are nearly always funny, like when he pooed his pants in Tesco, and when he mistook a stranger for his dad and followed him up the escalator at the airport. It makes me think what it might be like to have a real dad and go on holiday with him. I wouldn't lose—

'Ready, Sam?' Reilly's dad makes me jump out of my thought.

'Yes.' I open the box and see all the grey pieces of plastic inside.

'Just pull the parts away from the frame gently,' he says. 'You too, Bug, only don't go sticking any of them up your nose this time.'

We all laugh.

Reilly's dad doesn't match many of the things on my perfect parent list – he wears glasses and he looks nothing like me for a start. Plus he doesn't have a BMW M5. But I'd love to have a dad to build things with, and play with, but most of all I'd love to have a dad who cares about his son as much as Reilly's dad does. As I arrange all the parts in a line on the rug, like Reilly's dad has in his room, I hope that maybe I will find someone like him tomorrow.

CHAPTER 21

WASHING CARS

'Do you think this will work?'

'Of course,' says Leah. 'You love cars, and people need their cars washed. What could go wrong?'

'Everything,' I say.

Leah shakes her head as we push our bikes onto the Downs with all the posh houses around its edge. When Leah said bring a bucket and a sponge, I didn't think she meant this. And I'm not sure it'll work because surely anyone who lives here has chauffeurs or professional valets to clean their cars, not two eleven-year-old kids with buckets and sponges hanging from their handlebars.

We rest next to a postbox and I try to pick a house, but it's hard when most of them are surrounded by walls with big gates.

How am I going to meet prospective parents when I can't get in? But I have to, because after seeing Reilly with his dad on the iPad last night, it's made me want to find my perfect parents even more. It was hard to get out this morning though. I think Reilly's mum believed me when I said I was meeting Leah to do a school project, but she did tell me not to be gone too long.

'Ah! Look at her.' Leah nudges my arm. 'She's so cute.'

I look behind me, where a little girl is holding onto the strings of a kite, a woman beside her.

'Ready?' says the woman.

The girl nods. The woman throws the kite into the air. It catches in the wind, dipping left and right. 'Pull the string, Amelia,' the woman shouts. 'Pull the string.'

Amelia pulls the string and takes a step backwards. The kite darts up and down.

The little girl takes another step and trips. For a moment I think she's going to fall over, but then the woman bends down and catches her in her arms. The kite smashes into the ground.

'Again,' says Amelia, grinning. 'Again.'

I remember trying to fly a kite. I remember watching it fly up in front of a tower block. It was with my mum, but I don't know when or where. There was a red slide, and a see-saw and some swings. And someone else was there. I don't know who. But sometimes when I think about it at night, I can hear my mum's voice shouting, 'Yes, Sammy. Yes, Sammy!' and then laughing. And I walked backwards as the kite zipped around in the sky. One step, then another, until the grass ran out and I was standing on concrete and I fell and let go of the kite. I don't remember hitting the ground, but I've still got the scar, right here, at the back of my head, a ridge where I had six stitches.

'You all right, Sam?'

I take my hand down from my head and see Leah looking right at me. 'Yeah,' I say. 'I was just thinking.'

'You were miles away.'

'Yeah,' I say. 'I was.'

'So which one shall we start with?' Leah points at the houses. 'The one with the Range Rover?'

'No, we won't be able to reach the roof. I was thinking that one.'

I nod at a man wearing a blue shirt and jeans who's walking around a car in a driveway. Just the sight of the car gets my heart thumping.

'Good choice,' says Leah. 'He looks the right age. And his hair is the same colour as yours.'

'It's not that,' I say. 'He's got a BMW M5!'

'Sam!' Leah shakes her head.

'Plus this one doesn't have electronic gates.' I push my bike forward. 'So what do we say to him?'

'We?' asks Leah, surprised.

'Yes. You're coming, aren't you?'

'No, Sam,' she says. 'You've got to do this on your own.'

I panic at the thought of that. 'But you're good at talking to people. All my words will come out wrong.'

'Don't overthink it – if you can act on stage in front of loads of people, you can talk to *one* person. Besides, it's you who's searching for perfect parents, not me. And if I did go, they're *bound* to like me more.'

'Thanks a lot.'

'No worries.' Leah grins. 'I'm going to message Hattie for a bit. Oh no!'

'What?'

‘I’ve only got five per cent battery.’

‘At least that will stop you sending so many messages,’ I say.

‘Yeah, I suppose. Here, take my bucket and sponge too. Makes it look like you’re a doubly hard worker.’

I hang Leah’s bucket on my handlebars and take a deep breath.

‘Okay. Wish me luck.’

My feet crunch on the gravel as I walk up the drive. The man has walked down the side of his house, but he’s left the gate open like he’s going to come back. I keep walking. *This is it, Sam*, I think to myself. *There’s no turning back.*

I stop by the car. I’ve only stood this close to a BMW M5 in a Tesco car park. Its top speed is limited to 154 miles per hour, but it can do 190, and it does 0–60 in 3.1 seconds. At least that’s what it said in one of Reilly’s dad’s car magazines. I rest my bike on the gravel, then peer through the driver’s window. It’s got leather seats and paddle shifters, so you don’t have to take your hands off the steering wheel to change gear. And there’s—

‘Can I help you?’

I jump and spin around. The man walks across the gravel towards me with a cup of coffee in his hand.

‘Umm . . . Umm . . . Y-yes . . .’ I stammer. ‘I was just . . .’

‘You’ve been watching the house.’ The man nods across the road, towards where Leah is sitting. ‘You and your friend.’

‘Ah . . . Yes,’ I say. ‘We’ve been . . . I mean, I’ve been . . . Do you want your car washed?’ I blurt.

The man takes a sip of his coffee. I try to think of something to say to fill the silence.

'It's a nice car,' I say.

'It is.'

'Top speed it's allowed to do is a hundred and fifty-four miles per hour and it does nought to sixty in three point one seconds.'

'Sounds more like you're going to drive it than wash it,' says the man.

'Sorry.' I smile. 'I just like cars. Especially BMW M5s.'

'Well, you've certainly come prepared.' The man nods at my two buckets. 'What are you raising money for?'

'Sorry?'

'I'm guessing you're fundraising. We get Scouts round here raising money for trips or sometimes for Comic Relief.'

'Oh.' My brain scrambles for thoughts. 'It's for the school library. Yes, the school library. We don't have many books.'

The man makes an *mmm* sound, like he's trying to work me out. 'You're quite young to be doing it on your own.'

'I'm twelve,' I lie. 'I just need to grow a bit more, and I came with a friend.'

I point at Leah. She smiles, waves, then looks back at her phone.

The man nods. 'Okay,' he suddenly says. 'It is for a good cause, and the car does need doing. How much do you want?'

'Umm.' I look at the car. 'I don't know really. I hadn't thought about that.'

The man smiles. 'Well, you're not going to get many books if you don't charge any money. Tell you what, I'll provide the water and shampoo, and I'll pay you five pounds. Deal?'

'Deal.' I nod.

'Good,' he says. 'I'll go and get the stuff.' He goes to walk round the side of the house, then suddenly stops.

'What's your name, by the way?'

'Sam,' I say. 'Sam – little c, big C – McCann.'

The man smiles. 'Well, Sam,' he says. 'Just give me a few minutes.' He walks away and my phone buzzes in my pocket.

Yes, Sam ☺

I glance across at Leah.

He seems nice.

Yes, I reply.

☺☺ Wahoo! ☺

I hear the crunch of gravel.

Got to go, catch you later.

The man comes around the side of the house with a bottle of car shampoo in one hand and dragging a hose with the other.

'Here,' he says. 'You'll need this.'

'Thanks,' I say, looking at the end of the hose. I've no idea what to do as I've never cleaned a car before.

The man looks at me like he's guessed this. He points the nozzle of the hose into the bucket. 'Just twist it. And when you rinse, make sure you aim it at the car otherwise you'll get soaked. Oh, and only use two capfuls of shampoo at a time.'

Washing a car suddenly feels complicated.

The man rubs his hands. 'Right,' he says. 'I'll leave you to it. I'll be back out in about half an hour.'

'Okay.' As he walks away, I reach down and turn on the hose. I fill the bucket with water, and look at the car. Where do I start? The back, the front, the doors or the wheels? I'm too small to reach the roof, but maybe the man will help me when he comes back out. I pour some shampoo in the bucket, then turn off the hose. Still don't know where to start. I message Leah.

Do I start at the top or the bottom?

No idea . . . Just do the bits that are dirty ☺

Thanks, that helps!

I put my phone in my pocket and look at the car again. The wheels. I'll start with the wheels. I soak the sponge and begin cleaning. I'm not getting to know the man but at least this is a start. It's like when I meet someone for the first time. I don't talk to them loads straight away. I just stay quiet, try to decide if I like them, and then if I do, I talk, and if I still like them they might become my friend. It must be the same if you're looking for a new parent.

As I scrub another wheel, I glance around the garden. It would be great to live here, and to run around on the grass. It's big enough to play tag, even hide and seek. It would take ages for anyone to find me in the bushes or behind the trees. As I carry the bucket to the next wheel, I notice the man through the window. He's looking right at me as he talks on the phone. He waves. I wave back, then bend down, start to scrub another wheel. Who is he talking to? I scrub the wheel. Has he seen the poster I delivered last week? Has he worked out that it is me? But why's he on the phone? I didn't put a phone number down. Could he be calling the police, or the foster agency? I glance up again. The man is still talking but it could be to anyone. If Leah was here, she'd say I'm overreacting, that I have to trust people sometimes.

The man turns away from the window. I stand up and look around the garden again. It's as big as I've ever wanted, with a nice car just like I imagined, and the man seemed friendly. I wish he wasn't on the phone. I wish . . .

I wish I knew whether to stay or run.

The gate latch clicks open. He said he'd be back in half an hour and it's only been five minutes. I can't risk getting into trouble with the authorities and getting moved again. Reilly's mum is a pain, but I like Reilly, and school. And I want be in *Bugsy Malone*, and still be able to see Leah. Suddenly there are lots of reasons I don't want to move.

'Sam!' The man comes around the corner.

I can't . . . I can't . . .

I drop the sponge, grab my bike and run.

CHAPTER 22

THE RAINBOW HOUSES

The rainbow houses glisten in the sun. I've been here for two hours. So far, I've sat on the swings, sat at the bottom of the slide, walked round the edge of the park ten times and stopped by four gates. But I still haven't plucked up enough courage to walk up someone's path and knock on their front door and say, 'Hey, I'm Sam McCann, can I wash your car?' Washing cars is even harder than making first impressions and introducing myself. I smiled at the woman who walked by with her black Labrador. I smiled at the man who jogged past in a Rovers shirt and I smiled at the man and woman who came along the path pushing their baby in a pram. I've smiled and smiled and smiled, even though I don't feel like that inside.

After I ran from the man with the BMW M5, I cycled as fast as I could away from The Clift, past Leah. I thought she'd follow, but when I finally decided I was safe and looked behind me, she was nowhere to be seen. I was going to sneak back to The Clift but I was scared there might be police circling round in their cars. Maybe I was stupid to think the man would call the police. I overreacted. He was probably just talking to his partner, checking what time they would be home, like Reilly's mum does with his dad.

That's when I started cycling again. I was aiming to get back to the cycle track, but somehow ended up in Montville, where me and Leah delivered the rest of my posters.

I check my phone for the tenth time. Leah hasn't even seen my messages. She's either busy chatting to Hattie or her battery must have died. I wish she was here now, so we could talk about what just happened. I was stupid to think that a posh person from The Clift would want to adopt me. But maybe I've got more of a chance with the rainbow houses. They are nothing like the houses on my top ten things list. They aren't massive with big driveways and swimming pools, and they don't have huge gardens. They're arranged around a large square of grass, like they share it, because they've only got space for dustbins and a bike outside the front doors. They don't have a garage either, so definitely no basketball hoop.

There aren't any cars from my list here either, just Ford Focuses and Volkswagen Golfs, white vans and pickup trucks.

I check my phone again. Still no reply from Leah. The tick hasn't turned to green.

Over by the red house, an old woman walks into the park with a little white Scottie dog. She lets it off the lead and the dog sniffs round trees and bins as she walks slowly along the path towards me. She might not have a car to wash, and she's *definitely* too old to be my mum, but it doesn't hurt to practise my first impressions.

The Scottie dog sniffs the bench, then edges towards my feet. I put my hands in my pockets. Scottie dogs seem friendly, but it's hard to tell because their tails are too short to wag.

'It's all right.' The old lady stops beside me. 'He doesn't bite.'

I smile nervously.

'His name's George,' the old lady says.

It's ages since I googled it, but my list about first impressions flashes through my head: *Smile, shake hands, listen to the reply, build rapport.*

I reach down cautiously and rub George's head.

'Hi, George,' I say clearly.

'You look like you've been busy.' The old lady nods at my buckets.

'Yeah,' I say. 'I've been washing cars. I was thinking of cleaning some round here.'

'Well.' The old lady smiles. 'There are plenty to choose from.'

I look at the cars and try to think of what to say next. What was on the list? Number five. Pay a compliment.

'I like your blue coat,' I blurt.

'Oh, bless you,' the old lady says. 'It's an old mac I wear when I come here. This is where I met my George. We'd sit on the bench over there nearly every day before he died.'

'But he's not dead,' I say, tickling George under his chin.

'Oh no, my love,' the old lady chuckles. 'I meant my husband George. I miss him a lot. That's why I got this George. He doesn't replace him, but at least I still get to say his name every day. My children think I'm silly.' She looks at the sky, like George might be up there. 'Anyway,' she says, looking back at me. 'I suppose I'd best get on. Looks like it might rain again.'

I peer up as a dark cloud creeps over the top of the rainbow houses. I've not cleaned a car but at least I've spoken to someone, even if the lady now has a sad look on her face. It's like she misses someone in her life as much as I want someone in mine.

The old lady shuffles past me, then bends down and puts the lead on George.

'I don't think you're silly,' I say.

'What's that?' she says, turning around.

'You said your children think you're silly . . . for calling your dog George. But I don't think you are.'

'Aw, thank you, my love . . . What's your name?'

'Sam – little c, big C – McCann, but you can call me Sam.'

The old lady smiles again. 'Well, nice to meet you, Sam – little c, big C – McCann. I'm Mrs Shepherd. Maybe I'll see you again.'

'Hope so.' I smile back. I might have got my list a bit backwards, but I think I've just found my perfect gran.

My phone buzzes in my pocket. Leah? No, Reilly's mum. What can she want? She'll be checking on me again.

I sigh.

Hi Sam. We've got meatballs for tea. Be home for five. We're going to the beach tomorrow if the weather's still okay!

The beach, that's all I need. The last time we went to Swanage there were traffic jams, and Reilly felt sick when we reached a windy bit of the road. We had to keep pulling over to check he was okay. His mum said it was because he'd had too much milk with his Frosties that morning, but I think it was the Haribo we'd been eating because I could see all the pink bits in the gravel when he was sick in a layby. His mum told me off for laughing, but I wasn't, it was just my grin getting me into trouble again.

Reilly was okay when we got there. We had a picnic on the beach, and we played cricket with a group of other kids and their parents. I scored twelve runs until I whacked the ball too high and Reilly's dad caught it. Someone shouted, 'Hard luck,' and when I handed the bat to the next man, he rubbed my head and said, 'Hey, you need to have a word with your dad, and get him to drop it next time!'

He was smiling, but when I snapped back, 'He's not my dad!' he stopped and gave me a weird look. I think Reilly's dad must have heard me because he was shaking his head, but I didn't care. 'Well, you're not,' I said under my breath. I walked off along the beach while they kept playing. Out the corner of my eye I saw Reilly's mum coming after me, checking I didn't go too far. Being a foster-kid is like being kept on a hundred-metre leash, with someone watching you all the time.

My pocket buzzes again. I think it's Reilly's mum wanting a reply but it's a message from Leah.

Hey, sorry. Battery dead. Lost you when you cycled off.

Thought so.

I'm home now. What happened?

Long story. Tell you when I see you. I'm at the rainbow houses ☺

What are you doing there?

Trying to wash cars, of course.

Good luck x

Thanks.

I look at the houses. I've been here so long that people are coming home from work, looking for spaces to park. This would be a good time to ask if they want their cars washed. That way, I wouldn't have to knock on doors. I pick up my bike. My front tyre squelches on the tarmac – a puncture, that's all I need. I cross the road.

A man gets out of a blue Peugeot. He glances at me. *This is it*, I think. I could ask now: 'Hi, my name's Sam. Would you like me to wash your car?' The man reaches into the boot, pulls out two bags of shopping and jams a huge pack of toilet roll under his arm.

I stop my bike.

'Hi,' I say. 'W . . . w . . . would you like me to wash your car?'

The man glances at my buckets, then walks towards his house.

'Not now, mate,' he says. 'I'm a bit busy.' He kicks the gate closed and goes inside.

My face burns up with embarrassment, but at least I finally asked. There are more people arriving home all the time. Getting out of cars I'm too tired to clean, walking into houses with doors I'm too nervous to knock on. The Perfect Parent Project was a great idea, but I didn't think it would be this hard!

I wheel my bike along the pavement in front of the houses, glancing into windows as I pass. Most of the front rooms are empty except for an old man at number 28, sitting in his chair with a cup of tea as he watches TV. Three windows later an old lady sits doing the same. No perfect parents but enough perfect grandparents to fill a football team. At the next window, number 36, I see a boy sitting on a sofa, looking at his phone. I stop. He looks about the same age as me, doing what I do – sitting in front of the TV with his phone. I wonder what he's playing, maybe Minecraft Parkour or Sushi Monster, or perhaps he's messaging a friend. I walk slowly past, watching him as I go. It must be a game because his thumbs are pressing the buttons like he's getting ready to run and jump four blocks. Then suddenly he stops and looks up. I back away, crouch down behind a wheelie bin, then peer over the top. A man wearing a blue sweatshirt walks into the room, holding a parcel, then a woman follows behind, carrying a cake with candles. It must be his mum and dad. The boy's face cracks into a smile. His mum and dad open their mouths. The candles flicker and light their faces. I'm too far away to hear but I can tell they are singing 'Happy Birthday'. I imagine them in my head. I smile. Imagine I am the boy. Imagine them singing my name.

Happy birthday to you,
Happy birthday to you,
Happy birthday, dear Sam,
Happy birthday to you.

The boy stands up and blows out the candles. His mum puts the cake down and gives him a hug. I feel warm, like she's just hugged me. It's a perfect family – a perfect family that I've only seen in films or sitting around a table in one of Reilly's mum's cooking magazines.

The boy looks up at his dad. His dad bends down, ruffles the boy's hair, hands him the parcel. *I think this is what you want.* The boy smiles. *Yes, I think this is what he wants.*

A square box wrapped in blue paper.

I know that box.

I know what's in there.

It's the same as the one Reilly was given at Christmas.

It's the same box that Daniel had in the house I was in before that.

It's an Xbox One.

The boy pulls excitedly at the paper.

It's an Xbox One, I say to myself.

The boy throws the last piece of paper on the floor.

'It's an Xbox One!' he shouts.

See. Told you.

COVERING MY TRACKS

'So how was the Roman Empire?' asks Reilly's mum.

'What?'

'Your project, with Leah.'

'Oh,' I say. 'It was good.'

'Did you know they invented concrete?'

'No,' I say. 'We haven't got to that stuff yet. We're just doing the bit about baths and colosseums.' I stuff a forkful of spaghetti in my mouth, hoping I don't look guilty. 'Leah says hi.'

'That's nice,' says Reilly's mum. 'But, Sam, please try not to talk with a mouthful of food. And, Reilly, don't wipe your mouth with your sleeve.'

'Okay, I'll use Sam's then?' Reilly reaches across the table for my arm.

'No, don't be silly. Use kitchen roll.'

Good one, Reilly. We exchange smirks then shovel more spaghetti.

I want to go to Reilly's bedroom and message Leah about the boy in the rainbow houses, but now Reilly's mum has asked one question, there's bound to be more.

'So how was Leah?'

'Okay,' I say.

'It's good you spend time with her. You should invite her round. I've only seen her once since parents' evening, and that was just a flying visit when she dropped off the books you'd left at school.'

I stop eating. 'Why?'

Reilly's mum smiles. 'Well, you know. You obviously like her because you spend a lot of time—'

'We're just friends,' I cut her off. It's like she wants to know about everything in my life.

'Mum, Sam—'

Reilly's mum frowns. 'Not now, Reilly, I'm talking to Sam.'

'But . . .'

'I said, not now, Reilly. And don't talk with your mouth full, either.'

Reilly chomps on his spaghetti. For a moment I think he's derailed his mum's thoughts but she's like a snake with her questions, circling around me, closing in, waiting to take a bite . . .

'Maybe she could come for tea one night, Sam.'

There.

'What do you think?'

'Yeah and she could play Ace Pilot with us,' says Reilly.

'No,' says his mum. 'They'll be doing their project. What was it on again, Sam?'

'You know what it's on,' I snap. 'I told you, Romans.'

'Sam! There's no need to be rude.'

'Well, you want to know everything.'

'Mum?'

'Not now, Reilly.'

'But I want to tell you. Sam said I look like a jellyfish.'

Reilly's mum shakes her head. 'Well, that's nice, Reilly,' she says. 'But I need Sam to know I only ask where he is because I care.'

'That's what you always say.'

'I know,' says Reilly's mum. 'But it's my job to know you're safe.'

'Well, I am,' I say. 'I was just with Leah, doing our project.' I put my knife and fork down and push my chair away from the table.

'Okay, okay,' says Reilly's mum. 'I didn't say I didn't believe you, but you know how it is. I have to do the diary at the end of every day. I can't just put, "Sam went out and I never saw him all day." How would that make me look?'

'Like you don't care,' I mumble.

'Exactly,' says Reilly's mum. 'And we do care – Tom and I both do. I know how it must feel, like we're checking on you all the time. It can't be nice.'

'It isn't,' I say.

'No,' Reilly's mum says softly. She stares at me for a long time, then says, 'Sam, are you okay?'

I nod.

'Only you seem a little . . .'

'I'm fine,' I say, looking at my plate. I've still got some spaghetti left but I don't want to sit here. It's like being in the hot seat at drama club. I glance up at Reilly, hoping that any minute he'll blurt out,

'Can we play Ace Pilot?' and get me away from the table. But he just keeps eating and his mum keeps staring at me. I look at my plate, then around the room, anywhere but her – at the picture of Reilly and his mum and dad on the log flume at Thorpe Park, and the one of Reilly grinning with a Winnie-the-Pooh rucksack on his back taken by the front door on his first day at school. At the notches on the door where his dad measures him when he comes home. It's all Reilly, Reilly, Reilly. We're even eating Reilly's favourite food – meatballs. There are no pictures of me because no one ever takes them, and I don't have any notches on the door because I move before anyone can make a mark, and I don't have favourite food because it tastes different in every house. I bet the boy at the rainbow houses doesn't get this. I bet he doesn't get interrogated with twenty questions when he gets home every night.

Reilly's mum continues eating but I can still sense her looking at me, like she's wondering what I'm thinking. And for a moment I think of telling her about the pictures, and the food, and the notches on the door. But what would she say? That I could make notches too, if that would make me feel better? But it isn't her job to make me feel better, and even if I did mark my height, she'd use a pencil so she could wipe it off after I'm gone. Maybe none of that matters anyway, because I might just have found my perfect parents at the rainbow houses.

Reilly's mum puts her knife and fork down on her plate.

Here it comes. Another question.

'Sam?' There, I knew it. 'Have you ever been to the Roman Baths?'

'No,' I say.

'Would you like to go during the holiday?'

I shrug.

'Is it in Disneyland?' asks Reilly.

Oh brilliant, Reilly. I choke on my spaghetti.

'No, Reilly.' His mum picks up her plate. 'It's not in Disneyland. It's in Bath.'

Reilly's head moves from side to side like he's swinging his legs under the table.

'So is that a yes, Sam? Maybe when Reilly's dad gets back?'

'I don't know,' I say. 'I've got things to do. I'm going to Lewis's house to practise *Bugsy*.'

'Come on, Sam,' says Reilly excitedly. 'Let's go swimming. We can go on the inflatable whale.'

'It's not that sort of bath,' says his mum with a smile, then she looks at me and says, 'It's nice you're doing things, but don't forget me and Reilly would like to see you too.' She picks up her plate and stands.

'Can me and Sam play Ace Pilot now?' Reilly jumps down from the table.

'Yes!' I see my chance to escape at last. 'Come on, Reilly, let's go.'

'Don't you want dessert?'

'No,' me and Reilly shout as we bomb out of the door.

'Okay, but only half an hour,' says his mum from the kitchen. 'And, Sam?'

'Yeah?'

'Don't forget Steve is coming by in the morning.'

Ace Pilot starts to load as I sit on the bottom bunk. Reilly's kneeling down in front of me, fingers twitching, getting ready to select his weapons.

I message Leah.

Hey, I think I found them! The perfect family.

No way! Do you really think so?

Could be. Saw a boy opening an Xbox.

You can't choose someone because of an Xbox!

Wasn't just that.

What did they look like?

I try to remember what they looked like, but I was too focused on the boy and his Xbox to notice. I do remember his dad was wearing a blue sweatshirt, and I think he had dark hair like mine, and his mum's hair was tied back in a ponytail.

They looked nice, I type.

Just nice?

I was watching the boy.

Okay, so if they're nice, we need to get you back there. Tomorrow?

Can't. Lewis messaged to ask me to go to his for Bugsy. I've actually got to go this time or Reilly's mum will get suspicious and not let me go anywhere.

Okay, day after.

Yeah. But what are we going to do?

Don't worry. Leave it with me ☺

'Sam.' Reilly turns around. 'Can you help me again?'

'Yes.' I smile. 'Sit beside me and watch.'

Reilly jumps up and sits down next to me on the bunk. He doesn't care that his knee touches mine, or that his elbow is digging into my belly. He doesn't think that he's too close, or can't ever hug me. I'm glad he hasn't read the foster-parent rule book.

I press play. Reilly rests his head on my shoulder. I want to rest mine against his but I'm not sure I should. *I do like you Reilly*, I think to myself. I'm glad you have your perfect family. I do want to play Ace Pilot, and I do want to go places with you, but I hope you don't mind that I'd like to find my perfect family too.

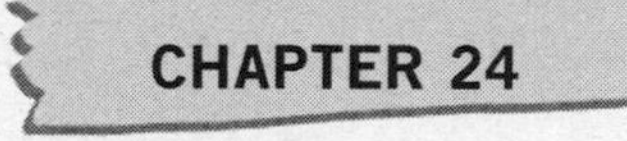

ROCK STAR STEVE *IS* A ROCK STAR

'She's only trying to help, Sam,' says Rock Star Steve.

I watch the wipers flick back and forth in his car.

'She's poking her nose in,' I say, nodding at Reilly's house. 'I bet she's watching us now. She wants to know where I am all the time. That's the only reason she wants me to go to the Roman Baths with them.'

'I'm sure it's not,' says Rock Star Steve.

'It is,' I say. 'Anyway, I told her you'd take me.'

'To the Roman Baths?'

'Yeah, but we don't actually have to go. I just said it.'

'Well, we could, of course,' Rock Star Steve says brightly. 'But maybe you should give Sarah a chance, mate. And try not to get so worked up. I mean, we can all get angry and frustrated, but we have to know when to stop.'

‘I know.’

‘So what are you going to do?’

‘Say I’m sorry?’ I look across at Rock Star Steve.

‘Well, I think that would be a good start,’ he says. ‘But you’ve got to mean it.’

‘But it’s not like they really care,’ I say.

‘You know, Sam.’ Rock Star Steve gives me his serious look. ‘Sarah and Tom *do* like you – they don’t just look after you because it’s a job.’

‘That’s what you always say.’

‘I’m saying it because it’s true. Only you’re getting too emotional and angry to see it. You have to stop thinking they don’t care, that they see you as a burden. Yeah?’ Rock Star Steve stops talking and looks at me like he means it.

I stare out of the windscreen, watching the wiper blades flick. Rock Star Steve doesn’t go quiet very often, but when he does, I know it’s to give me time to think. We meet like this once a week. Sometimes we’ll be in Starbucks, or Nando’s, or just walking in a park, but today we went for a drive and now we’re sitting outside Reilly’s house with the rain pouring down. Rock Star Steve is only trying to help, just as he’s done for four years. He helped by taking me to the cinema when I left Brad and Angie’s. And he helped by meeting me every day for a week when Ralph and Jean let me go. He can be serious, sometimes, but he makes me laugh too, even if it’s just me smiling at his snakeskin shoes. But we’re not laughing or smiling now. Rock Star Steve said Reilly’s mum and dad like me, but I’m not sure I believe him, and even if I did trust them, just for one second, they’d change their minds, and I’d have to start trying to trust someone all over again.

I glance up at Reilly's bedroom window. For all I know, Reilly's mum could be in there packing up my stuff right now. I look across at Rock Star Steve.

'Are you going to move me?' I say quietly. 'Because if you are, can I say goodbye to Reilly? Or could I move somewhere close, so I can come back and visit him?'

Rock Star Steve shakes his head slowly and smiles.

'No, Sam.' He turns to me. 'You're not being moved. That's not what this is about. This is about helping you realize that some people want to keep you. Some people actually like Sam – little c, big C – McCann and don't want to let him go.'

I smile. I like it when he calls me that; it makes me feel warm inside, like I'm special. Maybe that's what Reilly feels when his dad calls him Bug.

'See.' He reaches over and rubs my hair. 'That's the Sam I know. You've got to keep that smile, mate. It's much easier than frowning. It takes forty-three muscles to frown, but only seventeen to smile.'

'Is that true?' I ask.

'Yes. So do more of it.'

'Yeah,' I say. 'I'll try.'

'Good man. Now there is something else I'd like to chat to you about.'

'What, another thing?' I say defensively.

'No.' Rock Star Steve holds his hand up to calm me. 'It's nothing serious. It's just I've been talking to Gemma ... You remember Gemma?'

'Yes, she's the one I did the life stories with last year. I said I didn't want to do it again.'

'Yes, I know,' says Rock Star Steve. 'But you're a year older now, and I thought maybe we could try again. Revisiting your life story might help you find out a little bit more about yourself, help you understand what's going on.'

'No.' I shake my head. 'I don't want to. I've tried three times now, and it doesn't help.'

'I know it didn't go great last time, but Gemma could help you. Even revisiting a few little things – pictures, memories of the past – might help you settle at home.'

I glance out of the window, then look back at Rock Star Steve. 'I did think about something the other day,' I say.

'Really, what was that?'

'I was somewhere, and I saw a girl flying a kite. I think I had a kite once, and I walked backwards and fell off a wall.'

Rock Star Steve nods, like he just made a note in his head. 'See, Sam. That's exactly the sort of thing Gemma can help you with. Shall we give it a go?'

'No,' I say.

'Well, don't just say no. Have a think about it.' Rock Star Steve looks at me for a long time. 'Remember, it's not just about finding out about your parents, it's about finding out little bits about yourself.'

I nod. I'll think about it, but I'm still not saying yes. I stare out of the windscreen though the rain. I've thought about finding out more about my parents loads of times. Sometimes I want to know everything, but sometimes I don't want to know anything, because Mum stopped seeing me, and I never knew my dad. Why should I want to know anything about them if they don't want anything to do with me?

Rock Star Steve leans forward and presses the air-con button to demist the windscreen.

'You don't have to say now. But just think . . . Anyway,' he suddenly says brightly. 'I hear someone's about to be in a musical!'

'How do you know?' I turn to him.

'Sarah told me.'

'Oh, of course.' I sigh.

'Sam, she wasn't talking behind your back. She told me you'd got a suit, and I asked why. That's how it came out. So tell me about it. Come on!'

'Well, it's true.' I feel my face light up. 'I'm going to be in *Bugsy Malone*, or at least I think I am. I'm going to a friend's house this morning to practise and we've got the auditions the week after the holidays.'

'That's brilliant.' Rock Star Steve nods. 'I'm really pleased.'

'Me too,' I say. 'I googled it last night. I wanted to watch the film but it cost five pounds to download, so I found a script instead.'

'Well done.' Rock Star Steve smiles. 'You'll love it. I did.'

'You did *Bugsy*?'

'No, not *Bugsy*, but I used to be in plays and musicals at school.'

'Really?'

'Yes! Don't look so surprised, Sam. I sing, and play guitar a bit. Not so much now, but I was one of the T-Birds in my village's production of *Grease*.'

'I've not seen that,' I say.

'Look it up when you get back in.' He glances at the clock on the dashboard. 'Listen, I've got to go now, but this has been great.'

'Yeah,' I say. 'It has.' I didn't like talking about life stories, but I like being with Rock Star Steve so much that I don't want to leave.

'Maybe you could drop me off at Lewis's,' I say, trying to make my time with him longer. 'It's not far away.'

'I would, Sam, but maybe this is the sort of thing you should let Sarah help with, so she feels included, not shut out.'

'Okay,' I say. 'If you think so.'

'But look,' Rock Star Steve says brightly, like he heard the disappointment in my voice. 'I'll meet you the same time next week, and remember, I'm always at the end of the phone. You've got my number.'

I laugh inside. 'Yeah, I have.' I do have his number, but he doesn't know I have it saved as Rock Star Steve.

'Good, and next time we'll do something fun, and not sit here in the rain.'

'But I liked it,' I say.

'Yeah.' Rock Star Steve smiles. 'Me too.'

I reach for the door handle and step out.

'Oh, one sec, Sam.'

I stop dead. *Please don't ask me about life stories again.*

I turn and squint through the rain.

Rock Star Steve leans across the passenger seat.

'Sam,' he says in an American accent, 'remember, Charlie Yonkers! It's a double cross!'

'What?' I say, confused.

'Charlie Yonkers,' says Rock Star Steve. '*Bugsy Malone*.'

'Oh.' I grin. 'I don't know the story.'

'Never mind.' Rock Star Steve reaches for the handbrake. 'You will.'

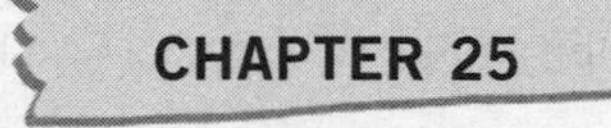

CHAPTER 25

THIS IS WHY I DON'T WANT TO DO MY LIFE STORY

The satnav said it should only take ten minutes to get to Lewis's house, but we've been sitting in traffic for ages. I only asked Reilly's mum to drive me because Rock Star Steve suggested it, but also, I thought if she drops me off maybe she'll believe me when I say I'm going to Lewis's house in the future, even if I'm not.

Reilly's sitting beside me playing Splatoon on his Nintendo. His mum has been asking me how things went with Rock Star Steve. She thinks I've been quiet ever since I saw him, and I have. I hated the last time I saw Gemma, and I don't want to do it again.

I can remember the room. There was a coffee machine in the corner, and two green sofas. And a green folder on the table. Gemma smiled as she put her glasses on and said softly, 'Remember, Sam, this is your life story. We'll work through it together.'

I don't like it when people talk softly. It means there's a secret, or I've done something wrong.

On the front of the folder there was a drawing of a boy and a girl and behind them were six adults: two that looked like parents and four older ones that could have been grandparents. Around the people were doodles of tennis rackets and footballs. In the middle was a dotted line, with my scrawly writing above it: 'Sam McCann – My Life Story'. I wrote it when I was six.

Gemma opened the folder. I didn't need to look to know what was in it – a photo of my mum with me in her arms on a hospital bed. A photo of me in a pushchair in a park when I was two. A photo of me and my mum in a room with paintings of flowers on the walls. I'm smiling but Mum is staring blankly at the camera like she didn't know it was there. That's all the photos I have of me and Mum. It's like someone lost the camera when I was four.

Gemma asked me what I was thinking. I was thinking, *I've not seen my mum for two years. She feels like a stranger.*

Gemma turned to the next page. On it I'd written a list of my interests and hobbies – playing catch, and watching *Shaun the Sheep* and *Fireman Sam*. Then I'd drawn a blue car with a stick person driving – me. That had been two years ago, and now when I looked at them, they just felt silly.

Gemma said maybe we should update it.

I told her I didn't have anything new to put in it.

'But you could have, Sam,' she said. 'If you think about it. What about all the places you've been? The new people you've met?'

'There's no point,' I said. 'Everything I have just gets taken away.'

'But that's why we put things in the book, Sam. So we can remember them. And it's not just you. I've got an album of photos of my gran and grampy. Pictures help us remember places and people. They remind us of where we come from.'

'So why didn't my mum take them, or keep them? Why don't I have any photos of *my* grandparents?' Gemma was only trying to help, but I could feel my anger building inside. All my mum had to do was pick up a camera and point it, but she couldn't even do that.

Gemma looked at me like she knew what I was thinking.

'Your mum was very young, Sam, when she had you. And I think maybe she had problems with her parents too. But that doesn't mean you shouldn't fill this book with pictures of yourself, and your friends. This book is about finding out about you as much as it is about finding out about your family.'

I turned the next page. It was totally blank.

'See,' said Gemma, 'perhaps you could draw pictures of yourself here?'

'I'm ten,' I said.

I flipped to the next page and saw the two Christmas cards Mum had sent me, and the cards of boys on bikes that she sent me for my seventh and eighth birthdays. She promised she would see me every month when she gave me away, but I could only remember seeing her twice since then. I shook my head, as if to rid myself of the thoughts.

'Shall we talk about Mum?' asked Gemma in that soft voice again.

'There's no point,' I said. 'You only tell me the same thing. That she had problems and wasn't well enough to look after me. And you can't tell me anything about my dad.'

'I know, Sam. But we can still talk, and I can try to help you understand.'

Gemma stared at me.

I felt hot. I felt cold. I felt as if the walls were closing in and I wanted to leave.

But there was something in the folder that I had to read even though I knew it would hurt.

I slid the folder towards me and flicked to the back. A blue envelope, with *Sam* written on the front. I picked it up. I'd read it lots of times before, but still my hands were shaking.

Gemma reached out, like she wanted to help.

It's my letter. I want to do it myself.

I slid my fingers under the flap of the envelope and pulled the letter out.

The paper was shaking, I was shaking, as the writing turned blurry.

I wiped my tears on my sleeve.

Sam, it isn't because Mummy doesn't love you. It's because Mummy needs help.

She only wrote that one line but I read it ten times.

Sam, it isn't because Mummy doesn't love you. It's because Mummy needs help.

it isn't because . . .

'Sam.' That was Gemma. 'Are you okay? Let's chat about it. Ask me anything. I'm here to help.'

I stared at the letter.

'Why didn't she want me?' I whispered.

'Your mum was going through some bad things,' said Gemma. 'She needed help, just like she says in the letter.'

'But she still doesn't see me,' I said. 'Not even for an afternoon.'

'I know, but we are still trying. Mum's still trying.'

No. I shook my head. I didn't think my mum was trying at all.

I slid the letter back in the envelope. Reading it didn't help. Writing my life story didn't help. It just reminded me of what I didn't have – a mum and dad.

'You have reached your destination,' the voice on the satnav says.

'Sam, are you okay?' I look up and see Reilly's mum glancing at me with a concerned look on her face. 'Only we're here.'

I look out of the window and see the pink blossom tree that Lewis told me to look out for.

I reach for the door.

'Sam,' says Reilly's mum. 'Are you sure everything's all right?'

Sam, it isn't because Mummy doesn't love you. It's because Mummy needs help.

Block it out, Sam. Block it out. It only hurts.

'Yeah,' I say. 'I'm fine.'

CHAPTER 26

CUSTARD PIES AND SPLURGE GUNS

My stomach flips over with nerves as I walk up Lewis's garden path. Maybe I could just go to Eric. I could get a copy of the play and learn all the lines there on my own over Easter. Yes, I could do—

'Hi, Sam, in here!' Lewis is standing in the hallway. It's too late to turn back.

'Hi!' I say.

Lewis smiles, and I think how much younger he looks wearing a T-shirt and shorts instead of school uniform. 'We're just in the front room,' he says.

I walk past photographs of Lewis and what must be his family on the walls.

Amala and Rhian are sitting on the sofa.

'Hi, Sam,' they say at the same time.

‘Hi,’ I reply.

‘We were just waiting for you.’ Lewis walks over to the TV. ‘We thought we’d watch the film then chat about it after.’

‘Okay.’ I nod nervously, not sure where to sit down. I knew it would be weird meeting them out of school, but it’s even weirder to see Amala and Rhian wearing make-up and normal clothes.

‘I’ll get you a Coke,’ says Lewis. He walks past me into the kitchen.

For a moment I think about following him, but then Amala says, ‘So, Sam, what have you been up to?’

‘Up to?’ I reply.

‘So far, in the holidays.’

‘Oh,’ I say. ‘Nothing much. Just been at home.’

‘Me too,’ says Amala. ‘My mum is driving me mad, trying to get me to tidy my room and stuff.’

‘And mine.’ Rhian rolls her eyes. ‘She’s always telling me to get off the phone. What about your mum?’

‘Umm, yeah,’ I say. ‘Mine does that too.’ I was anxious about coming, and now I’m anxious about the questions. When we’re at school no one asks me about home – it’s mostly about lessons or complaining about homework. I’ve never done this before. I wish Lewis would hurry up with my drink. It doesn’t take this long to get a Coke out of the fridge. I hear a *pushhht* sound in the kitchen, like Lewis has one of those posh machines for making coffee.

‘So what part do you want to be?’ asks Amala.

‘I don’t know,’ I say. ‘I’ve read the first two scenes and all I know is I want to be in it.’

They both grin, like I said something funny, or something wrong.

Or maybe it's because they've found out that I'm a foster-kid. I knew this was a mistake. I've only been here for two minutes but already I want to leave.

'Here you go, Sam,' says Lewis.

I turn around.

'Tha—'

Lewis pushes a plate into my face.

My mouth and eyes fill with foam. Lewis and the girls burst out laughing. I bend over, trying to wipe the foam away.

'Welcome to *Bugsy Malone*,' says Lewis.

I wipe my mouth on my sleeve, then clean my eyes. Amala and Rhian are curled up laughing on the sofa.

'What are you doing?' I turn to Lewis.

'Custard pies,' he says. 'They throw them in *Bugsy Malone*. Only I didn't have any custard so I used Dad's shaving foam.'

'It's okay,' says Amala. 'He did it to us too.'

I force a smile. I thought for a second they were picking on me, but they were just including me in the fun.

Lewis hands me a towel.

'Sorry,' he says, grinning. 'You can get your own back on me, only with custard.'

I wipe my face again.

'Come on,' he says. 'Let's watch the film.'

Amala and Rhian slide towards one end of the sofa. I sit down next to them. Lewis picks up the remote control and sits down next to me.

'All right?' he asks.

'No,' I say, licking my lips. 'All I can taste is soap.'

He laughs. 'It goes after a while. Here.' He hands me a Coke. 'This'll help.'

I take the can.

'Okay,' Lewis says, 'shall we take notes, like Mr Powell said, or just watch?'

'Just watch!' Me, Amala and Rhian say at the same time.

'I was joking.' Lewis grins.

He points the remote at the TV and presses play.

I take a sip of my Coke as the film starts. A piano plays as an old car weaves down a winding road, but I'm not really watching it. It's weird being in somebody else's house, with just friends. I've been to birthday parties when I was at primary school, but they were held in halls where the whole class was invited and even then loads of parents were about. And the foster-kid playdates don't really count because that's just a group of foster-kids sitting in a room, not knowing what to say to each other.

I look around Lewis's living room. It's way bigger than the one at Reilly's house and it feels like it's got twice as many photos. Lewis and who I think must be his younger brother and sister on a giant banana being towed by a boat. Lewis with a rucksack on his back walking up a mountain path. Lewis in his school photo, with a huge grin and gaps between his teeth.

Lewis nudges me. 'Don't you want to watch the film?' he says quietly.

'Yeah,' I say. 'I was just . . .'

Lewis glances at his school photo. 'I know. It's so embarrassing. There are pictures of me everywhere – up the stairs, on the landing, even in the bathroom. Mum hasn't stopped taking them ever since Dad bought her a new camera.'

I smile and take another sip of my drink.

'Have you got any brothers or sisters?' he asks.

I freeze.

'Are you two going to talk all the way through it?' asks Amala.

I breathe with relief.

'Sorry.' Lewis rolls his eyes at me, like he thinks I sighed. 'Chat later,' he whispers.

I nod and hope he forgets to ask that question when we do.

Back on the TV the car stops outside a shop and two children dressed as adults get out. At school I only ever talk about what I've watched on TV, or what I've done at the weekend. I never tell anyone about my family. Conversations just stop awkwardly when someone asks, like Lewis just did. That's why, apart from Leah, I don't have any real friends at school.

I take a sip of Coke, then look back at Lewis, who's now watching the film. Maybe I could tell him something about myself. If we both get into *Bugsy Malone* we're going to be spending a lot of time together rehearsing and he'll think it's weird if I don't say anything, especially if I never invite him to Reilly's house.

I lean towards him.

'I've got a brother,' I say.

'What?' He looks at me like he hadn't asked the question.

'You asked if I had a brother or a sister. I've got a little brother.'

'Cool. What's his name?'

'Reilly. He's six.'

'Seb's eight, and Rosie's six,' he says, nodding at the picture of them on the giant banana. 'That's just before we all fell off.'

I smile.

'Have you ever been on one?' asks Lewis.

Amala leans forward and scowls at us.

Me and Lewis exchange glances and look back at the TV. The boy and girl dressed like adults walk into a bar where a band is playing, and girls are dancing on a stage.

I look back at the photograph of Lewis and his brother and sister bouncing across the waves in their red life jackets. I can't see their faces properly, but I bet they're laughing. If it were me and Reilly, we'd be laughing too, so much that our hands would go weak and we'd not be able to hold on, and the banana would flip over a wave and toss us both into the sea. We'd spit out water and I'd swim over to Reilly and check he was okay. And he'd laugh as we waited for the boat to turn round and get us so we could climb back on the banana again.

We all agreed *Bugsy Malone* was great, although it was a bit weird with kids dressing up as adults, and running around shooting each other with splurge guns. That's what we said while we were eating the pizza that Lewis got out of the freezer. His mum ate with us too, said we could help ourselves to drink and biscuits, but could we be quiet at two p.m. because she had a Skype meeting. I didn't see her after that. If that was Reilly's mum, she would have been in and out checking on us all afternoon.

After the film, we chose our parts, or at least the parts we'd like, because we still had to do the auditions. Amala said she'd like to be

Tallulah so she could dance and get to sing a song on her own. I chose Dandy Dan and Lewis wanted Bugsy. Then we realized what Mr Powell meant when he said that most of the parts were boys so we'd have to change some boys' roles to girls. Which was great because that meant that Rhian chose Fat Sam. She stuffed a cushion up her jumper, and Amala drew a moustache on her with an eyebrow pencil. Lewis looked up the lyrics for the Fat Sam Speakeasy song and they danced around the room singing.

I sat on the sofa watching them. I love drama at school, and I can sing and dance okay, but it was in Lewis's house and it felt weird to join in.

Then they got to the chorus:

'Da da da da da da.

Da da da da da da.'

And Lewis and Amala pulled me up. They were laughing so much that I couldn't help joining in.

'Da da da da da da.

Da da da da da da.'

At the end Lewis said we should get together again next week and that in the meantime, because the play was set in America, we should practise talking in American accents. Amala said she would ask her mum if we could go to hers, and Rhian said she was going to Cornwall with her dads for two days but she would be back Monday so maybe we could go to hers the next day. For a moment I felt jealous she was going away, or maybe it was because she has two dads and I don't even have one. Then they all looked at me. I said I'd ask my parents, but that they wouldn't want to come to mine because my brother would get in the way. Lewis's mum must have overheard us chatting, because she came in and said it was fine to go there again. I sighed with relief when she said that, because if they all turned up at Reilly's house they'd only have to take one look at the photos on the fridge to realize that I didn't belong there at all.

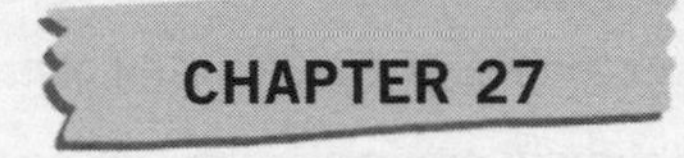

A GOOD DAY

I'm sitting in the lounge with my notebook. After Reilly's mum picked me up from Lewis's, we collected one of Reilly's friends to come over for tea. Reilly just asked if they could have a sleepover, but his mum said that would mean me sleeping on the sofa. I thought Reilly would get upset, but he just went, 'Okay,' then bombed upstairs back to his friend in his room. I felt a bit guilty because I'm the reason his friend couldn't stay, but it does mean that apart from the toilet, I've got no place to sit on my own.

'There you go.' Reilly's mum comes in and puts a glass of orange juice on the table in front of me.

'Thanks,' I say.

She sits down. 'Oh. Nice to rest at last.' She takes a sip of her coffee.

I look at my notebook.

'What are you up to?' she asks. 'Learning your lines for *Bugsy*?'

'Yeah.' I nod, quickly. 'Something like that.'

'You had a good time,' she says. 'I can tell.'

'Yeah, I did. Everyone was totally into it. We learned all the lines to one of the songs, and danced around.' I stop talking because the more I tell Reilly's mum the more questions she will ask.

'Well, I think it's lovely,' she says, taking another sip of her coffee. 'Maybe we could read some characters out together.'

'Maybe,' I say. 'But it's not been decided who we're going to be yet.'

'All right.' She smiles. 'But maybe when you do have a part, we could.'

She picks up the remote and turns on the TV. I hate it when I'm alone with her because there's no Reilly to help me evade her questions, and she always takes the opportunity to talk about foster-kid stuff, things she doesn't want Reilly to hear. Like whether I'm interested in a foster-kid meet-up at Longleat, or Weymouth, or wherever the next meeting is. But luckily all she seems to want to do now is watch *The Great British Bake Off*, the show she always records. I think of getting up and going into the dining room, but I'm going to try to meet the boy in the red house tomorrow, and his mum and dad, and I don't know how long that will take. Maybe I should sit with Reilly's mum, so she doesn't get too mad if I come back late.

A man on the TV says the contestants' challenge this week is to make profiteroles. Reilly's mum sits back in her chair. I did enjoy myself at Lewis's but on the way home I couldn't stop thinking about the boy and what questions I need to ask him. I open my book and look at the notes I made in the car:

Ten Questions to Ask the Boy in the Red House

1. What's your name?
2. How old are you?
3. Which school do you go to?
4. What games do you play on your Xbox One?
5. What are your mum's and dad's names?
6. How old are they? (Preferably about Reilly's mum and dad's age, but with Rock Star Steve's personality, though not as old as him obvs ◡̈)
7. What do they do for work?
8. Do they have a BMW M5 parked in a garage somewhere? (If yes, can we go and see it?)
9. How many bedrooms does your house have? (If two, I don't mind sharing. If three, I don't mind if you keep the Xbox in yours.)
10. Do your parents want any more children?

I scrub the last one out. I can't ask that. He'd think it was weird. He might even guess what I'm up to. Leah said in one of her messages that we have to plan carefully so as not to arouse suspicion.

10. Do you have a brother or a sister? (If yes, argh! If no, would you like one?)

Reilly's mum chuckles. I glance up from my notebook. 'She does make me laugh,' she says, nodding at a short woman with curly hair on TV. 'I can't remember what else she used to be in, but I liked her in that too.' I feel like I should say something, but I've never seen the woman, and I can't even heat up baked beans let alone make profiteroles.

Reilly's mum takes another sip of coffee. She looks tired. I've never noticed it before, but maybe that's because I never sit with her. It must be hard looking after Reilly. He's always running around. It must be even harder looking after someone like me. Sometimes I wonder what made her want to look after a foster-kid. Does she have a friend that did it? Or did she see something on TV or in a magazine? I wonder if she did it for Reilly, because he hasn't got a brother or sister. Maybe she doesn't want any more children of her own and she thought he might like the company.

An advert for washing powder comes on TV.

Reilly's mum catches me looking at her and smiles.

'You okay, Sam?'

'Yeah,' I say. I look down at my notebook, then back up at her. She's going to ask me something. I know she is, like how did it go with Rock Star Steve.

She puts her mug down on the coffee table. Here she goes.

'Tom is always saying I should go on *Bake Off*,' she says.

'Sorry?' I say, surprised.

'Tom thinks I should go on *Bake Off*.'

'Yeah. You should.'

Reilly's mum's face lights up. She didn't expect me to say that, and neither did I. But it's nice to see her smile. I haven't seen her smile for a while.

‘Your cakes are lovely,’ I say. ‘Especially the chocolate one.’

‘Ah, thanks, Sam.’ She beams. ‘That’s very kind.’ She looks back at the TV as *Bake Off* comes back on. ‘Mind you,’ she says, ‘Tom says I’m too bossy to go on there.’

‘Well,’ I say. ‘That’s true.’

‘You’re not supposed to agree!’ She pretends to look hurt.

I smile. *Today ended up being a good day*, I think to myself. *A really good day.*

THE BOY AT THE RAINBOW HOUSES

'Urgh! Sam.'

'What?'

'The rain's getting in.' Leah squirms. 'Next time you choose a den, can you make sure it has a proper roof?' She rolls over and shows me the back of her jeans. 'It looks like I've peed myself.'

I laugh.

'It's not funny,' she says. 'How come you always get the dry bit?'

'Cos I'm here so much, I know where the leaks are.'

'Well, I'm not staying here . . . Swap places.'

We shuffle around in Eric, until Leah is satisfied she's sitting in a dry bit, then she asks, 'So tell me about it.'

'It was good. Lewis pranked me by throwing a custard pie in my face. And I've got to practise talking in an American accent.'

'No, dopey. I meant when you scoped the boy and his birthday out.'

'You make it sound like I was spying.'

'Well, you were, sort of. And this *is* a mission.'

'True.'

'So what happened? All you told me was he got an Xbox One. What were his parents like?'

'Well, they seemed mighty nice,' I say in an American accent. 'They eat turkey and pecan pie.'

Leah laughs. 'Sam,' she says. 'It's good, but I can't take you seriously when you talk like that.'

'Okay.' I smile. 'They seemed nice, but I can't really explain why.'

'Well, think about it. While I clean the lenses on my binoculars.'

'You haven't got binoculars,' I laugh.

'No, I actually have.' Leah reaches into her bag and pulls out a pair of binoculars. 'Mum had them in the loft. She says they belonged to my great-granddad. He used to watch birds.'

I shake my head, disbelieving. As she pulls off the black lens caps, I think about the boy in the red house. How he seemed to have no idea his mum and dad were coming in with his cake and present. I feel myself smile as I picture the amazed look on his face. An Xbox One. 'It's an Xbox One!' It must be brilliant to be given a surprise like that.

'So.' Leah wipes the lenses with a cloth. 'What made them so nice?'

'That they were so thoughtful,' I say. 'Or maybe that when he opened up the Xbox One they were as happy as he was. Only thing is . . .'

'What?'

'I'm not sure I look like them. Even if they wanted me, no one would believe they were my mum and dad.'

'You worry too much,' says Leah.

'Easy for you to say. You live with your mum and you look just like her.'

'I know, unfortunately,' says Leah, laughing. 'But not all families look like each other.'

'You look just like Mollie too,' I say. 'And Reilly's family look the same.'

'Well my Uncle Pete looks nothing like my other uncles. My gran says he was like a carrot growing in a field of parsnips.'

I laugh. 'What does that even mean?'

'Don't know.' Leah smiles. 'But he does have red hair.' Leah clips the lens caps back on. 'Come on,' she says, pushing herself up.

'Where are you going?'

'It's obvious. I didn't bring these to zoom in on your zits. We've got to get you over there. It sounds like you've found your perfect parents. Now all you've got to do is let them know that you're perfect for them.'

'But what do I say? "Hi, I saw you give your son a present and I think you'll be great parents for me." They'll just think I'm after an Xbox.'

'No,' Leah laughs. 'You don't speak to his parents, you speak to the boy, make friends, and *then* you get to speak to them. It's how my mum met my dad. Wait, maybe that's not the best example given the way things turned out. Anyway, we need to get going.'

'What, right now?'

'Yeah,' says Leah. 'You want to be in *Bugsy Malone*, don't you? This could be your way to stay.'

I check my phone for the time.

'How long have we got?' asks Leah.

‘About four hours,’ I say. ‘I told Reilly’s mum I was going to yours but I didn’t want to upset her so I said I’d be back just after lunch.’

‘Good thinking. You’ll never meet your perfect parents if you get grounded.’

I stand up. My stomach flips over. Suddenly everything seems real. I’m going to meet actual people, not celebrity couples I’ve picked out on the internet or in magazines.

Leah sits on the top of Eric, and looks back at me.

‘What are you waiting for?’ she asks.

‘I don’t know.’ I take a deep breath. ‘I’m not sure.’

‘It’s okay,’ says Leah gently. ‘I know this is a big step. I’d be nervous too, but this is what we’ve planned for.’

‘You’re right. Let’s go.’

I put my hands on the edge of Eric and pull myself up.

It’s rained so hard that the rainbow houses look like their paint has run. I’m on my bike at the top of the square, scanning the houses with Leah. We’ve taken it in turns to zoom in on the boy’s red house, but we’ve not seen anyone go in or come out and the front rooms are too dark to see inside. We did see his neighbour come out to put some cans in the recycling bin. Leah wonders if they might have gone out before we got here, but their red car is parked outside. I told her that the boy’s probably playing on his Xbox in his bedroom. I know I would be if my parents had bought me one – I’d stay in all day and all night, all week, and when I finally came out, I’d be blinking and staggering around like a zombie.

Two boys enter the square carrying skateboards. Leah tracks them with the binoculars as they skate across the path.

I glance over to my left and smile.

Leah takes her binoculars down.

'What are you smiling at?' she asks.

'The old lady I told you about,' I say. 'My perfect gran.'

Mrs Shepherd walks along the pavement, maybe heading towards the shops. She's wearing a floppy blue rain hat and raincoat, like she's expecting a monsoon.

'Sam!' Leah grins. 'She looks so cute. And look at her dog's little jacket.'

'I know. He's cute too.'

Mrs Shepherd looks over and waves. I wave back.

'She's lovely,' Leah says quietly. 'But since when did you like Scottie dogs?'

I smile. 'Since my perfect gran had one.'

Leah shakes her head. 'Sam McCann. What are you like?'

I shrug.

'I think I just saw him!' Leah nods across the square. 'The boy, in the top window. Must be his bedroom. Wait there!' She reaches down for her bag.

'What is it?' I ask.

She pulls a red Frisbee out of her bag. 'Here,' she says. 'We've wasted enough time.'

'Where did this come from?' I say, taking it.

'Forward planning, Sam. Now just go down there and throw it about.'

'What? On my own?'

'Yes.'

'But I'll look like Sam no-mates.'

'So what's new?' Leah laughs. 'Quick, go. I think he's still there.'

I look at the red house, in the top window.

'I can't see anyone,' I say. 'And besides, I'm going to look weird throwing a Frisbee to no one.'

'We can't just sit around waiting for something to happen. So just go.' Leah gently pushes me in the back.

'Okay,' I say. 'I'm going. I'll take the Frisbee.'

'Good.' Leah holds up the binoculars. 'And remember, I vill be vatching you,' she says in a strange accent. 'So don't go scratching yourself, or picking your nose.'

'You're weird.' I laugh as I head across the grass. But if the boy in the red house is anything like me, he won't come out.

I stop about fifty metres in front of the boy's house, and raise my arm. I glance over at Leah and see her watching me. I imagine her giggling at me, or telling me to imagine I've got an invisible dog. I throw the Frisbee up in the air, then catch it. I do it again, and again, all the time checking over to Leah and across at the red house.

My phone buzzes in my pocket.

Keep going. Something will happen soon.

Hope so, because this feels weird.

I throw the Frisbee again once I've sent the message.

On the way here, me and Leah talked about what the boy's parents might be called and what they did for work. Leah thought their names would be Dom and Fiona and he'd be a computer wizard who had a huge bank of screens in his office, and she'd be an art teacher or would work in a gallery. Or maybe they're popstars, tired of being followed by reporters, so they've hidden away in a row of terraced houses where no one would ever think they'd live. I said that would be cool, but very unlikely.

I keep throwing the Frisbee.

My pocket buzzes again.

Sam!

I'm trying!

No. The eagle has landed.

What?

He's here!

I turn and look around. A boy in a blue hoody is standing next to me.

'All right?' he says.

'Uh, yeah,' I say, putting my phone away. I try to figure out if it's the boy from the red house, but I'm worried if I stare too long he'll think I'm weird.

'Do you live around here?' he asks.

'Yeah,' I say. 'I do. I just moved in.' I look down at my Frisbee. Why did I say that?

'Thought so,' says the boy. 'I've seen you hanging around.'

'Yeah,' I say, hoping he doesn't mean when I was snooping through his window. 'There's nothing much to do though.' I hold up my Frisbee. 'There's no one around.'

The boy smiles. 'New school too then?'

'Yeah,' I say. 'Dunham High.' I blurt out the name of my real school without thinking.

'Dunham High?' the boy says, surprised. 'That's miles away.'

'It is,' I say, trying to cover my tracks. 'What I meant was, that's the school I used to go to, but now I'll be going to a new one round here. How long have you lived here?' I ask, changing the subject from me to him.

'Oh, I'm just visiting during the holidays. I do it every year.'

'So you don't—'

'No, I don't live here.' The boy nods at the red house. 'That's my auntie and uncle's place.'

'Oh . . . right.' My heart sinks into the ground. 'So they aren't . . . they aren't your parents?'

'No, but it's okay,' the boy says brightly, like he's noticed my disappointment. 'My Auntie Michelle and Uncle Dave are cool. Dave takes me to the football, and they bought me an Xbox One for my birthday, so I don't have to bring the one I got at home any more.'

'You've . . . you've . . .' My mind's still struggling to catch up. Not his parents. Not his parents. 'You've got two Xbox Ones?' I say eventually.

'Yeah, but I busted one of the controllers at home, so maybe I'll just swap them. I'm Josh, by the way.' He looks at me.

'Oh, I'm Sam,' I say. 'Sam – little c, big C . . .' My words fade away, not that Josh seems to notice.

He just says, 'Cool, Sam,' then smiles.

You seem nice, I think to myself. *But I've come here to meet your parents who aren't even your parents.*

I glance over at Leah, wishing I had a microphone hidden on my sweatshirt and an earpiece in my ear. Leah waves at me. *No!* I think. *They aren't his parents.*

'Sam?'

'Sorry.'

'I asked you where you live?' says Josh. 'You said you just moved in?'

I glance in Leah's direction, panicking. No microphone. No earpiece. She's too far away to help me.

'I . . . I . . . I just moved around the corner,' I say eventually.

'Cool,' says Josh. 'I don't know anyone round here, and that lot are too old.' He nods at the boys on the skateboards walking back through the lane. 'Wanna throw this for a bit?' He takes my Frisbee.

'Uh, yes,' I say. I might be panicking, but Josh doesn't seem to have noticed.

It's worked. I'm talking to the boy from the red house. I take my phone out of my pocket to send Leah a message, but then Josh shouts, 'Sam! Catch!'

I duck and the Frisbee whooshes past my head.

'Sorry,' says Josh. 'Thought you were ready.'

'It's okay,' I say, running after the Frisbee. When I reach it, I look at my phone and send a message to Leah, saying thanks. I look up to the top of the square for her reaction, but she's already gone.

CHAPTER 29

JOSH

Josh can run 100 metres in 14.3 seconds.

Josh can drink a can of Coke in one go.

Josh goes to school on the other side of town.

Josh doesn't play football much, because his school plays rugby.

Josh is on level nine of Star Race 3000.

Josh's phone number is 07705482093, and while Reilly is having a shower, I've been on the bottom bunk messaging. Josh loves cars. His favourite is the E-Type Jag, because his granddad always wanted one. It did 0–60 in 7.6 seconds and had a top speed of 153 miles per hour. I was going to message that the BMW M5 is a lot quicker, but it was his granddad's dream car, so I just said I thought it was cool we were both into fast cars. He said maybe we could play Top Trumps, but he wouldn't find his dad's Renault Megane in there. I told him we wouldn't find my dad's VW Golf in there either. I felt a bit bad lying about that, and also the fib about me moving schools, but I just want to be his friend, then meet his auntie and uncle. That's all.

I just told him I can't meet tomorrow because I'm meeting Lewis, Amala and the others for drama.

My phone buzzes.

Cool, Josh replies. Come over on Friday.

I smile then run through the rest of the things I learned about him today.

His mum and dad both work for the Ministry of Defence. They aren't spies but they aren't allowed to talk about work, although Josh says the bits he hears are boring.

Josh is really good at climbing. I found that out when he climbed the tree in the park after I threw the Frisbee too high by mistake. That's when we stopped playing and sat down on the swings.

'What about your auntie and uncle?' I asked. My list of questions had disappeared from my head when Josh told me they weren't his parents, but now they were back.

'My auntie works in accounts at thc arts college, and my uncle used to be a fireman but he's a fire-safety consultant now,' he said.

'Have they got a BMW M5?'

'No,' Josh laughed. 'Uncle Dave drives that van.' He pointed at a red van with 'Fire Protection Services' on the side. 'And Auntie Michelle drives that beaten-up Ford Fiesta.'

'Oh,' I said, 'and how old—'

'Is that what your mum and dad drive?' Josh cut me off. 'A BMW M5?'

'No, it's just my favourite car,' I said.

Josh smiled. 'And what do your parents do?'

My head flashed with panic. 'Oh, boring jobs,' I said eventually. 'Do you like cycling?' I asked, switching the subject. 'I do. I like acting too. I'm hoping to get a part in the school production of *Bugsy Malone*.'

'Cool,' said Josh. 'Can you do an American accent? They all talk in American accents.'

'Not very well,' I said. 'I'm still practising.'

I looked at his uncle and auntie's house. I was already feeling like me and Josh were becoming friends, even though I had told him lies. He was nice, which made me think maybe his auntie and uncle would be nice too. All I had to do was work out a way I could get to meet them. That's when Josh said, 'I need to pee. Auntie Michelle tells me off if I go against the tree. You coming?'

'I don't need to go,' I said.

'Okay,' said Josh. 'But we could get a drink anyway.'

That's when I followed him across the grass. I was actually going into the house. And it still makes me excited when I think about it now.

'Reilly!' I jump as Reilly's mum shouts up the stairs. 'Get out of the shower now, otherwise you'll use up all the hot water for Sam.'

'Okay!' Reilly shouts back.

My phone buzzes. This time it's Leah.

How did it go?

Great. I can't stop myself smiling as I type. His name is Josh and he's really cool.

Did you meet his mum and dad?

No, that's the only problem, they're his aunt and uncle. But I went in the house!

And?!

I just stood in the hallway.

Sam!

I was nervous.

Did they speak to you?

No. They were in another room, but I heard their voices. They sounded nice.

Are you going to see them again? Leah's typing excitedly, faster than I can reply.

Hope so, got drama tomorrow, so day after. Not sure what I'll say to them though.

You'll be okay, just do one of your lists.

I smile. I love how Leah is always looking out for me. If I do get to meet my perfect parents, I'm not going to leave her out.

OK, I type. Good idea.

Cool. Btw, Mum's got a new boyfriend.

Great.

Not really!

Why?

He's got a round head and ears like a jug ☹

☹

Message tomorrow.

Yep.

I pick up my notebook.

Top Ten Questions I'm Going to Ask
Josh's Auntie and Uncle

1. Do you like having Josh stay with you?
2. If yes, do you wish he could stay more often?
3. If no, can I stay instead ◡̈
4. Do you like Nand—

Reilly bombs into the room with wet hair wearing only his pyjama bottoms.

I snap my notebook shut.

'What are you doing?' he asks.

'Nothing. Just doodling.'

'Sometimes I doodle at school,' he says, looking serious. 'But

Miss James told me off for drawing a chicken on a table with my crayon.'

I smile and slide my notebook under my pillow.

'Reilly, are you out yet?' his mum shouts.

'Yes!'

'Good, make sure you dry yourself properly. I'll be up in a minute to say goodnight.'

Water trickles down Reilly's face.

'I think you'd better get the towel,' I say.

'Yeah.' Reilly runs out. Five seconds later he's back.

'Will you do it, Sam?' He holds out the towel. 'Do that thing that Dad does – put the towel around my head and pull it backwards and forwards like brushes in the car wash.'

'Okay,' I say. 'Stand still.'

I put the towel around the back of his head and hold the ends.

Reilly starts to giggle.

I love that he always seems so happy, and for once, I feel happy too, because today I made a new friend and I almost got to meet what I hope could be my perfect parents. I've just got to make sure that the next time I go I do.

PICTURES OF ME

'Please come with us, Sam,' says Reilly the next morning.

'Yes, come on, Sam,' says his mum. 'It feels like we've not seen you all week, what with your project with Leah and *Bugsy Malone*.'

'But I told you, I'm going to Lewis's.'

'Well, what about tomorrow? I've got to do a bit of shopping, but we could go and do something after, before Reilly's dad gets back?'

'Yeah, come on, Sam.' Reilly jumps up off his bed in his *Sharkasaurus* pyjamas. 'We could go to the sports centre, see if we can do taekwondo.' He holds his hands out in front of him and kicks the air. 'You get a cool gown and belt.' Reilly spins, and kicks again.

His mum shakes her head. 'Reilly, mind what you're doing, you'll knock over your TV. And that's really not what I had in mind. I told you, the gown and belt are expensive, and the lessons are forty-five pounds.'

'That's not lots,' says Reilly.

'It is when you multiply it by two. I was thinking more like a walk and an ice cream down by the docks. What do you think, Sam?'

'What?' I look up from the TV.

'Sam,' says Reilly's mum, rolling her eyes. 'Are you even listening?'

I look back at the screen, pretending she's not there.

'Reilly, can you go to the toilet?' she says.

'I've already been.'

'Well, go again, and get some clean clothes out of your cupboard at the same time. And put those pyjamas in the washing machine – you've been living in them for days.'

Reilly huffs.

'Reilly!'

He turns and I listen to his feet thud out across the landing. His mum looks at me.

I prcss the controller buttons, make my plane rise in the sky.

Reilly's mum sits down beside me. 'Sam, would it do any harm to come with us tomorrow? You know how much Reilly likes being with you.'

'I know,' I say. 'But I really want to go to Lewis's.'

'Two days in a row?' Her voice rises in surprise.

I should have said I was meeting Leah for the school project, but my lies are confusing me now. 'It's because we all want to make sure we get the best parts,' I blurt. 'And we won't get them if we don't practise.'

My plane levels out and I cut the engines, ready to dive. If I play long enough she'll give up and leave, but she's still looking at me like she wants a long conversation.

'Sam,' she says quietly. 'It's Reilly's birthday next week and I was thinking this might be a chance for you two to do something he could remember together.'

'I might be busy with stuff,' I say.

'Then we'll choose a time when you're not.' Reilly's mum glances at the wardrobe door covered in *Transformers* posters. 'I thought maybe we'd get a photo of you with him, like that one he did with his cousin last year in the photo booth.'

I glance up, looking at the picture of Reilly grinning with his front tooth missing. Next to him is his cousin, leaning her head in like she thinks she'll be out of frame. It looks like they're having fun. But why does she suddenly want me to have my photograph taken? Pictures are to remind you of people and places, like the ones I've got of Mum in my life story folder. Pictures aren't always happy like Reilly and his cousin. Pictures are so people remember what you look like after you've gone.

I press X and stop my plane. 'I'm going to Lewis's. Today and tomorrow.'

'What?' Reilly's mum shakes her head like there's a bee in her hair. 'Why, Sam? I just said it'd be nice to get a picture of you. Maybe we could get you some posters too.' She turns and looks at the pieces of Blu Tack above the bed. 'I know you won't want *Transformers*, but it might be fun to have pictures of some of the things you like, like cars or—'

'No,' I snap. 'I don't want any pictures or posters.' I stand up.

'Sam.' Reilly's mum pushes herself up off the bunk. 'What's wrong?'

'It's nothing,' I say. 'I just have to get to Lewis's.'

'But you're not wearing your suit,' she says.

'I don't have to wear it every time.'

I head towards the door, just as Reilly bombs past, still wearing his *Sharkasaurus* pyjama top.

'Can I keep on this bit?' he says.

His mum sighs, like she gives up.

'It doesn't stink.' Reilly sniffs his pyjama top. 'Does it, Sam?'

'No, Reilly,' I say. 'It doesn't smell. Anyway, I'm going now.'

'But we've not finished talking,' says Reilly's mum.

I walk past her. She looks as confused as I feel.

Posters are fun, she said, but what's the point of putting them up when I'll have to take them back down?

CHAPTER 31

WHY CAN'T I SAY 'BEST FRIEND'?

'I won't be a minute.' I'm in Eric, changing out of my suit. I'd thought about wearing it to meet Josh's auntie and uncle, but Josh might think it's a bit weird, especially if he's wearing his hoody and jeans. At least Reilly's mum believed I was going to practise *Bugsy* when she saw me.

But I did feel bad when she told me I looked smart.

I stuff my suit in my bag, reach for the rope and pull myself up.

'You are, by the way.'

'I am what?' I say, flipping my legs over the top of Eric.

'Overthinking,' says Leah. 'Reilly's mum is right. Those photo booths *are* fun. Hattie and I did it once. We put on our mums' dresses and wore loads of make-up.'

'Well, I'm definitely not doing that!'

Leah laughs. 'But maybe you should think about it.'

'It's too late.' I jump down and pick up my bike. 'They're doing it today, before Reilly's dad comes back.'

'Won't you get into trouble if you're not home when he arrives?'

'He's not back until later,' I say. 'Besides, there's no way I would miss out on this.' I nod down the alley. 'Come on. I get to meet my perfect parents today!'

Leah smiles. 'It's good you're excited. Maybe it's better to look forward to the future, and not think about the past. That's what my mum says whenever she has a break-up. Doesn't stop her texting them while she's watching telly though.'

I shake my head as we wheel our bikes down the high street towards the cycle path.

'What?' asks Leah.

'Nothing,' I say. 'Just you do say some random things.'

Leah shrugs. 'That's me. Anyway, how did *Bugsy* go yesterday?'

'It was good. We looked at the script and acted out the characters in American accents. Lewis was Bugsy, Amala was Tallulah and I played Fat Sam.'

'Oh cool, let's hear it then.'

'What?'

'Your American accent!'

'What now?' I say, looking up and down the street. 'Right here?'

'Yeah, why not? You need to practise if you want a part.'

'Okay.' I lean my bike against an estate agent's window. 'But this feels a bit weird, doing it here. You have to imagine I'm wearing a gangster hat, and my suit.'

'Sam, just do it!'

'Okay, okay.' I take a deep breath. 'You ready?'

'Yep.'

I get my head into character. ‘Someone once said, “If it was raining brains, Roxy Robinson wouldn’t even get wet,”’ I say in my best American accent.

Leah laughs. ‘That’s brilliant. Do some more.’

‘I haven’t remembered the lines yet.’

‘Say anything.’

‘All right.’ I hold my arms out, spread my fingers. ‘Well, my name is Sam and I’m a here with my friend a Leah, and we walking down the sidewalk to find me perfect parents.’

Leah’s whole face creases up. ‘Oh god, Sam. You sound more like a rapper than a gangster.’

‘Yeah. I think it needs more practice. We all do, that’s why we’re going to meet up at least once more during the holidays.’

‘At least once?’ says Leah. ‘But with that *and* finding your perfect parents, you’re not going to have any time left to meet me.’

‘I will,’ I say, picking up my bike.

‘I was joking,’ she says. ‘You know how much I want you to do both.’

We wheel our bikes along the pavement. For a moment Leah is quiet as she glances in shop windows. I hope she was joking about me not having enough time to see her. I always will – none of this would be happening if it wasn’t for her. She’s the best friend I’ve ever had. I wish I could tell her. Maybe I should. I know I’d like it if she said it to me.

We stop at a crossing. I reach out and press the button. I glance at Leah as the traffic rushes by. She’s looking straight across the road, waiting for the red man to turn green.

I could tell her now, but I'm frightened she'll laugh.

'What are you looking at?' she says, turning to me.

'Nothing,' I say. 'I was just thinking . . . I know you said you were joking, but I will have time to see you. Even if Josh's auntie and uncle are my perfect parents, I'll ride over to yours.'

'I know you will.' She smiles.

I look at her. *Tell her now, Sam*, I say in my head. *Tell her she's the best friend you've ever had.*

'Leah . . .'

'Yeah.'

'Did you know . . . Do you know . . .'

'We can go.'

The traffic stops. The red man has turned green. We wheel our bikes across the road, up onto the pavement that leads to the cycle path.

Leah climbs onto her bike, putting one foot on a pedal. I do the same.

'What were you going to say?' She looks across at me.

'Say?'

'At the crossing?'

I was going to say you are my best friend, the best I've ever had.

'Oh, that,' I say like it's not important. 'I just wanted to say . . .' *You're my best friend.* 'I just wanted to say . . . I'm really grateful you're doing this for me.'

Leah chuckles. 'That's okay. I'm only coming to check that Josh isn't an axe murderer, or a weirdo who'll lock you up in the basement.'

I laugh nervously. Why couldn't I just say it?

Leah pushes down on her pedal. 'Come on,' she says, 'we'll never find your perfect parents if we sit here.'

I pedal after her. Why couldn't I say it? I hear kids say it at school all the time.

'My best friend came over.'

'Jamala is my best friend.'

'Reece is my best friend.'

You're my best friend . . . It's only four words. Was I worried Leah wouldn't say it back? Or because every time I get to like someone, they get taken away?

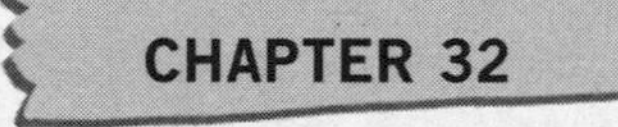

CHAPTER 32

THE PERFECT PARENT PROJECT STAGE THREE

Josh is already waiting in the middle of the square when we get there. I'm glad I ditched the suit because Josh is wearing a T-shirt and trainers and I'd have felt even more edgy that I already am. We got on great last time, but now there's a chance of meeting his auntie and uncle, my stomach keeps flipping over and over.

Me and Leah wheel our bikes into the park in the square.

'It's okay, Sam,' she whispers. 'He doesn't look much like an axe murderer. Don't think he'd squash a fly.'

I go to laugh, but all that comes out is a nervous grunt.

Josh runs over to us.

'Hi,' he says.

'Hi,' me and Leah say at the same time, as we lay our bikes on the grass.

'This is Leah,' I say, standing up. 'Leah, this is Josh.'

They both nod at each other.

I don't know what to say next. I've never been in the middle of two friends. But my stomach is flipping double with the awkward silence. I need to think of something to break it.

'How do the owners choose the colours of the houses?' I blurt. 'I like them, but who decides?'

'Don't know.' Josh looks around the square. 'I think they can do what they want? Oh, nice trainers.'

'Thanks.' Leah looks down at her feet. 'Bit random, but thanks.'

We all laugh. I think we are all as nervous as each other but I relax when I spot Leah giving me a secret thumbs up to say she thinks Josh is okay.

'So do you live round here too?' asks Josh.

I look at Leah, panicking. She just smiles calmly and says, 'Yeah. I live in the same road as Sam.'

'Cool,' says Josh, looking at his Frisbee. 'Did you want to play with us?'

'No thanks.' Leah takes her phone out of her bag. 'Oh, I've got a message,' she says.

'Have you?' I know she thinks Josh is okay, but I didn't think she'd leave as quickly as this.

'Yeah. I've got to go – I've got to go – home. Yes, home. Mum thinks our puppy has swallowed a sock and she wants me to go to the vet's with her.'

'A sock?' says Josh.

'Yeah,' says Leah. 'He eats anything that's hanging around. He's a Dalmatian.'

‘And Dalmatians eat socks?’

‘Yeah. At least this one does.’ Leah winks at me. Josh looks at her strangely.

‘I’ve got a fly in my eye,’ she says like she knows he spotted her.

‘Let’s see,’ Josh says.

‘No, I think I got it,’ Leah says, hurriedly picking up her bike. ‘I’ve got to go. Message you later, Sam. That’s if you *axe*-ually get a signal from the basement.’

I smile inside at how weird she’s being.

Leah smirks as she walks away.

‘What was all that about?’ says Josh.

‘Nothing,’ I say. ‘She just watches way too many films.’

‘But she seems cool.’

‘Yeah.’ I smile as Leah walks her bike out of the square. ‘She is.’

‘Just a bit weird.’

I laugh. ‘She’s not like that all the time.’

Josh holds up the Frisbee.

‘Did you want to play this for a bit?’ hc asks.

‘Yeah,’ I say. ‘But I’m not very good at it. You saw me the other day . . .’

‘That’s okay,’ says Josh. ‘I used to be the same, until Uncle Dave taught me to throw by flicking my wrist not using my arm. He might play when he gets back.’

My heart sinks as I glance across at the red house.

‘Have they gone out then?’

‘Yeah,’ says Josh. ‘Only for a bit I think – depends how long Auntie Michelle spends chatting at the till.’

I smile with relief. I didn't come all this way for them not to be in.

Josh steps away from me. 'We'll start off close together until you get used to it, then gradually move further apart.'

He walks the width of a tennis court away, then throws the Frisbee. I catch it, then throw it back.

Josh catches it above his head and grins. 'See, you're not so rubbish.'

I laugh. 'Well, I thought I was.'

'Catch!'

I move to my left and catch the Frisbee just above the grass, then send it back.

Josh jumps in the air, catching it above his head. 'Let's move further apart.'

I back towards his house, and suddenly feel guilty. Josh could actually be my friend, and I feel bad for using him just so I can meet his auntie and uncle. Even though it makes me nervous, I can't stop wishing I could keep walking – all the way across the grass, over the road, through the gate to his uncle and auntie's door.

'They're back!' Josh runs towards me. 'Come on, Sam,' he says. 'Auntie Michelle is bound to have got some Coke and sausage rolls.'

I spin around and see Josh's auntie and uncle getting out of a red Fiesta.

Josh runs ahead of me as they lift the boot. I can't see his uncle properly because he's wearing a baseball cap, but his auntie looks a lot different, her hair hanging loose over what looks like a university sweatshirt. They wave at Josh as he crosses the road towards them. I stay on the grass as Josh points at something in the boot. His auntie taps his hand. I think she says, 'No, that's not yours!' and they all laugh and start carrying the shopping into the house. I've only seen Josh's auntie and uncle for a few seconds on Josh's birthday, but they look as friendly and happy now as they did then.

I sit down on the grass and wait as they take the shopping away. I've got a little longer to prepare myself to meet them, but then Josh runs out and shouts, 'Sam, what are you doing there? I told you, we're having Coke and sausage rolls.'

My heart thuds in my chest, through my neck, into my head. *This is it. This is it.*

I stand up and brush the grass off my jeans. *First impressions count*, I say to myself. This is the first time I'll meet the people who could be my perfect parents. I wait for Josh to turn away, then I brush grass off my elbows, lick my palms and flatten my hair.

My legs are moving, but I don't remember starting to walk.

I'm across the grass, the road.

I'm at the gate.

I'm through the door into the hall.

I hear voices, but everything is a blur.

Until I'm in the kitchen, heart booming, face to face with Josh's uncle.

'Oh, hi, Sam. Here you go.' He holds out a can of Coke.

'Thanks,' I say. 'I mean, thank you.' I take the can, trying to calm down, but my hands are shaking too much to flip the ring.

'Here.' Dave holds out his hand. 'Let me do it. I didn't realize the can was that cold.'

'No . . . No . . .' I cross my legs. 'I . . . I . . . I think I need to go to the toilet.'

'What?' says Michelle. 'You mean you don't do it behind the tree, like Josh?'

'Hey!' says Josh. 'That was only once, and I *was* five.'

They all laugh, then Josh's auntie says softly, 'It's up the top of the stairs, Sam, straight ahead.'

'Thanks.' I put the can down on the worktop and walk back out into the hall. As I go up the stairs, I hear Michelle say, 'He seems nice, Josh.' She says something else but I don't hear it, because I'm already heading into the bathroom.

I close the door behind me, spin around and catch myself in the mirror. My face is scrunched up, full of panic. I take a deep breath. 'You've got to do this, Sam,' I say to myself in the mirror. 'You have to do this.' But even when I say it a second time in an American accent, it doesn't sound convincing.

I fumble for my phone to message Leah.

I'm so nervous.

Have you met them?

Sort of. I'm in the bathroom.

What are you doing there?

I needed to pee, but now I'm here, I don't.

☺

It's not funny. What do I do?

Just be yourself. They'll love you.

Okay.

Now go back down. And don't forget to flush.

But I haven't done anything.

Do it anyway. You've been in there so long they'll think you've done a number two ☺

I turn and flush the toilet.

'So, Sam,' says Dave. 'You just moved in around the corner?'

'Uh . . . yes,' I say.

'What, Malvern Street?'

'Yeah,' I say cautiously. 'Malvern Street.'

'And how do you like it?' asks Michelle.

'It's good,' I say, glancing at Josh and wondering what else he told his auntie and uncle.

'Mum and Dad got a lot of decorating to do?' asks Michelle.

'A little,' I say. 'They're doing my bedroom at the moment.'

'Oh lovely. And I guess they've got work too.'

'Yeah,' I say, taking another sip of Coke. Josh's auntie is nice, but she's firing questions out of a machine gun. I just wish I could find the answers as fast.

'What do they do?'

What do they do? My brain's blank with panic. What did I tell Josh when I first met him? I have to say the same thing.

'Well,' I say. 'They . . .'

'Chelle.' Dave jumps in and saves me. 'The poor kid just wants to drink, not answer twenty questions.'

'Sorry.' Michelle smiles at me. 'Was only being friendly.'

'More like nosey,' says Dave.

'Oi!' Michelle nudges him. 'I just want to get to know Josh's new friend.'

I smile, try to relax, but Josh's auntie is back at me again.

'They're nice houses on Malvern. Has yours got an attic room, Sam? My friend Jackie lives at number sixteen. What number are you?'

'Umm . . . ninety-six,' I say, thinking of a number far away from Michelle's friend.

'Oh, right. That must be at the other end of the street.'

'Yes,' I say. 'It is.'

'Maybe we could go around later,' says Josh.

What? No? My head rings like an alarm bell just went off.

'Uh, we could, we could.' I search my brain in panic. 'But it's like your auntie said, we're decorating. There are paint pots and bits of wallpaper everywhere.'

'See, told you,' says Michelle. 'Oh, and you can call me Michelle, Sam. But not *you*.' She wraps her arm around Josh's shoulders and hugs him. 'My little Joshie can still call me auntie when he's thirty!' She kisses Josh on the head.

'Aww.' Josh ruffles his hair.

'Chelle,' says Dave. 'Leave him alone.'

I smile and take a sip from my Coke. Josh does the same. Dave and Michelle look at us.

'Well, this is nice,' says Michelle. 'I'm glad Josh has met someone his own age. We always wonder if he gets bored when he comes here.'

'The only thing anyone gets bored of is your questions,' Dave laughs.

I realize I've not asked any questions myself, but I don't know what to ask. Then I notice Michelle's sweatshirt.

'Is that where you went to university?'

Michelle looks down. 'Chicago? No.' She smiles. 'We just went there for a holiday.'

I look at the ground, feeling stupid for asking a silly question. Then Dave jumps in like he noticed my awkwardness.

'Come on, you two.' He nods towards the front door. 'I'll help you escape. It's your holidays after all, not an interrogation! Frisbee or football?'

'Frisbee,' says Josh.

We put our cans down on the counter and walk into the hall. As I wriggle my feet into my trainers by the door, I spot Dave and Michelle hugging in the kitchen.

'Go on,' says Michelle, pushing Dave away. 'It's obvious I come second to Frisbee.'

'Third,' says Dave, walking into the hall, 'after football.'

Michelle picks up a can and pretends to throw it. Dave laughs and I smile as he jogs past me out into the street. I look back at Michelle. She's still smiling as she puts the cans in the bin and pours coffee down the sink. *This is what a family is like*, I think. *They don't just exist in adverts and films on TV.*

Michelle looks up and catches me watching her.

'You okay, Sam?' she asks.

'I was just . . .' I squirm my left foot into my trainer. 'I should undo the laces really.'

'Yes,' says Michelle. 'I bet that's what your mum says too.'

'Yeah,' I say. 'Sort of.'

Michelle picks up a cloth and wipes the counter down. 'Still here?' she says, looking up at me. 'Something wrong?'

'No,' I say. 'I was just thinking,' I say as my foot slips into my trainer.

'What about?'

'When you went to America, did you go to Disneyland?'

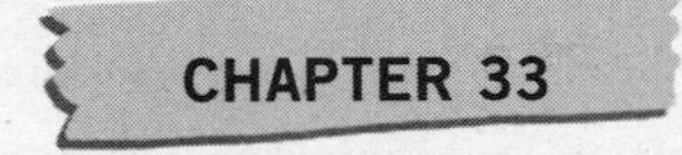

OVERTHINKING

'Hiiiiii ... yah!' Reilly jumps into his bedroom wearing taekwondo robes. 'What do you think?'

'They're cool, Reilly.' I smile. 'But I don't think the top's supposed to go down to your knees.'

'Mum said they were second-hand.'

'Must have belonged to a giant.'

Reilly looks down at his arms. 'Really?'

'Yeah,' I say. 'The one at the top of Jack's beanstalk.'

Reilly laughs. 'Mum says I can keep them on and show Dad when he comes home. I'm going to ask Mum how long he'll be. You coming?'

'No,' I say. 'I've got to change out of this suit.'

'Okay.' Reilly spins around and leaves.

I take my suit jacket off and lay it on my bed. Reilly jumps down the stairs, then I hear his mum shout, 'Reilly, calm down!'

He's as excited about his dad coming home as I was about meeting

Michelle and Dave. In the afternoon, we sat in the garden for ages talking about things they had done together last summer, like when they got trapped by the tide while walking to an island in Cornwall, and when Josh got lost in the Chamber of Secrets at Harry Potter World. All the time they were talking I was thinking how much I wished I could have gone with them and how if they did turn out to be my perfect parents then I probably wouldn't get to go to those places anyway because they'd already been. Eventually they started to ask about the places I'd visited. I said I'd not been to many because my mum and dad worked lots. Then Michelle looked at me for a long time and I didn't know if she was waiting for me to say something else or if she knew something was up.

'Choo . . . wah!'

I'm startled out of my thoughts as Reilly springs into the room, aiming a taekwondo kick at the TV.

I can't help smiling at him. He's trying to sound as tough as a lion, but his kicks wouldn't hurt a mouse.

'Dad's home in half an hour. And Mum says we're having a movie night!'

'Cool,' I say. 'Which film?'

'Don't know, but Dad's bought it.' He picks up a controller and hands it to me.

'Is half an hour long enough to get me to level four?'

'Yeah.' I smile. Reilly's attention span is like a puppy's.

I press X and fly the plane off an aircraft carrier, into the sky. I tilt the wings from side to side and take the plane up through the clouds. Everything is quiet and still as I wait for the enemy planes to arrive.

All the time, Reilly's sitting beside me, picking his nose. Sometimes I wonder what it must be like to be him. He has no worries. If he had to keep a diary like I do, it would just be: went to school, came home, played Ace Pilot (or taekwondo), then went to bed. And the next day he would write exactly the same again. But today he could write: Dad came home. I wonder what that feels like for him. I like his dad even if he's quite strict about some stuff. We always have to get to the table on time to eat. He says we all have to be punctual because if you are late in the air force, you don't just risk missing your dinner, you risk missing your plane.

'Enemy at three o'clock!' Reilly nudges me. 'Sam, argh!'

The room lights up white as my plane crashes then burns on the TV screen.

'They got you!' shouts Reilly.

I stare at the screen.

'Try again, Sam,' he says. 'Again.'

'Okay.' The game reloads.

But I can't concentrate. Michelle and Dave seem nice, but what if they don't want a son? I've only got a few days left of the holiday – I need to find my perfect parents soon. *Bugsy* is starting next term. Wait … what if Reilly's dad is coming home to talk about me? Him coming back, and Reilly's mum trying to get me to have my picture taken. It all adds up. I could be gone before the auditions even start.

I put the controller beside me on the bed.

Reilly looks up.

'What's wrong, Sam?' he asks.

'Nothing.'

'Did you want to watch a film with me now? We could watch *The Lion King*.'

'No, it's okay,' I say.

'Or we could—'

My phone buzzes on the table. Me and Reilly look at it at the same time.

'Is that your girlfriend?' he says.

'Oi!' I rub his head. 'She's not my girlfriend.'

'Mum says she is. Says she thinks it's cute.'

'Cute?' I reach for my phone. 'I don't think your mum would say anything to do with me was cute.'

'She did!' Reilly jumps up and dances in the middle of the room. 'Sam and Leah, sitting in a tree, K-I-S-I—'

'That's not right,' I laugh. 'It's K-I-S-S . . . and we're not!'

'Are.' Reilly pokes his tongue out. 'Sam and Leah, sitting in a tree, K-I-S-S-I-N-G.'

I jump up and grab him.

'Take it back,' I say as I tickle him. 'Take it back.'

'No.' Reilly wriggles. I tickle him more. Spit dribbles out of Reilly's mouth as he giggles. 'Okay, Sam!' he says. 'It's not true. It's not true.'

I let go of him and we stand up, trying not to laugh as we catch our breaths. Reilly's face cracks into a grin. 'Sam and Leah, sitting in the tree . . .'

I reach out. Reilly bolts for the door, but he's too slow. I grab him and tickle him some more.

I love Reilly. It doesn't matter if I find my perfect parents, or if his mum and dad get rid of me first. I'm going to miss him loads.

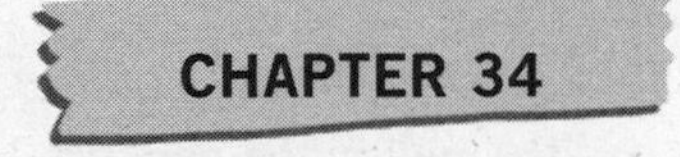

CHAPTER 34

WHEN REILLY'S DAD COMES HOME

When Reilly's dad comes home, Reilly hides in the downstairs toilet. And when his dad walks through the hall, Reilly jumps out and shouts, 'Surprise! Did you see me?' and nearly knocks the popcorn out of his dad's hands.

When Reilly's dad comes home, Reilly runs around the living room with his arms out wide, pretending to be a fighter pilot.

When Reilly's dad comes home, he picks Reilly up, runs out into the hall and turns the fighter pilot into a fighter bomber.

BOOM, BOOM!

When Reilly's dad comes home, he hugs Reilly, and he hugs Reilly's mum, and I think that they are never going to let go.

When Reilly's dad comes home, he looks at me standing at the top of the stairs and smiles and says, 'Hi, Sam, how are you doing?'

And I smile back and say, 'I'm doing fine.'

And then they all look at me and Reilly's mum says, 'Come on down, Sam. It's movie night.'

And Reilly holds up a giant packet of M&Ms and says, 'We got your favourite, Sam, so they melt in the popcorn.'

I look down at them. *This is a perfect family*, I think to myself. *This is a perfect family, but I don't think there's a space for me in it.* And it goes around and around in my head until Reilly shouts, 'Sam's got a girlfriend. Sam's got a girlfriend!'

'I haven't,' I say.

'Has.'

'That's enough, Reilly.' His dad sits down on the bottom stair. 'How's *Bugsy* going, Sam?'

'Okay,' I say.

'He's been with his friends acting all day,' Reilly's mum jumps in. I feel bad lying to Reilly's dad, but at least it wasn't me who said it.

'Good stuff,' he says, untying his laces. 'Any other news?'

'Not really,' I say. Then Reilly's mum says she's got plenty, that Laura and somebody else they know are getting married and asked her to do the cake, but I'm not really listening. I do have news; I've got lots of news and new people in my life – I've got a grandma who walks her dog in the park. I've a new friend called Josh and he's got an uncle and auntie who I hope will be my perfect parents and one day soon I hope I will go and live with them in their red house. That is my news, but I can't tell anyone about it.

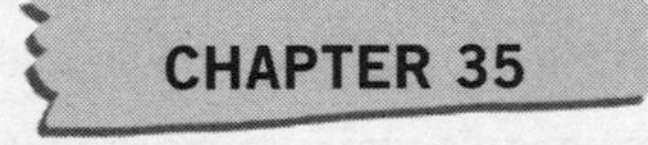

MY IMAGINARY BROTHER

Everyone is downstairs watching *Guardians of the Galaxy*. I love this film, especially Groot, but I'd rather be on my phone. I'm telling Leah all about my day. And also Josh has messaged to ask me to go over again tomorrow, but I told him I was going to visit my gran with my parents. I couldn't tell him it's because I might not be able to get away so easily now that Reilly's dad is back.

I hear the sound of Reilly laughing downstairs. Little giggles joined together like machine-gun fire. They must have got to the bit where Rocket Raccoon jumps on Groots's shoulders. Part of me wants to go down and watch it with Reilly, but it'd be weird because he'll be sitting cuddled up with his mum and dad on the sofa and I'd have to sit on my own in a chair.

I hold my phone against my chest. Sometimes I imagine that I have a real brother or sister and one day they'll come for me. They will be older than me, maybe sixteen – old enough to ask the authorities if they have any other family. And the authorities will tell them they have a brother and they'll try to find me, but it might take them a while because I've moved around so much. I will be sitting in a bedroom somewhere and I'll hear a car pull up outside, and I'll look out of the window and watch two people walk up the path. One of them will be Rock Star Steve with his spikey hair but the other one I won't know because they'll be wearing a baseball cap back to front. The foster-parent will open the door and I'll hear Rock Star Steve talking but it'll be so quiet I won't be able to make out the words. So I'll sneak along the landing to the top of the stairs and peer down but all I'll see will be Rock Star Steve's snakeskin shoes and beside them a pair of white trainers.

'Is Sam here?' Rock Star Steve will ask, and the foster-parent won't have to answer because, for once, instead of running away, I'll be halfway down the stairs. Rock Star Steve will smile and I'll glance at the person next to him and they'll smile and take off their baseball cap. I'll gasp because it's like I'm looking at a taller, older me in a mirror.

And I'll walk down the stairs and now he'll be grinning, and I'll see his brown eyes and he'll say, 'Hi, I'm Ross – little c, big C – McCann and I think I've found my brother.'

'Sam . . . Sam.'

I jump out of my dream.

Reilly's mum is standing in the middle of the room with a tub of popcorn in one hand and a piece of Reilly's dad's helicopter cake in the other.

'I thought maybe you'd like some,' she says.

'I'm not hungry,' I say.

'Then I'll just leave it here.'

'Okay,' I say, as she puts the popcorn and cake on my bedside cabinet.

I wait for her to go, but she bends down and says, 'Sam, are you all right?' as if I'm ill.

'I'm fine.'

Reilly's mum's still there. 'Sam, we've been thinking, we've not seen much of you this holiday, and now Dad's back we thought perhaps we might all go to the Roman Baths tomorrow.'

'But I can't,' I say.

'It can't be *Bugsy* again.'

'No. But I was going to see Leah. Can't we go the next day?'

'Not really – Reilly's nan and granddad are coming on Sunday.'

'Again?'

'It's only once a month, and this is Easter Sunday.'

I roll my eyes. It's so boring when Reilly's nan and granddad visit.

'Look,' says Reilly's mum, like she's suddenly had a great idea. 'How about Leah comes with us too? That way you can work on your project.'

I feel bad that she believes my story about the fake project. I look at the popcorn box.

'Come on,' she says. 'Reilly would love it. You know how much he enjoys doing things with you. What do you think?'

I think no, but she'll never go away if I say that. Maybe I should make her happy and go to the Roman Baths. That way she might not get on my case when I go back to the rainbow houses.

'Okay,' I sigh.

'And Leah?'

Going with Leah would be fun, but she talks so much she might let the Perfect Parent Project out of the bag.

'No,' I say. 'I'll come on my own.'

'Great.' Reilly's mum claps her hands like she's just made her best cake. 'I'll go down and tell Reilly. He'll be pleased . . . Are you sure you won't join us for the film?'

'Yes. I'm sure.'

'Okay.' Reilly's mum turns, then stops. 'Sam, you do know I want you to come down. You are part of the family.'

'Yeah,' I sigh again. 'I know that.'

She gives me a smile, like the one Mrs Sorrell gives me at school, then leaves.

I lie back on my bed, wishing I could return to my dream about my brother, like it was as easy as pressing play on the TV. But maybe I shouldn't do that anyway, because all it does is make me upset that if I do have a brother, he never came for me today.

CHAPTER 36

CATCHING UP WITH LEAH

How were the Roman Baths?

Reilly was sick.

What?

Went all over the floor. And my trainers.

Eew.

Too much Easter egg . . . and hot dog and onions.

Aww. Poor Reilly. Is he okay now?

Yep. He's in bed, above me. Hope he isn't sick again!

How many eggs did you get?

One. M&Ms. You?

None, Mum thinks it's better to buy presents so she's taking me to get a piercing tomorrow. You want to come?

I've got to stay here. Reilly's grandma and granddad are coming over.

You've DEFINITELY got to stay. Reilly's mum will ground you if you're not there.

We've got a family meeting too, after they've gone.

☹

I look at my screen. This means I won't have seen Josh for two days. He'll think I'm avoiding him, or he might just forget about me. Maybe I could sneak out in the afternoon.

Don't even think about it!

How did you know what I was thinking?

Because I know you. Just don't worry about it. I'll work it out.

How?

Doesn't matter. But I will. Gotta go now. Going to watch Love Actually with Mum. Jug-ears has gone away for Easter. Enjoy the grandparents. Bye x

Bye.

XXXXXXXXXXX

Stop doing that!

☺

THIS IS WHAT IT'S LIKE WHEN REILLY'S GRANDPARENTS VISIT

Reilly puts on clothes he hates.

Reilly's mum and dad spend the morning cooking roast dinner and get red, hot and stressy. Me and Reilly lay the table, then keep out of the way, watching TV or sitting in his room playing Ace Pilot on the Xbox.

When the doorbell rings, Reilly runs downstairs. He tells me to follow, but I stay up on the landing while he opens the door.

And he says, 'Hey, Nan. Hi, Granddad!'

And his nan goes, 'Oh my goodness, Reilly, haven't you grown! Gerald, hasn't he grown?' Even though they were here only four weeks ago.

And his granddad hands Reilly's dad a pack of beer and goes, 'Oooh, yes, Reilly, you're nearly as tall as me, or am I shrinking?'

Everyone laughs. Then Reilly's mum walks into the hall and says, 'Reilly, don't just stand there. Let them in. Take your nan's coat.'

And Reilly's nan goes to take it off but before she does she hands Reilly a carrier bag.

'It's your Easter egg,' she says. 'And something else.'

Reilly pulls out a box and smiles, because his egg has got his name written on the front. And then he pulls out the something else and shouts, '*Toy Story 4*. I got *Toy Story 4* pyjamas!'

And his nan goes, 'Yes, I picked them up from ASDA.'

Then Reilly holds the pyjamas up to me and says, 'It's Forky, Sam! Look!'

His granddad hands him another box and says, 'We thought we'd give you this now, because we won't be here for your birthday.'

Reilly rips the paper off and shouts, 'It's a Lego helicopter, Sam. We've got to make it. Will you help me?'

I take a step forward, even though I don't want to, and Reilly's nan looks up and says, 'Oh! I didn't see you there. I'm afraid we forgot an extra egg.'

'That's okay,' says Reilly's mum. 'Reilly can always share his.'

I smile and say it's okay, but in my head I'm thinking, *I know you just forgot my name again and I don't want pyjamas with a picture of a stupid cutlery character.*

Then Reilly's mum says, 'It's SAM, Mum, you remember. The great actor.'

'Oh, yes,' she says. I wait for her to say something about drama, but she turns to Reilly and asks, 'Oh, is that the jumper I bought you for Christmas? Very nice.'

Ten minutes later, Reilly's granddad and dad have opened their beer cans and we're all sitting at the table eating. They're talking about things that happened before I was here and people I've never met, and Reilly's granddad asks—

'How's Reilly doing at school? Does he still want to be a pilot?'

Reilly nods and glances at me as he eats, because I'm the only one who knows that he'll never become a pilot if he can't get off level three.

Then we eat the apple pie his nan brought.

Clear the table.

Load the dishwasher.

And sometimes I get in Reilly's nan's way, and she smiles and goes, 'Oops! Oops! Sorry . . .'

And in my head I go, *Sam, my name's Sam. But it's okay if you forget it, because tomorrow I'm going to see my perfect parents again, so I probably won't be here the next time you come.*

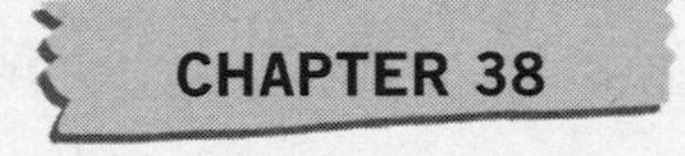

THE FAMILY MEETING WHERE I DO OKAY ☺

'You've been busy, but you're not getting home too late.' That's Reilly's mum.

'It's good you've got drama.' That's Reilly's dad.

'And it's good Sam's got a girlfriend.' That's Reilly.

'So does that mean I can go to Lewis's tomorrow?' That's me telling a lie.

'Ah, Sam . . .' Reilly's mum and dad say at the same time.

'But I did go to the Roman Baths.'

'Yes, you did.'

'And I did stay in all day today for Reilly's grandparents.'

'Yes, but, Sam,' says Reilly's mum, with a tired look on her face. 'Sometimes it would be nice if you stayed with us because you wanted to, not because you have to.'

'So does that mean I can go or not?'

'Maybe just for the morning.'

But that isn't long enough.

'I was hoping I'd meet Leah, after . . . for our project?'

'Where?'

'At her house.'

'But isn't her mum at work?'

'Yes,' I say. 'But her sister will be there to check we're okay. She's sixteen.'

'Maybe she could come here instead.'

'Yeah, Sam,' Reilly says. 'Let her come here. Let her come here!'

'I won't be able to concentrate.'

'He has got a point.' Reilly's dad glances at Reilly, who's doing his K-I-S-S-I-N-G face.

'Okay, but I don't want you out late. It would be nice to have tea together, while we're all here.'

'Okay,' I say out loud. *Yes! I'm going to Michelle and Dave's*, I say in my head.

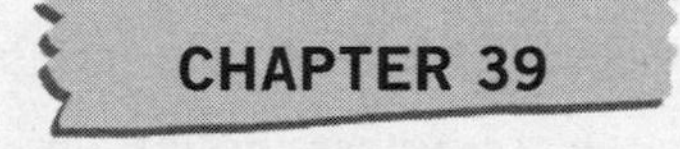

CHAPTER 39

THE PERFECT PARENT PROJECT STAGE FOUR

Josh is sitting on the wall outside his house when I get to the rainbow houses.

'Just be yourself, Sam,' is what Leah said to me, when I left her at her house this morning. 'Just be yourself and they are bound to like you.'

I wanted her to come with me, but her dad had arranged to meet her and Mollie. She hardly ever sees him, so I didn't want to stop that.

I take a deep breath, look across the square.

Just be yourself, Sam, I say in my head. *Just be yourself and they will like you.* I say it over and over. Because that's the aim of the Perfect Parent Project Stage Four: getting Michelle and Dave to like me.

I wheel my bike towards Josh.

Here we go, Sam. Just be yourself.

I keep walking.

Josh waves at me. I wait for him to jump down off the wall and meet me, but he sits and waits, with the door wide open behind him. There's no Frisbee. No football. Just a suitcase beside him on the ground.

Have Michelle and Dave changed their minds about having Josh to stay?

Is Josh homesick and wants to go home already?

I push my bike faster in panic. My Perfect Parent Project is going to fail before stage four has even started.

'What are you doing?' I say, catching my breath.

'What do you mean?'

'No football,' I puff. 'No Frisbee. Are you leaving?'

'No.' Josh narrows his brow. 'Why would you think that?'

I nod at the suitcase.

'Oh, that's nothing. Auntie Michelle was just throwing some stuff out for Uncle Dave to take to the dump.'

'Oh, cool,' I say with relief, hoping Josh didn't notice my panic. 'So we can still play Frisbee?'

'No, sorry. I should have messaged you. We're about to go out, but Auntie Michelle takes ages to get ready.'

'Oh,' I say, trying to hide my disappointment. 'Where are you going?'

'Bowling,' says Josh.

'Cool.'

'Would bc, but we're going with Uncle Dave's friends and their daughter Orla who is annoyingly good at bowling. That's not the worst thing though – all Dave and his friend do is talk about fire safety.'

‘Fire safety?’

‘Yeah, it’s his job. Uncle Dave and his friend go around to companies, talking about how not to let their buildings burn down. It was way more exciting when he was a fireman. He’s been on the news three times. Remember that fire at the cereal factory last year?’

I nod like I’m listening, but I’m still getting my head around the fact I’m not going to see them today.

‘Well, he helped put it out,’ says Josh. ‘It was cool, but Auntie Michelle got jealous when he was interviewed on TV and loads of women asked to be his friend on Facebook.’

‘Are you on about my job again?’ Dave comes to the doorway and looks at me. ‘Josh preferred it when I was putting out fires rather than trying to stop them in the first place,’ he says, rubbing Josh’s head. I smile as I pick up my bike.

‘I’d better be going,’ I say reluctantly.

‘Okay,’ says Dave. ‘Maybe catch up with Josh tomorrow, Sam. Or pop by later, as you’re only around the corner.’

‘Yeah,’ I say, ‘I will.’

‘Can Sam come with us?’ Josh suddenly says.

‘Well.’ Dave looks as surprised as I feel. ‘I don’t know, I hadn’t really . . .’

‘What’s that?’

Michelle walks through the hall, squeezing herself next to Dave in the doorway. Josh said she takes ages to get ready, but she’s dressed in a red tracksuit like she’s going to the gym.

‘Josh just asked if Sam could join us.’

Michelle and Dave exchange looks. I feel embarrassed that Josh asked, but it doesn't stop me from wanting to go.

'Please,' says Josh. 'Orla might be taking her friend so I won't have anyone to talk to.'

'Okay,' says Michelle, 'but, Sam, go and tell your mum first. Take Josh with you while I put my trainers on.'

'Cool!' says Josh, beaming at me. 'Come on, Sam.' He jumps down off the wall, ready to follow me to a house that doesn't exist in a street I don't live in.

'I . . . I . . . I'm not sure,' I say. 'I . . . I . . .' I tap my pocket in panic. 'Maybe I'll text her instead.'

'Why don't you give her a call?' says Dave. 'We're leaving now, and we'll have to turn back if she says no.'

'It's okay,' I say. 'I'm pretty sure she won't . . . but I will call, just in case.' I turn away, shielding my phone. I can't call Reilly's mum because she thinks I'm practising *Bugsy* this morning. There's only one person to call. I click on Leah's number.

Michelle comes out, closing the door behind her.

'He's calling his mum,' says Dave.

The dialling tone buzzes in my ear. Then: 'Hi, Sam, what's wrong? You never call me!'

'Hi, Mum,' I say. 'You know that boy I told you about?'

'Mum?' says Leah. 'Sam, why are you—'

'Yeah, that's right – Josh. Well, his auntie and uncle are taking him bowling. Can I go with them?'

'Sam, what are you on about? Oh, right!' Leah laughs, finally getting it.

I press my phone close to my ear so Michelle and Dave can't hear giggling.

'So it's okay?' I say. 'Isn't it?'

'Yes,' says Leah.

Dave walks to the passenger door of the car and holds up his hand. 'Tell her we'll be back about five,' he says, spreading his fingers.

'We'll be back at five,' I repeat.

'Okay,' says Leah. 'I'll come back to the park for you, but don't be late.'

'Okay, Mum.'

'Oh and, Sam,' says Leah. 'Are they listening?'

'Yes.'

'Okay. Just say bye and love you, Mum.'

'What?'

'Just do it, Sam – it's what I always say to my mum, even when sometimes I don't mean it.'

'Okay,' I say through gritted teeth. 'Bye . . . Love you . . . Mum.'

Leah giggles as I pull the phone away.

'She says thank you,' I say, turning to Dave.

'Great,' he says, looking into the car. 'Now all we've got to do is hope Michelle doesn't kill us with her driving!'

TEN PINS

'Where did you live before, Sam?' That was Michelle, in the car.

'Why did you move?' That was her too.

'Was it Mum and Dad's work?' Still Michelle.

'What is it that your mum and dad do again?' That was Dave.

'Um, I used to live in Devon,' I told them.

Michelle asked where exactly, because they go there on a lot on holidays.

'Brantwich,' I said.

'Oh, I don't think I've heard of it,' said Michelle, which wasn't surprising as neither had I until it popped into my head. I told her it's a very tiny village, so small that most people don't even know when they've driven through it. And we moved for Dad's work because hc's a private detective, but I'm not allowed to talk about that much. Then the car suddenly swerved, and Dave told Michelle that it might be better if she stopped talking and kept her eyes on the road. And I was glad because that was the end of her questions, but now I'm at the bowling alley, waiting to meet new people, and there'll be even more questions for sure. I just have to make sure I remember my lies.

'What shoe size, Sam?'

'Sorry?'

'Shoe size?' says Dave, looking down at me. 'You have to wear bowling shoes to play.'

We're at the counter inside the ten pin bowling complex. I'm surprised that we have to change shoes, but at least the first question is easy.

'Four,' I say.

The girl serving us puts our bowling shoes on the counter. Josh grabs two pairs. 'Come on, Sam,' he says. 'We'll change over here.'

I follow him through a crowd of people and we sit down on a row of seats next to a hot-dog stand. *This is just bowling*, I tell myself, *people do it all the time*, but that doesn't stop my hands from shaking as I pull off my shoes. It also doesn't stop me feeling embarrassed because Josh's Nike trainers look so new and clean next to mine.

'You all right, Sam?' Josh looks across at me as we tie our laces.

'Yeah,' I say. 'I'm just a bit nervous. I haven't played for a while.'

'How long?'

'Well, like never.'

'Really?' Josh sits up. 'Never?'

'No,' I say. I could have lied, but I'd look stupid when it's obvious I don't actually know what to do.

Josh smiles as we pick up our trainers. 'That's okay. We're not brilliant. Well, Auntie Michelle is quite good, but Uncle Dave has only just stopped using bumpers.'

'Hey! I heard that!' Dave says loudly from his seat opposite us.

Josh laughs. I smile. I love how they have little jokes together, like I do with Reilly.

We all take our street shoes and hand them back over the counter for safe-keeping. Then Dave steps behind us, puts one arm around Michelle's shoulder, the other around Josh's. 'And you, Sam,' he says, beckoning me.

I move closer to Josh and feel Dave's hand on my shoulder.

'Oh no.' Michelle rolls her eyes. 'Here we go. Team-talk time.'

Dave leans forward and groups us into a huddle. 'Okay, team, we've got Super Sam and Jumping Josh . . . and Dangerous Dave.'

'Who am I?' asks Michelle.

'No idea – I can't think of anything that starts with M. Now let's go beat this mob.'

Michelle shakes her head. 'I don't think you'll ever grow up.'

Dave grins.

Michelle wants him to grow up, but I hope he never will.

'This is Sam,' says Dave. 'He's a friend of Josh who's just moved in around the corner from us. Sam, this is Pav and Monika.'

I look at Dave's friends. Pav has a shaved head and a serious expression on his face, and Monika seems shy, but they both look friendly when they smile.

'Hi, Sam,' they say at the same time.

I nod, trying to be cool, but inside my heart is beating like a rabbit's.

'This is Orla,' says Monika, 'and her school friend, Freya.'

'Hi,' I say. Orla and Freya smile and look as awkward as I feel. It's as if everyone is looking at me, waiting for me to say something. I can't think of anything because I'm nervous, but also, I'm thinking that Freya looks just like a girl in Year Eight at my school.

'Right, team.' Dave rubs his hands together. 'I think it's time we kicked this lot's butt!'

Everyone laughs, then we walk across to our bowling lane. While the adults stand around talking, Josh picks up a ball.

'You should probably use the same one as me,' he says, 'because our hands are the same size.' He holds the ball out in front of me. 'You just put your thumb in this hole, then your middle finger and ring finger in these two holes. Try it.'

I take the ball and put my thumb and fingers in the holes just as Josh said. Out of the corner of my eye I see Orla and Freya whispering to each other as they watch me. For a moment I panic, but then I think that I don't know anything about kids in Year Eight, so how would they know anything about me? I catch Freya's eye and she quickly looks up at the scoreboard even though there's nothing there to see. Now I'm sure they were talking about me. It happens all the time. I can't hide being a foster-kid, no matter how much I try to cover it up or lie. They know what I am, just like I bet everyone at school does. Sometimes I feel like I'm wearing a T-shirt with 'I'm a foster-kid' written on the front. Leah and Rock Star Steve say it's not true. They say I'm imagining it, that people are just curious when they meet me – as they would be with anyone new.

'So have you got it, Sam?'

'What . . . ? Oh, yes.' I look at the ball, my fingers in the holes.

I sneak another look at the girl. Now I've seen her face properly I realize it's not the girl in Year Eight. I smile with relief, but it doesn't last for long because suddenly Dave says, 'Right, Sam, it looks like you're up.'

I glance up at the screen and see my name first on the list with Josh, Michelle and Dave written underneath. Josh has shown me how to hold the ball, but not how to let it go. I look across the other lanes, to see if there's anyone I can copy. A man three lanes away is standing with a ball held up to his chin. I go to do the same, but my fingers wobble weakly in the holes.

'Tell you what,' says Dave, 'I'll help . . . Orla, could you change the order on the board?'

I want to say I'm okay, but I've seen people fall over in films and fly down the lane in cartoons. Orla taps the screen and Josh's name flips with mine. I pass him the ball and he walks towards the lane.

Dave crouches beside me. 'Just watch what he does, Sam,' he says softly. 'See how he holds the ball below his knee, then swings it back and through? Now he's going to let it go.'

The ball rolls down the lane. Josh leans forward as it smashes into the pins.

'Yes! Six!' he says with a fist pump.

'Well done, Joshie,' says Michelle, giving him a high five.

'Now he's got another go,' says Dave.

'Okay,' I say. For a moment I feel confident, but then I spot Orla and Freya watching me and suddenly I feel six years old and my confidence disappears down a drain.

I sit and watch as Josh bowls another ball and knocks one more skittle over. The skittles re-stack as Monika walks past me. She bowls the first ball, knocks four over, then another two with her next ball.

'Okay, Sam,' says Michelle. 'Off you go.'

My stomach flips. I stand up. I want to impress Dave and Michelle and prove that I listened, but I'm so nervous it feels like my shoes are stuck to the boards with glue.

'You're good,' says Dave.

'Yeah,' says Josh. 'And remember, whatever happens Auntie Michelle will always be worse.'

'Oi.' Michelle gives Josh a fake glare.

I smile, then pick a ball up from the feeder and put my thumb and fingers in the holes.

'Ooh, he's a leftie,' says Pav with his serious look.

I stop. *Aren't I doing it right?* Dave never said I couldn't use my left hand.

I look around at the group. 'Is that okay?'

'Yeah, of course,' says Pav, smiling. 'I'm just saying you're left-handed. Are your mum and dad?'

'Are they what?'

'Left-handed?'

'I don't know.' I glance at Michelle and Dave as I realize my mistake. 'I mean, my dad is,' I say. 'Yeah, my dad is.' I turn towards the pins and hope no one noticed my mistake. Everyone knows if their mum and dad are right- or left-handed. They can tell when they see them write a letter, or play tennis or badminton, or by just laying their cutlery on the table. I don't know if my parents play sports and I've never seen my mum write a letter. I stare down the lane.

'You ready, Sam?' Dave steps beside me.

'Yes,' I say, even though I don't feel it. I lower the ball below my left knee. The pins are lined up at the end of the lane in front of me. *I'm left-handed*, I think to myself. *And I've never thought about why.*

I step onto the white line, swing the ball back behind me, swing it through and let go.

I DON'T KNOW . . .

I don't know why my hair is brown.

I don't know why I have a tiny mole on my wrist.

I don't know why my nose wrinkles up when I laugh, only that Leah says it does.

I don't know why I have brown eyes.

I don't know why I hate cheese but love tomatoes.

I don't know why I can run so fast but eat so slowly.

I don't know why I love cycling but am rubbish at swimming.

I don't know why apple juice brings me out in a rash.

I don't know why I kick a football with my right foot.

I don't know why I'm left-handed.

Why am I left-handed?

That's all I can think about in the car on the way back from bowling. Everyone else knows where they get their 'things' from. Reilly's face looks like his mum, but his hair is black like his dad's.

Reilly is good at writing because his granddad is. And he goes weak when he sees blood, just like his nan. That's what everyone says about Reilly. Reilly gets this from here. Reilly gets that from there. Reilly knows where everything comes from. He knows his whole life story. If he wanted to he could draw his family tree. I could draw mine too, but it would be like a pot plant with just me.

'Everything okay, Sam?' I see Michelle's eyes in the rear-view mirror.

'Yeah,' I say. 'I was just thinking it was a brilliant day.'

'It was,' she says.

'Yeah.' Dave looks over his shoulder. 'But I bet you wouldn't have said that if you hadn't knocked all those pins over.'

'Yeah,' says Josh. 'You were great. Hang on, I'll send you the picture the guy from the alley took.'

My phone vibrates. I look at the screen – it's me, Josh, Dave and Michelle, thumbs up, big smiles, and underneath Josh has typed 'THE WINNING TEAM! ☺'. I can't stop myself smiling. I really like Dave and I really like Michelle. They don't have a huge house, or a BMW M5, and they don't even seem that bothered about going to Disneyland, but it still feels like they've ticked every box on my list, and more. It isn't a team on my screen; it's like being part of a family. I turn and see Josh with his head down, looking at his phone. In the front Dave and Michelle are laughing like they are sharing a joke. I lean forward in my seat. The seat belt tightens across my chest but it's not tight enough to stop my words coming out.

'Thank you for taking me,' I say.

Dave turns around.

'No problem, Sam.' He smiles. 'Do you think your mum would mind if we dropped you back a little bit later?'

'Why, are we going to Wagamama?' Josh looks up and grins.

'That's what we were thinking,' says Michelle.

'Great,' says Josh. 'Do you like noodles, Sam? Uncle Dave hangs them from his nostrils and pretends he's a walrus.'

Dave laughs. 'I only did that when you were little! But, Sam, do you want to call your mum first and check it's okay?'

'I'll message her,' I say. 'She might be working.'

I take my phone out of my pocket. I've been enjoying myself so much, I've not checked my messages for ages – there's one from Leah, saying she hopes I'm having fun. Three from Reilly's mum, asking what time I'm going to be back, and reminding me we are all having tea together.

The last one says, Sam, if you don't reply soon, I'm going to have to call Steve.

She won't do that, I think to myself. She says it but never does. I message Leah.

Having a great time. Going to Wagamama.

My phone bleeps. Leah replies:

☺

'Yeah,' I say. 'Mum says it's fine.'

'Cool,' says Dave.

I look at Reilly's mum's messages again. I quickly send a reply.

Staying at Leah's for tea.

Then I turn my phone off and put it in my pocket.

CHAPTER 42

DIGGING HOLES IN WAGAMAMA

It's like we're sitting in our own little room where no one else can hear us.

I'm trying to pick up noodles with chopsticks but it's hard to concentrate when Dave and Michelle are making me laugh so much. Dave just told us how he left home when he was eighteen and joined the fire brigade. One of his first call-outs was to a fire at a clothing warehouse near Taunton. The flames were fifteen metres high and he and his crew had to pump thousands of litres of water from twelve engines before the fire died down. The next morning, it was Dave's job to walk through the wreckage of the warehouse to find out what had started it. Two of the dummies fell over and Dave was so scared that he ran out, thinking he was being chased by zombies.

Now Michelle is telling us about a time at her work when a

colleague put some money in a vending machine, pressed the button for a Mars Bar, but it didn't come out. So he tried to reach the Mars with his arm and got it jammed in the machine and they had to call the fire brigade out.

We laugh, then laugh even harder when Josh gives up using the chopsticks and sucks the noodles off his plate, making them disappear like wriggling worms. He chokes and laughs at the same time and for a moment it reminds me of Reilly doing the same with his spaghetti and I feel guilty that I'm having so much fun without him. That he's sitting on his own with his mum and dad right now. For a moment I feel bad that I'm not with him. But then I also don't want my time with Michelle and Dave to end.

I suck up more noodles, then sense Michelle looking across the table at me. I wipe my mouth on a napkin just in case that's the reason she's looking, but then she says, 'Listen to us, yapping about ourselves, Sam. What about you? I bet you've done some funny things.'

'Me?' I say nervously. 'I . . . I . . . There isn't much to tell.'

She smiles. 'There must be something. What about your hobbies – things you do and don't like to do?'

I try to pick up some noodles but they slip between the chopsticks. My face starts to burn. What can I say? I can't tell the truth – that I'm a foster-kid and they're part of my project to find perfect parents. I glance up and see them all looking at me, waiting for an answer.

'W . . . W . . . W . . .' I look down at my plate. 'Well, I'm rubbish at picking up worms.'

Everyone laughs.

I smile. I hope I've got out of the question by making a joke like I sometimes do in maths at school. But Michelle is still looking at me, waiting for a proper answer.

'I . . . I . . . I . . .'

'You like acting,' Josh jumps in. 'Don't you, Sam?'

I nod.

'He's going to be in *Bugsy Malone*.'

'Is that right?' says Michelle. 'That's great. What part have you got?'

'It hasn't been decided yet,' I say. 'It starts next term.'

'I'm sure you'll get a great part,' says Dave.

'Yes,' says Michelle. 'Does that mean you can dance and sing too?'

'Yes,' I say. 'Well, a bit.'

'Your mum and dad must be very proud,' she says. 'Are they musical too?' Michelle looks at me like she's expecting me to burst into song, but all I'm doing is trying to think. The questions are coming so fast that I'm scared of digging holes full of lies that I can't get out of. But I have to say something.

'Umm . . . my mum is,' I say. 'She went to acting school in London.'

'RADA?' asks Michelle.

I've never heard of it, but it sounds good. 'Yeah,' I say. 'I think that was it.'

'Lovely,' says Michelle. 'And does she still do it?'

'Little bit.' I pick up a noodle and put it in my mouth, hoping the questions might stop, or that Dave will jump in and tell us another story, but then he starts asking questions too!

'Would we have seen her in anything?' he asks.

'What about *Casualty*?' Michelle says. 'I think they film that round here.'

'No.' My mind scrambles for more lies. 'She gave it up when she had me.'

'Oh,' says Michelle, sounding disappointed.

I need to say something interesting. They'll never want me if I'm boring.

'She was in an advert once,' I blurt.

'Ooh, which one?' says Michelle.

'Umm . . . soap powder,' I say. 'But it's not on TV any more.' I suck on a noodle – too many questions, too many holes – and Michelle opens her mouth like she's going to ask another. I need to get her off my case, stop her talking about parents.

'I'd like to go to Disneyland,' I say.

Michelle and Dave laugh.

'Me too.' Josh looks hopefully at his auntie and uncle.

'You can give me that sad look all you want, matey,' says Dave. 'It costs a packet.'

'But it's worth it,' says Josh. 'My friend Kam went and he said the rides were amazing. And they went to Universal Studios.'

'Yes,' I say. 'I'd like to do that too.'

Dave grins and shakes his head slowly. That's when I notice Michelle smiling at me for too long. I look down and fiddle with my last noodle.

'Sam,' she says. 'That's the second time you've mentioned Disneyland.'

'I know,' I say. 'I think about it lots. I hope I'll go one day.'

'After a big Hollywood director sees you in *Bugsy Malone*,' says Josh, 'you'll be rich and famous. You won't have to catch a plane – you'll live so close you can just jump in a limo … Or get a police escort in your BMW M5.'

'Yeah.' I smile. 'That'd be cool.'

Dave and Michelle are in the front of the car listening to music, talking about people I don't know. Josh is sitting beside me, messaging someone on his phone. I'm leaning against the door, my head resting on the window. Apart from digging holes, it's been a perfect day. A perfect day with perfect parents. Now all I've got to do is think of a way that I can see them so I can have days like this all the time. Should I just turn up at their house in the morning and hope that if they're going out they'll take me with them again? Maybe I should have told them I like playing pitch and putt, or tennis. But that costs money. They paid for everything today. What if they expect me to pay them back? Most kids would go home and ask their parents for some money, but I can't do that. Even if I thought Reilly's mum would give me it, she'd want to know what it was for. I look at my phone and message Leah.

The Perfect Parent Project stage four. Mission complete ☺

They like you!

I think so!

See, Sam! You just had to be yourself.

☺

Even if you can be annoying ☺ x

Grr!

XXX

My phone buzzes with a message from Lewis.

Hey Sam, we're all meeting at Amala's the day after tomorrow. 11. Here's the address.

I click off the message. Trying to meet my perfect parents and keep drama going is getting complicated.

'So,' says Dave loudly.

Me and Josh look up.

'What do you think, boys?'

Michelle turns the music down.

'Help me paint the back fence?' says Dave.

'Who?' asks Josh.

'You two.' Dave's eyes catch mine in the rear-view mirror. 'You and Sam. I've been meaning to do it for ages, but it'll be much quicker if I have some help. What do you think?'

I look at Josh. *Say yes*, I think. *Say yes. We can do it, the two of us.*

'I'd like to,' I jump in before Josh can answer. 'It'll be fun.'

'Wait.' Josh looks at me, surprised. 'You haven't seen the fence; it goes on for miles!'

I shrug. I don't care how long the fence is. There aren't many days left of the holidays but I'd use them up if it meant spending all that time with Michelle and Dave.

'Come on, Joshie,' says Michelle. 'Sam's up for it.'

'Okay.' Josh grins. 'But how much are you going to pay us?'

Michelle laughs. 'You just got an Xbox!'

'Okay if we start tomorrow, Sam?'

'Yes,' I say. 'The sooner the better.'

Dave laughs. 'Well, you can't say you're not keen.'

I shouldn't have said that. I feel my face burn.

'Which number, Sam?' Dave suddenly shouts.

'Sorry?'

'Which number's your house?'

I look through the window. We've been chatting so much I hadn't realized we'd turned into the road where I pretend to live.

'Umm . . .' I try to think of a number as we drive past doorways and parked cars. Which number did I give Michelle when she asked? 'Oh,' I say. 'It's okay. You can drop me back at your house.'

'Don't be silly,' says Michelle. 'We're here now.'

Dave checks the rear-view mirror as the car slows to a crawl. 'This one?' He points at a house with a yellow skip outside filled with pieces of wood and old window frames.

This is getting worse by the second. I look at the skip, at the number on the door – 56. Maybe Michelle won't remember what I said. And the skip fits in with my lie about my parents decorating.

'Yeah,' I say. 'It's here.'

Dave starts to pull over. It's like he wants to stop for a while, even meet my mum and dad.

'It's all right,' I say quickly, 'you don't have to park. I'll just jump out.'

'Blimey,' says Dave. 'It's like you can't wait to get away from us, Sam.' Then he adds to Michelle, 'He's already reaching for the door handle!'

The car slows, then stops. Why does the perfect day have to end like this?

I flip the door handle.

'See you tomorrow,' says Josh.

'Yeah,' I say. 'See you.'

'And bring old clothes,' says Michelle. 'So you don't get your nice ones messed up. Actually,' she turns to Dave, 'maybe we should go and have a word with his mum, just so she knows where he'll be.'

'No,' I say. *Please just go. Please.* I'm running out of excuses. 'It's fine. She'll be busy, putting my little brother to bed.'

'Your brother,' says Michelle. 'You never . . .'

A man cycles by on a bike. My bike! I need it to get back to Reilly's.

'Wait,' I say. 'I need my bike. I left it at yours.'

'It'll still be there in the morning, Sam. I'll pop it in the shed.'

'No.' I search for another reason. 'I need it, I'm . . . I'm . . .' *Got it!* 'I need it early. I'm helping a boy next door do his paper round.'

'Then you'd better jump back in,' says Dave.

I sigh with relief as I sit back next to Josh. It's so hard telling lies and trying to cover my tracks.

Dave puts the car in gear, and we drive to the end of the street where I don't live.

CHAPTER 43

POLICE CAR RIDE

When the police car drove by, I saw the police officers looking out of the window at me. I looked at the ground and kept walking. I was cold, and tired, and my bike had got a puncture.

I wished I was in a bed. Even wished I was back at Reilly's house.

When the police car turned around, I kept walking.

When the police car stopped in front of me, I slowed down.

When the police officer got out of the car, she walked towards me and said softly, 'Are you Sam?'

And I nodded and looked at her shoes. I didn't want her to see that I was upset, that I was scared.

And she said, 'Sam McCann?'

And I mumbled, 'Yes. How did you know?'

'Your foster-parents have been looking for you everywhere. It's gone eight o'clock. They called us; they've been calling you. Don't you have your phone?'

‘Yes,’ I said. ‘But I haven’t looked at it.’

‘Then maybe you should now.’

I reached into my pocket, but I didn’t need to check it. It had buzzed ever since I left Michelle and Dave’s, but I’d ignored every one of the twelve messages and six calls. All of them Reilly’s mum. The police officer led me to the police car. Out of the corner of my eye, I saw a group of kids standing on the kerb outside a chip shop. I looked at them, pretended I wasn’t scared. And I wasn’t scared. I was embarrassed. All I’d done was get a puncture and I couldn’t call Reilly’s mum when I told her I was at Leah’s.

Another police officer put my bike in the boot while the first police officer sat in the back of the car with me. She made notes in her book, while I listened to the chatter of people talking on the police radio.

This was the third time I’ve been picked up in a police car. It happened to me once during the first week with Brad and Angie, but that was because I’d forgotten where their house was, and then at Ross and Kim’s. I didn’t get lost that time; I just didn’t like them.

The police officer told me she didn’t think that going missing was a good thing to do – not for my foster-parents and especially not for me. She told me I seemed like a nice kid, but I didn’t feel like one. Good kids don’t tell lies all the time. I rested my head against the window, watched the kids on the pavement joking and laughing. They were with friends, having fun. I was sitting in a police car with two officers, but I was alone. I had no one to talk to, no one to tell how I felt. Just a horrible aching feeling in my belly, because I had no real parents and no real home and it was too early in the Perfect Parent Project to think that Michelle and Dave were definitely the answer.

I looked at my phone, saw all the messages from Reilly's mum, getting angrier and angrier – until ten past seven when she must have called the police. I switched to a new message from Josh, with no words, just a selfie he took of me and him in Wagamama with Michelle and Dave holding their fingers up behind us, making us look like rabbits.

The kids on the pavement stared at me as the police car moved away and turned onto the high street. We passed people walking, or looking in shop windows as the street lights flickered on.

'We'll soon have you back home nice and safe and warm, Sam,' the police officer said.

I rested my head against the window – more people, more shops, more lights, all of them turning blurry. I didn't want to go back. There was no home; there was no place I felt safe and warm. All I knew was that I ached so much because I wanted it so bad. I wiped my tears on my arm.

'Hey, come on,' said the police officer. 'I'm sure we can sort this out.'

But she didn't know what it felt like not to belong anywhere. She didn't know what it's like to want something so much that you ache for ever inside.

CHAPTER 44

I'M IN TROUBLE

'Sam, it's quarter past eight!'

'I know. I said I'm sorry.'

'Yeah,' Reilly's dad sighs. 'But sorry isn't good enough. Sarah and I shouldn't be chasing around the streets looking for you; we shouldn't have to involve the police. She was worried sick. Now she's got a migraine. You know how hard Sarah works – the last thing she needs is you playing up as well.'

'But I messaged . . .' I say. 'I said I was having tea at Leah's.'

'But we called Leah's house. Mollie said you'd not been there all day.'

'We were there,' I lie. 'Mollie was watching films with her boyfriend.'

'Sam,' says Reilly's dad. 'I don't think that's the case, and that still doesn't explain why you were out so late. And when the police picked you up, you were a mile from here.'

'I know,' I say. 'That's what I'm trying to tell you.' What am I trying to tell him? 'Some kids took my bike from outside Leah's and we followed them, and when we eventually got the bike back, they'd let down the tyres.'

'Sam,' Reilly's dad snaps. 'You know what, I've heard enough.' His face turns red. 'As far as I can see, you're spinning more webs than Spider-Man. I think the best thing for you to do is go to bed and we'll talk about this in the morning.'

I like Reilly's dad. I didn't mean to upset him. I try to think of something to say that will calm him down.

'I am going,' I say. 'But I just wanted—'

'No, Sam.' Reilly's dad waves me away. 'Go. It's clear you just don't care.'

'I do,' I say under my breath.

'No, you really don't.' Reilly's dad rubs his forehead. 'Just go, and please don't disturb Reilly more than you already have.'

I catch Reilly's mum sitting on the sofa with her hand held up to her head. I didn't mean to give her a migraine or to make Reilly's dad this angry and tired. All I wanted to do was have a good time with Michelle and Dave. As I trudge up the stairs, I think about how everyone else at school can go bowling and to Wagamama with their friends. They don't have to explain where they are every second of every day. And they don't get picked up by a police car as they are walking home.

I open the bedroom door slowly. Reilly's on the top bunk with his head hidden behind a book, wearing his new pyjamas. I wait for him to put it down, but he must be as upset as his mum and dad because he doesn't move his book at all. I slip my trainers off. Reilly's dad says I don't care, but he's wrong. My heart wouldn't be thudding like crazy and my face wouldn't be burning if I didn't care. I walk along the edge of the bunks and *accidentally* knock the ladder with my hand, but still Reilly doesn't move. It's like the whole house is mad with me.

I lie back on my bed and stare at the slats.

I did message Reilly's mum. I said I was going to Leah's.

Reilly's mattress pings. I knew he wouldn't sulk for long.

'Sam,' he whispers as his jellyfish head hangs upside down over the side of the bed.

'Yes, Reilly,' I say, smiling.

'I'm not supposed to talk to you, but did the police use the siren?'

'No. No, Reilly, they didn't use a siren.'

'Lights then?'

'No. No lights.'

'So it wasn't exciting?'

'No, not really.'

'I've got taekwondo tomorrow!'

'Have you?'

'Yeah. Will you help me build my Lego helicopter after?'

'I'm not sure,' I say.

'Because you might be going out again?'

'Yeah. But maybe we could do some before I go.'

'Okay.'

Reilly flips back onto his bed. I don't want him to go to sleep unhappy, but I don't want to make promises I can't keep either.

'Reilly,' I whisper. 'I'm sorry, but I will try, even if it's not tomorrow.'

'It's all right,' he whispers between the wall and his mattress. 'I'll wait.'

I roll over on my side. I'm in trouble, but it was worth it to spend the day with Michelle and Dave. There's bound to be trouble in the morning though. I bet they call Rock Star Steve. I just hope he doesn't take me away. I don't want to stay here, but I can't go to Michelle and Dave's to live, not yet. I've only had one full day with them. I'm going to help them paint the fence, but I don't know if they like me enough yet.

The bunks shake as Reilly turns over.

'Night, Sam,' he says.

'Night, Reilly.'

Reilly is too young to understand how I feel. No one understands. I was so happy when I was out. It's like I'm a different person with two different lives. And I don't want this one. I want the one with a perfect family in a red house.

I close my eyes. Today was a perfect day but I wish it hadn't ended like this. And when I do go, I wish I could take Reilly with me.

CHAPTER 45

SOMETIMES I WISH ROCK STAR STEVE WAS MY DAD

I'm sitting in the lounge waiting for Rock Star Steve to turn up. I think things are going to kick off because Reilly's at a friend's house for the morning and his mum and dad are out in the back garden talking. It's like they're deliberately staying out of my way. They didn't say good morning when I came down, or even sit at the table with me while I was eating my cornflakes. I'm trying to be cool and pretend I don't care what they do, but I tossed and turned in my bed with worry all night. All I could think about was how Reilly's dad's face turned so red I thought his head was going to burst, and his mum was so upset she couldn't even look at me. I don't want to stay here, but I'm not ready to move. What if they move me to a school miles away, and I won't be able to do *Bugsy*, or see Leah? I definitely won't have the chance to get to know Michelle and Dave better.

Reilly's mum turns and looks at me through the window. *I know it*, I think. *I know you got Reilly out of the way while you get rid of me. But that's okay, I've packed some stuff just in case.*

I pick up my notebook. Sometimes the best way to cope is to pretend I don't care what they do.

My Top Dream Rides if I Ever Go to Disneyland

1. Guardians of the Galaxy – Mission: BREAKOUT!
2. Splash Mountain.
3. Matterhorn Bobsleds (first or last carriages are best).
4. Toy Story Midway Mania! (for Reilly if his mum and dad aren't too upset to let him go with me ☺).
5. Haunted Mansion.
6. Stealth.
7. Swarm (these last two are actually at Thorpe Park, but it's my dream top ride list and anything can happen in dreams).
8. Any other ride that I'm tall enough for and won't make me feel sick.

I'm thinking of the ninth ride when the doorbell rings. I think of getting up to answer, but Reilly's mum and dad are so anxious to get rid of me, they've already rushed through the hallway and beaten me to it.

I listen to them talking to Rock Star Steve in the hallway:

'Nice to see you.'

'Tom, how's work going?'

'Not so bad. It was nice to be back home, until . . .'

'Yes, I know. Maybe it's best we talk through here.'

Their voices fade away as they walk into the kitchen and close the door. And I think, *What's the point of talking? You're always talking. Just tell me I have to go.* Maybe I should run upstairs, grab my things, make my decision before they make theirs. But running away would mean more police, more trouble. And what if there's a chance, just a tiny chance, that they might let me stay? I'm so confused about what to do for the best. All I know is that I need to stick around long enough to see Michelle and Dave again.

The kitchen door clicks open. Their voices grow louder.

I pick up my pen.

Number nine . . . Number nine . . . Revenge of the Mummy. (It's actually at Universal Studios, but we could fly there afterwards.)

'Sam.'

I'm trying to be cool but my heart still stops as I look up and see Rock Star Steve smiling at me in the doorway.

'Come on,' he says. 'Let's have a chat.'

'Do I need to get my things?' I say. 'Do I need—?'

'Sam.' Rock Star Steve nods his head towards the stairs. 'Let's just go, mate.'

'Keep your head down.' That's what Rock Star Steve says to me in Pizza Hut. 'Just keep your head down, make more of an effort at home, try to spend more time with them. I know you're busy with *Bugsy* at the moment, but they'd appreciate it, and you'll feel better too. And when you're out, make sure you use that.' He points to my phone. 'It only takes a message or a call. And not a fib, either. You can't blame them for worrying. You know what it's like if you don't hear from your friends for a while. You worry too.'

I nod, but I'm confused. Rock Star Steve is talking like I'm staying. I look across at him. I'm scared to ask, but I need to know if I've got it wrong.

'So I'm not leaving?' I wince, dreading the answer.

'No, you're not leaving.'

'And I don't have to say goodbye to Reilly?'

'No.'

I take a bite of pizza in relief.

'It's okay, you know, if I do have to move,' I say, once I've swallowed. 'I don't want to stay there anyway.'

Rock Star Steve shakes his head. 'Sam,' he says. 'You don't have to keep doing this.'

'What?'

'This.' He holds out his hands. 'This *I don't care* thing you do. You do care. I know you. You pretend you don't, but you do. It's okay to get upset. It's okay to show your feelings.'

I look back at my plate and pick up another slice of pizza. On the next table I notice a woman looking at me and Rock Star Steve. She's been doing it since we got here. I think she thinks Rock Star Steve is my dad. It's the way she smiles at me when I accidentally catch her looking. It's the way she smiled when I went to the toilet and when I came back again. It's happened before. It must be because he's got brown hair and brown eyes like me, even if his skin is browner. Sometimes I imagine telling people that he's brown because he spends a lot of time in the sun in Los Angeles in his snakeskin shoes. And I'm pale because I have to stay at home to go to school in England, but when he's away we Skype and WhatsApp and he sends me videos of him singing and playing guitar, and he's famous and goes on American TV shows.

The woman smiles at me again, then looks at Rock Star Steve, but he's wiping his hands in a napkin, looking at me.

'So what do you think, Sam?' he says.

I lean forward. 'I think that woman fancies you.'

Rock Star Steve chuckles. 'Come on, let's concentrate on you. Are you going to keep your head down?'

'Suppose so,' I say.

'Look.' Rock Star Steve interlocks his fingers, like he's going to say something serious. 'You may not think it, but Tom and Sarah have a lot of time for you. But I have the feeling there's something else going on with you, something that's not about them at all.'

Yes, there is. I've found my perfect parents and there are only five days of the holidays left to get to know them.

'No,' I say. 'I'm fine.'

'Are you sure?'

I nod.

'You know I'm always on your side, Sam. Yes, I'm here to help Sarah and Tom, but above all else, I'm batting for you.'

'And I'm okay,' I say.

Rock Star Steve nods slowly, like he doesn't believe me.

I pick up my glass.

'So what are you going to do?' says Rock Star Steve.

'Go and get a refill of Coke,' I say.

'No.' Rock Star Steve smiles. 'I meant what are you going to do today?'

Helping my perfect parents paint a fence, I think to myself.

'I promised Reilly I'd help him with his Lego helicopter later,' I say out loud.

'That's good.'

'Can I get a refill now?' I want Coke but I also need to reply to Josh to tell him what time I'll be there. I've been so worried about leaving I forgot.

'No, just hold on a minute, Sam,' says Rock Star Steve. 'Look, I've been thinking. Your life story . . .'

'I'm still not doing that,' I say.

'Yeah, I know. I was going to say that you didn't get on with your life story, but maybe there's something else we can do. You mentioned that you had memories of playing in a park, with a kite.'

'Yes.' I lift my hand and feel the scar on my head. 'My mum was there, but I can't remember much else. Only the swing and see-saw, and the tower blocks.'

'How about if I took you back there? I think I know where it is.'

I stare at my empty cup. I don't remember much about where I grew up. I don't know if I want to go or not, only that it makes me feel anxious inside.

'Is my mum still there?' I say tentatively. Part of me wants him to say yes, but the rest of me thinks that even if she is she'll just let me go again.

'No. She's not there.' Rock Star Steve picks up his napkin and wipes his hands. 'But it might help you get a better idea of where you came from. We could walk around the area, maybe even go to the hospital where you were born. I still go back to the village I grew up in even though my parents don't live there. Those little parts of our lives that we like to remember, happy times, can help us when we're not feeling so good.'

'I don't know if I was happy back then,' I say.

'But don't you think it's worth a try?'

I glance out of the window. A man stops with a pushchair. He opens a packet of sweets, bends down and gives them to a toddler. I smile as the toddler swings his legs as he puts the sweets in his mouth. I don't remember many things from when I was that young. Gemma tried to help me to, but I think I blocked a lot out because of the stuff that made me feel bad. But the park with the kite doesn't make me feel bad, it just makes me feel like someone cared about me. I wish I could feel that again, even if my mum isn't there.

'Okay,' I say. 'I'll do it. But with you, not Gemma.'

'Sure.' Rock Star Steve nods like I just made *him* happy. 'Sure. I'll fix it up.'

'So can I get a refill now?'

'Yeah,' he says. 'You go ahead.'

I stand up. The woman smiles at me. As I fill my glass, I look back at Rock Star Steve squinting as he types something into his phone. I like Rock Star Steve. He's the best social worker I've had, but he feels like a friend. Sometimes, I wonder what it would be like if he was my dad. He would still take me to places like this, and to the cinema, and he'd come and watch me in *Bugsy* in the school hall. I might be embarrassed if he turned up in his snakeskin shoes, but he could put his feet under the chair in front so no one could see them. And afterwards he would come backstage and hug me and say well done, and I'd introduce him to Mr Powell. 'This is my dad,' I'd say. 'He plays guitar and sings, and he was in *Grease* in his village musical.' I wonder what it would be like to say those words. 'This is my dad.' I could say them to the waiter, to the chef behind the counter, even to the woman who has been watching us ever since we got here. 'This is my dad. This is my dad.'

Cold Coke spills over the top of my glass onto my fingers.

I pull my glass away.

Rock Star Steve is looking at his phone. He'll be checking his messages from the office – messages from his colleagues about other foster-kids like me. I was stupid to even think he could be my dad. He's great, but this is his job, and one day, like me, he could get moved on. And I'll have to learn to trust someone all over again.

KEEPING MY HEAD DOWN ☺

Are you grounded?

No. But Rock Star Steve says I should do more stuff with Reilly's mum and dad.

Probably a good idea. How are you going to go back to Michelle and Dave's?

I told Josh I'd go tomorrow instead of today, but that's when I said I'd meet Lewis and the others at Amala's. It's getting too complicated. I don't even think I'll be allowed out anyway. Reilly's mum is watching me like a hawk after last night.

Going to be hard doing both, anyway.

I know. But I've got to try. How did it go with your dad?

He didn't turn up. Said his car had to go to the garage.

Sorry.

It's okay. He says he'll make up for it by taking me and Mollie to the cinema tomorrow.

Cool.

'Hiiiiii-yaaaaa!'

I jump as Reilly bounces into the room wearing his taekwondo outfit.

'Hi, Sam,' he says, aiming a kick. 'What are you doing?'

'Just messaging.'

'Okay. Want to do some taekwondo? Mr Philips teached me some new moves.'

'It's taught,' I say. 'Or you learned.'

'Okay, Mr Philips learned me new moves. Get up. I'll show you.'

I smile. Reilly's so excited that I can't help but join in.

'All right,' I say.

I message Leah, Got to go, speak later, then stand up.

'Go on then.'

'Cool,' says Reilly. 'So, just stand like this.' He puts his left leg out in front of him. 'You do it too, Sam.'

I stand beside him and put my left leg out.

'You've got to keep your back straight,' he tells me. 'Mr Philips says it will get easier when we build our core muscles, but I don't know what they are. Then do this.' Reilly lifts his right arm in front of him. 'This is the fist punch. Hi-ya!'

'Do I have to make that noise?' I ask.

'No,' Reilly says seriously. 'But I always do.' He puts his feet back together then does the move again. I do the same. It feels a bit stupid but before I know it me and Reilly are moving around his bedroom doing the fist punch and shouting, 'Hi-ya!' at exactly the same time.

'You should come, Sam,' Reilly says between moves. 'It's good, and you don't get wet when it rains like you do on your bike. Hi-ya!'

'It's okay,' I say. 'Hi-ya! I like my bike and besides your mum wouldn't . . . Hi-ya!'

'Reilly's mum wouldn't what?'

I stop dead. Reilly's mum is standing in the doorway, smiling.

'It's all right, Sam, don't look so worried,' she says. 'I'm pleased to see you having a good time.'

I glance at Reilly as I catch my breath. I don't like it when his mum catches me having fun. She'll think I'm happy here and that she made it that way.

'What were you going to say, Sam?' she says. 'That I wouldn't pay for taekwondo lessons?'

'Yes,' I say.

'Well, I would. If that's something you wanted to do. I know one person who wouldn't mind.'

'Yeah.' Reilly beams. 'Go on, Sam!'

'No,' I say, sitting down on the bottom bunk. 'I don't think so. I've got lots of other stuff of my own to do.'

'Aww, Mum,' says Reilly, disappointed. 'Tell him, Mum – tell him it's okay.'

'Sam has to do what he wants,' says his mum, like I'm not here. 'Just as long as he knows I would . . . Anyway.' She looks at me through the rungs of the bunk ladder. 'That's not why I came in. I just wanted to remind you to do your diary, Sam, like we agreed.'

I stare ahead.

'Sam, did you hear me?'

'Yes,' I mumble.

'Good,' says Reilly's mum. 'Then I'll go and do mine.' She walks out of the room and I listen to her footsteps on the stairs. I sigh.

'It's okay, Sam,' says Reilly. 'I'm getting tired too. Do you want some juice?'

'No thanks,' I say.

Reilly darts out of the room like nothing happened, but we both know something has. Why does his mum always have to do that? It's like she's the fun police, waiting for me and Reilly to have a laugh and then coming in and killing it dead. And she does it every day.

Reilly's dad knows how to fit rotor blades in real life.

Reilly's dad knows the four controls of the helicopter: collective pitch, throttle, anti-torque and cyclic pitch.

And this afternoon, Reilly's dad put two cushions on the floor, pretended they were pedals. Then he held a sink plunger and pretended it was the joystick. And he put a fan on the coffee table.

Reilly's dad said the sofa was the cockpit and got two alarm clocks and said they were the speedometer and altimeter.

Then he said we should sit next to him.

I didn't want to, but Reilly said he wouldn't do it if I didn't.

Reilly's dad told us to button our seat belts, then he pressed the cushions with his feet, pulled at the sink plunger and we took off and hovered in the living room with the wind from the fan blowing our hair.

Reilly started laughing.

Reilly's dad flew us out of the window, up into the air, past the light bulbs in the lamp post, up over the roofs, until we were so high we could see parks and fields and the golf course, and people's heads so small they looked like ants walking around.

Reilly's dad told us to be careful, to hold onto the side, but if we liked we could lean out of the window and wave to our friends.

That's what Reilly did. I just sat on my hands.

Then Reilly's dad took us up into the clouds, told us we could fly because the rotating blades create a downwards force that tilts us backwards and forwards to make us go up and down, and the rotor on the back spins us round.

Reilly's dad said we could have a go.

Reilly said he was rubbish; he'd make us crash, but Sam is good.

Reilly's dad handed me the sink plunger. I wanted to do it, but I felt embarrassed.

Reilly's dad said that was fine and he flew us safely back to the ground.

I wish I'd held the plunger. I wish I'd landed us back in the living room, because today, Reilly's dad wasn't just Reilly's dad.

He was very, very cool.

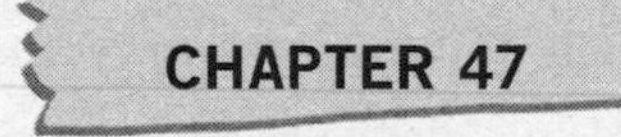

NOOOOO!

The problem with Reilly's dad having fun with us is that now Reilly's mum thinks it would be nice if we could all play a game together after tea.

That's why we're sitting in the living room.

That's why we're playing charades.

Reilly's dad guessed that I was making pizza. Reilly's mum guessed that I was raking leaves, but no one guessed Reilly's dad was riding a carousel, even though he made us all laugh when he pretended to get off and stumbled around the living room, like he was drunk.

Now it's Reilly's turn and that's why he's running around, cupping his hands and pretending to throw something.

'Cowpat throwing,' his dad guesses.

'Noo!' Reilly giggles. He bends down, cups his hands and pretends to throw something again.

'Sowing seeds,' guesses his mum.

'Nooo!'

'Throwing water over yourself,' I guess.

Reilly shakes his head. 'No. Do you give up?'

'No,' says Reilly's dad, leaning forward on the sofa. 'But, Reilly, you are supposed to help us – let us know if we are close.'

'Okay, okay.' He jumps up and down. 'Then Sam was close.'

'Throwing water over yourself?' says Reilly's dad.

'Yes,' says Reilly.

Reilly's mum smiles. 'Just do it one more time, Reilly.'

Reilly bends down, scoops his hands and throws something.

'Ah,' I say. 'I've got it. You're washing a car.'

'No.' Reilly grins. 'Do you give up? Can I tell you?'

'I think you'd better,' says his dad.

'Washing an elephant,' says Reilly.

We all laugh.

'Well,' says his mum, 'I don't think we'd ever have got that! Your go, Sam.'

I reach across and pick up a card.

BE A SPIDER SPINNING A WEB

'Got it?' asks Reilly's dad.

I nod, then get down on the floor. *How can I be a spider when they've got eight legs?*

I turn around in a circle, like I'm spinning a web.

'A dog, chasing its tail,' guesses Reilly's mum.

I shake my head.

'Dog having a poo,' says Reilly.

'Bug,' says his dad. 'Not everything has to do with poo.'

I crawl towards Reilly and spread my fingers on his knees.

I creep my fingers up his legs, over his body. He giggles. His mum and dad start laughing.

I try to pull an angry spider look but I can't keep a straight face.

'No idea,' says Reilly's mum.

'You've got me,' says his dad.

I crawl my fingers up over Reilly's shoulders and scramble his hair.

'Spider!' shouts Reilly. 'Spider.'

'Yes,' I say. I'm having so much fun I've forgotten that it was actually a spider spinning a web.

'Okay.' Reilly's mum looks at her watch. 'I think you'd better get ready for bed now. But maybe we could do it again tomorrow.' She glances at me and says, 'Maybe after Sam gets back from his drama.'

'Okay!' Reilly scoops up the cards. I'd help him put them in the box, but I can't believe what his mum just said.

'Do you mean it?' I say. It must be a trick. Maybe she thinks that if she says I can go, I won't want to.

Or maybe she's just given up.

'Yes,' she says. 'Today's been great, all of us together. Maybe when you get back from drama we could act out bits of the play with you.'

I smile. I think Rock Star Steve must have had the same chat about being more interested in me as he did with me about them.

'Okay,' I say.

Reilly puts the last of the cards in the box.

'Come on, Sam,' he says. 'Race you upstairs.' He bolts for the door. I chase after him. He giggles and shouts, 'Beat you, beat you!' as we run up the stairs. He darts into his room. 'This is our den!' He jumps onto the bottom bunk. We look at each other, trying to catch our breaths.

'Let's play hide and seek, Sam,' he says.

'Your mum said you had to get ready for bed.'

'I will,' he says. 'After.'

'All right. But you're not allowed in your mum and dad's bedroom. I never go in there.'

'Okay.' Reilly jumps off the bed. 'Count to twenty,' he says. 'And no peeping.'

I lie face down on my bed, pulling the pillow over my head.

'One, two, three ...' My voice is muffled as I count out loud. I thought I wouldn't enjoy today, but it's actually been quite fun. Even Reilly's mum joined in. But it's not the same feeling I get when I'm with Michelle and Dave. With Reilly's mum and dad, I still feel like I'm watching a roller coaster; with Michelle and Dave I feel like I'm on the ride.

'Eighteen, nineteen, twenty.' I push myself up off the bed. 'Coming, Reilly,' I shout. 'Ready or not.'

Reilly isn't hiding in the bath.

Reilly isn't behind the laundry basket.

Reilly isn't behind the curtain on the landing.

Reilly isn't in the utility room.

Reilly isn't under the dining room table.

And when I walk into the living room and see his mum and dad cuddled up on the sofa, they tell me that he isn't there either.

But I still check behind the door, and the chair, and the curtains. And they smile and say, 'See, Sam, we did tell you.'

And I know they aren't lying because if Reilly was in here, I would be able to hear him giggling. As I go out into the hall, I sense them looking at me, like they haven't seen me having such a good time before.

I check behind the coats again, then thud back up the stairs, so Reilly can hear me coming. I imagine him curled up somewhere, trying not to laugh. But where is he? I'd normally have found him by now.

'Reilly,' I shout. 'I said you can't hide in your mum and dad's bedroom.'

No answer.

I check his bedroom again, under my bed, even in the wardrobe – although he can't fit in there because there are so many toys. The only room left is his mum's office. I only go in there if she calls me in to do some foster-parent and foster-child 'let's work together' worksheets on the computer.

I edge my way in.

Ah, there he is.

I spot Reilly to my right, hiding between the filing cabinet and the wall. I smile. I don't want his fun to be over. I'm not sure I want it to end either.

I walk towards his mum's desk, pretending I can't see him. The computer is turned off, but beside the keyboard is a brochure. I walk closer.

Everything You Want to See and Do in Disneyland

I put my hand on the cover. There are pictures of children laughing as they go down a log flume and older children and adults with their mouths wide open like they are screaming on a roller coaster.

Reilly giggles behind me.

I flip the first page of the brochure.

Contents:

1. Disneyland itself
2. Places to stay
3. Things to do
4. Other attractions

They're going to Disneyland, I say in my head.

'They're going to Disneyland,' I whisper.

Reilly giggles again, but I can't turn round, because there's a piece of paper poking out of the next page.

I turn the page over. It's a note in Reilly's mum's handwriting:

Check best month for flights?
Check school holidays
Check if we need a car
Check insurance

Check, check, check, lots of things to check.

My eyes jump to the bottom.

Tom ✓

Sarah ✓

Reilly ✓

Sam X

What?! I stare at the X. They're going to Disneyland. They're going to Disneyland without me!

WHISPERS

'Sam won't play with me.'

'What's that?' says Reilly's mum.

'Sam won't play with me. He's gone to bed.'

I hear footsteps coming up the stairs.

'What's going on?' whispers Reilly's dad.

'Reilly says Sam's gone to bed and isn't talking to him.'

'Just leave him for a bit – there might be things going on that we don't know about. Maybe I'll talk to him in the morning.'

'Yes, but what a shame; we had such a lovely day.'

Footsteps move away. Reilly comes into his bedroom.

'Sam, do you want a fruit gum? Sam, what's wrong?'

Your mum and dad are taking you to Disneyland without me, Reilly. That's what's wrong. They're leaving me behind.

It happens every time.

I roll over and face the wall. Reilly's mum wanted me to put photographs and posters on it, so I felt like one of the family. And Rock Star Steve said they care about me. But if they cared about me, they wouldn't go to see Mickey Mouse and ride on Star Wars Hyperspace Mountain while I'm stuck in a bedroom with a respite family in Weston-Super-Mare.

I should have known. That's why they've been so nice today; that's why Reilly's mum has been smiley, smiley, smiley and is letting me go to drama tomorrow. Well, I don't care. They can go to Disneyland as a family – it's only Paris, anyway. Besides, now I've found Michelle and Dave I can go with a family of my own. But what do I say to them tomorrow? Leah said I should just be me, but does that mean I should tell them the truth? *Hi, you know I said I live round the corner and my mum is an actress and my dad is a private detective? Well, that was all lies.* They'd never trust me enough to ever let me in their house again. But I have to come up with something because Josh will be going back to school soon and I won't have a reason to go there. Everything is going wrong. I'm not going to be able to see Michelle and Dave enough, and the family I'm staying with are going to leave me behind and go to Disneyland.

CHAPTER 49

THE PERFECT PARENT PROJECT STAGE FIVE

Michelle and Dave's red house shines bright in the sun. I'm on the pavement outside, stamping my feet and rubbing my hands, but I can't get warm. Josh messaged and said they were making an early-early start, but I've been here for twenty minutes watching the closed curtains in their bedroom window and they still haven't moved. It was hard getting out of the house. I don't think Reilly's mum believed me when I said I was going to drama this early, but I don't care what she thinks – not now they're going to Disneyland without me. Eventually she said I could go, as long as I text her every hour.

I stamp my feet again and blow into my hands.

Come on.

Come on.

You've got to get up soon.

Why am I so cold? Why can't I stop my teeth from chattering?

I wish I could talk to Leah, but she must still be in bed because she hasn't responded to my message about Reilly's mum and dad taking him to Disneyland. She doesn't know I have to speed the Perfect Parent Project up. I've changed my mind a hundred times about what I'm going to say when Michelle or Dave eventually open the door. Right now I'm thinking I might say, 'Hi, I've come to help you paint your fence, and if you let me live with you, can we also go to Disneyland?' But I can't say that – they hardly know me. I'm just Sam – little c, big C – McCann, who has told them more lies than truths.

'Hello, dear. You're up bright and early.' I jump as Mrs Shepherd and George walk towards me. 'He got me up,' she says, nodding at George. 'Been scratching at the door since eight.'

I smile. I haven't been scratching at the door to get out, but I do know how George feels.

I look back at Michelle and Dave's house. The curtains are still closed; they haven't moved a millimetre.

'She's probably sleeping in.'

'Who?'

'Michelle. You'd better not knock, but I saw young David out there with his paint and brushes over an hour ago. Just go down to the corner.' Mrs Shepherd points down the park. 'Then turn left and there's a lane that takes you round the back of the houses.'

'Thanks,' I say.

Mrs Shepherd nods. 'Go on then,' she says to me, like she knows I'm hesitating. 'You know he doesn't bite. David, I mean, not George.'

I smile nervously, then walk down the path in the direction she pointed. As I cross the road, I feel even colder. It's just a man and a woman, I tell myself. I've met loads of them, lived with loads of them. But Michelle and Dave feel different. They're fun, and they love Josh, and I think they must like me otherwise they wouldn't have invited me here. But I've only got five days left of the holidays, and it might be even less, because if Reilly's mum and dad aren't taking me to Disneyland, they obviously don't want me at all.

I walk along a narrow lane between rows of wooden fences and gates. Above them the backs of the rainbow houses are dark and grey and all look the same. Some of the gates have numbers, others just have a dirty mark where the numbers used to be. I pass number twenty-four, blank, blank, thirty, blank, blank. I stop at number thirty-six. This is the one. I peer through the gap between the gate and the fence. Dave's crouched down over a pot of paint with his T-shirt creeping up his back. And Josh is by his side with a paintbrush in his hand.

Do they really need my help, or were they just feeling sorry for me?

I'll turn back.

They don't need me.

No, Sam, I tell myself, *but you need them. Just push the gate. All you've got to do is push the gate open and everything will be okay.*

I put my hand gently on a black ring handle and gently turn it. The latch clicks loudly and makes me jump.

You've started, Sam, now just push it open.

'Hey!' Dave turns around. 'I'm glad you came. We only did a couple of panels yesterday, so we need the help.'

'Yeah, we do.' Josh turns around with blue paint smudged on his cheek.

Dave shakes his head. 'An hour, Sam, we've been doing it for an hour today, and he's already complaining.'

Josh shrugs.

I try to smile, try to close the gate, but my jaw is frozen, and my feet are stuck to the path. It's only been two days since I was last here, but it feels like I need to get to know them all over again.

'Come on, Sam.' Dave smiles as if he knows I'm nervous, then holds out a brush. 'You can use this one. You don't have to be too fussy with it, just start at the top of each panel and work your way down.'

I walk towards him and take the brush.

'Like this,' says Dave. He bends down and dips his brush in the tin. 'Maybe halfway, so you don't overload it, otherwise you'll end up like Josh, with more paint on his clothes than on the fence.'

I smile. I spent all night and all morning planning what to say, but now no words will come out of my mouth. I'm glad Josh is here, and luckily Dave seems to have enough words for all of us. I dip my brush in the blue paint then stand in front of the fence, but I can't work out if I'm supposed to paint from side to side or up and down.

'Here, Sam,' says Dave. He puts his brush on the fence. 'Side to side, in the direction of the slats. Otherwise it'll leak through to the other side.'

I do as he says and the fence panel changes from brown to blue.

'Yeah, that's it.' Dave grins across at me. 'And don't ask why she wanted it painted blue.' He glances back at the house then adds quietly, 'But it's okay, cos if I do this for her, the deal is she goes and gets me a fifty-five-inch TV later.'

'I'm going to pick it up with Auntie Michelle,' says Josh. 'So we can watch *Spider-Man: Into the Spider-Verse* after we've finished this.'

'Cool,' I say.

'So we're all happy.' Dave grins.

Yeah, I think to myself. *We're all happy. Not like at Reilly's house where his mum is always stressed and busy and his dad is away all the time and even when he is back they pretend to be happy when really they're thinking of getting rid of me.*

I feel bad for thinking it, but I'm even happier when Josh leaves to pick up the TV. I've been painting for two hours and my arms feel like they're going to fall off, but I'm not going to stop because I get to talk to Dave on my own now. He tells me about how he was good at football at school, okay at rugby and rubbish at cricket, but he was brilliant at climbing ropes in the gym which is why he thinks he ended up in the fire brigade. I nod and keep painting. Dave says his favourite sweets are marshmallows, his favourite meal is Sunday roast at his dad's and his worst meal is Sunday roast cooked by Michelle, because the potatoes are too big and her gravy is as runny as water. Oh, and his favourite football team is Chelsea, and he had a replica shirt when he was younger but he never wore it because he was chubby and it gave him man boobs. Then he looks at me and says, 'And what about you, Sam?'

Suddenly it's my turn to speak, but I can't think of anything, because all my notes on meeting my perfect parents have been about them, not me. So I look down at my shirt and say, 'Well, I think I'm too skinny to have man boobs.'

Dave laughs so much he misses the pot with his brush.

'No, Sam,' he says, 'I meant what things do you like and dislike? You can't just let me yabber on all the time.'

Well, yes, I could.

I dip my brush in the pot, then spread paint onto the fence. I don't mind if he keeps talking because if I start I might make a mistake and say something I shouldn't. All I want is to ask him if he'd like to be a dad, and if he'd like me as his son. But that would be weird and it would surprise him cos it would be like going from 0–60 in 3.2 seconds in a BMW 5.

'I'm okay at football,' I say slowly, 'but I'm not good enough to play in the school team. We only play tag rugby and we've never played cricket.'

'Not even on the beach?' asks Dave.

'No,' I say. I don't really count the time with Reilly's mum and dad because I walked off after five minutes.

'I used to go to the beach with my mum and dad and brother, and all our cousins, and we'd start playing and before you knew it other kids would join in and we'd have enough for two full teams. Kids don't seem to do that these days. I bet you're like Josh, just wanting to stay in and play computer games.'

'A bit,' I say. 'But you did buy Josh an Xbox One.'

'Yeah, true,' Dave laughs. 'But that was Michelle's idea. She loves him, and money grows holes in her pockets. Not that I'm complaining – I am getting that TV after all.' He glances at his watch like he's wondering how long they've been gone, and I think, however long it is, please let it be longer, because I'm loving talking to him.

If he was my dad maybe he'd give up his fire prevention job and we could go around in a white van doing odd jobs like this for people.

Dave dips his paintbrush in the tin and spreads it on the fence.

'So what about your favourite food and stuff?' he says.

'I don't have favourite foods,' I say, 'but I do love Snickers and McDonald's. Just not at the same time.'

'No,' says Dave, 'that doesn't sound great.' He smiles and starts painting again.

The day is going even better than I planned. For the last ten minutes I've been talking to an adult, saying the things I want, without them stopping and writing down every word in a notebook or diary. Being with Dave is like being with Rock Star Steve without his notes, without thinking he's going to use them against me. Being with Dave is like being with a best friend who is way older than me. *Is this what having a dad is like?* I think to myself. *Like having a best friend who is older?*

I keep painting and tell Dave more about myself. That I like acting, and I love cycling, even if my bike is a bit too small for me. I tell him I had a puncture, but I think I made a rubbish job of mending it, because it's gone flat again. He says maybe he could take a look at it for me. All the time we move along the fence, moving the pot as we go. Then Dave says, 'Watch where you're stepping, Sam. I think Michelle has planted some carrots around here somewhere.'

'Oh,' I say. 'I hate carrots. I hate all vegetables.'

'Blimey,' says Dave. 'I bet your mum loves you!'

Dave's words land like a bomb in my head.

Mum . . . Loves . . . You.

Mum . . . Loves . . . You.

I stop painting. I've heard all the words before but never in the same sentence.

My hand starts to shake.

Mum . . . Loves . . . You.

How could my mum have loved me when she gave me away?

'Sam, are you okay? Sam . . . ?'

I can see and hear Dave, but all I do is stand still with paint dripping down my hand.

'Sam?' Dave takes the brush from me. 'Mate, you look very pale.'

I stare down at my hand.

'Let's go inside,' says Dave. 'And we'll wash that off.'

I don't remember walking up the path. I don't remember sitting on the stool. But I do remember Dave pouring me orange juice and giving me a chocolate muffin and asking, 'Are you feeling better, Sam?'

And I remember nodding and seeing Dave smile and lift his hand. I remember thinking, *He's going to ruffle my hair, like he does to Josh*. I remember closing my eyes, waiting for his hand to land, but then Dave reaching behind me to close a cupboard.

I thought you were going to ruffle my hair, I said to him, in my head.

I wish you had.

CHAPTER 50

UH OH!

'What's he done to you, Sam? Was he working you too hard?'

'He must have just been hungry,' says Dave, sipping his coffee. 'One minute we were chatting about veg, the next he looks like he's seen a ghost.'

'And you gave him a chocolate muffin?' says Michelle.

Josh grins. 'Told you we should have brought back McDonald's.'

'Aww.' Michelle looks at me like she's thinking of buying me in a shop. 'Bless you. Sam, you've got to say if you're feeling ill next time.'

I swallow. 'I'm okay. I don't know what it was.'

'Don't worry about it,' says Michelle, pouring water into her mug. 'Probably just your age. When I was eleven, we had a boy in our class, Tim Flower, who fainted and fell into the stream on a geography field trip at Castle Combe.'

'What's a geography field trip got to do with this?' says Dave.

'I'm just saying it's his age,' says Michelle. 'When boys' bodies start to do different things. You know . . . hormones.'

Dave grins. 'I'm pretty sure Sam doesn't want to talk about hormones with us.'

They both laugh and I don't understand why. I'm just glad they are thinking more about Tim Flower than they are about me.

'You like pizza, Sam?' Michelle opens the freezer door.

'Yes,' I nod.

'Great,' says Dave, rubbing his hands. 'Josh and I will get the TV out of the car and unbox it.'

'No,' says Michelle. 'Fence first, that was the deal.'

'But we can't just leave it in the car – it might get stolen. And Josh has only got a few more days left to watch it.'

'Six days,' says Josh. 'School's got in-service training on Monday.'

For a moment I think I've got an extra day too, but then I remember we don't go to the same school.

'Anybody would think you don't want to go home, Joshie,' says Michelle.

Josh smiles. 'I do. Mum's cooking is way better.'

'Oi!' Michelle clicks a button on the cooker. 'For that, Sam's getting your share of the pizza.'

'Good luck with that, Sam.' Dave grins. 'Come on, Josh.' He puts his hand on Josh's shoulder and leads him into the hall.

Michelle puts the pizza in the oven, then turns and looks at me.

I take another bite of muffin.

'So, Sam,' she says. 'What are your mum and dad doing for the rest of holidays?'

'Nothing much,' I say. 'Just decorating, like you said.'

'And what about your brother?'

'Who?' I say, choking on my muffin. How does she know about the brother I sometimes imagine I have?

'Your brother. You said your mum would be busy putting him to bed when we dropped you off the other night.'

'Oh.' I smile with fake relief. 'That brother.'

'Blimey,' Michelle laughs, 'he won't be pleased you forgot him.'

'No, I hadn't forgotten him. It's just that . . .'

'Just what?'

My mind searches for a lie.

'Well . . .' I say, still searching. 'He's not actually my real brother. Mum and Dad, they look after him.'

'What,' says Michelle, 'like foster-parents?'

'Yeah, that's it. Foster-parents. He's only been with us a few months, but I like him.'

'What's his name?'

I can't remember what name I said before, or if I even gave a name.

'Reilly,' I say. 'He's six and plays Ace Pilot all the time.'

Michelle smiles like the teachers who know I'm a foster-kid at school do. 'I just think it's lovely that people do that. You should be very proud of your parents, Sam. And of yourself.' She puts her arm around my shoulder, which makes me feel warm inside. 'Not everyone can share their home and welcome someone into their family like that. I bet you're great with him.'

'Not really,' I say. 'But I did help him get to level four on Ace Pilot.'

Michelle smiles, then looks towards the front door where Dave is walking backwards through the hall.

'Pop it down here, Josh,' he says. 'I'll take Sam home as he's not well, then we'll get back to the fence. That okay, Sam?'

My heart jumps into my throat. First lying about Reilly, now this.

'No,' I say quickly. 'I was just hungry, and besides, it's only around the corner.'

Dave looks at me and I can't tell if he's thinking of something to say to me or trying to work me out, like Rock Star Steve does – asking me questions, then looking out of the car window, waiting for me to talk and fill the silence.

'Really,' I say. 'I'm okay. I could paint the fence right now if I wanted.'

No one talks. I hate the silence. I fiddle with the crumbs on my plate.

There's a clunk as Michelle puts her mug down on the counter.

'Sam?' she says.

'Yeah.' I look up and see Michelle, Dave and Josh staring like they've had a secret meeting about me.

'What's wrong?' I say. 'What have I done? Have I got chocolate on my face?'

'No,' says Michelle. 'It's not that.'

'What is it then?'

'Sam,' says Dave. 'Where do you really live?'

'I told you.' My face burns. 'I live around the corner, number ninety-six.'

'No, Sam,' says Michelle. 'You don't.'

'How do you know?'

'Because there isn't a ninety-six.'

I'M SORRY, LEAH

'It feels like we're criminals,' says Leah as we sit inside Eric.

'I know,' I say. 'I'm starting to feel like one, I'm telling so many lies.'

'So what happened?' she asks. 'Your message didn't make sense.'

'Sorry, I was so panicked. It's just they found out I didn't live in that road.'

'What?' Leah looks at me.

I gulp like I did when I was caught out. 'See, I told you it was bad. Michelle keeps asking so many questions. I feel like she knows.'

'But she can't do. What did you tell them?'

'I was so shocked I couldn't think at first. I hoped Dave would say something funny to get me out of it, but all three of them just stood staring at me. Then out of nowhere I told them I lived in Bedwin Flats. You know, the grotty ones down by the river. I told them I was too embarrassed to say I lived there. And now I feel bad I said that.'

'Don't be,' says Leah. 'Mum says the council are going to knock them down, they're that horrible.'

'Dave was nice about it. He said it's okay to lie about where you live. Nobody is going to die. He said that sometimes we're embarrassed about our real situations, and we want people to think we have more than we do, but there's nothing to be ashamed of, living in a council flat. But I lost the afternoon with them. I was stressing so much that I told them I felt ill again, and needed to go home.'

'Ill again?'

I move some cardboard to make us more comfortable and tell Leah what happened in the garden when Dave said he bet my mum loved me. Leah says she doesn't blame me, that she might have done the same. Then I tell her that I'm panicking because we're getting towards the end of the holidays and it feels like we're running out of time. I'll have no reason to go back there after Josh has gone. And by the time the summer holidays come around, I'll have been moved and Michelle and Dave will have forgotten I ever existed.

'Sam,' Leah says quietly. 'Listen to me. It's obvious they like you or they'd never have taken you bowling. When my mum and dad were together, we didn't take people we didn't like anywhere with us. Apart from when we took Laura Thompson to Legoland, and that was only cos she had half-price vouchers because her auntie worked there. Anyway, I've already thought about how you can spend more time at their house. You've just got to ask for a sleepover.'

'A sleepover? But I've never had a sleepover.'

'Sam,' Leah sighs. 'It's easy – it's just like sleeping in your bed but in someone else's house.'

'Yeah, but how do I ask?'

'Oh, you just go, "Hey, Josh, how about we have a sleepover at your auntie and uncle's at the weekend."'

'Just like that?'

'Yep.' Leah grins. 'Just like that.'

My phone buzzes.

'Reilly's mum?' asks Leah.

'Shouldn't be,' I say, squeezing my hand into my pocket. 'I'm not due back until . . . Oh . . .' I look at the message.

'Who is it?'

'Lewis,' I say sheepishly. 'I missed drama practice this morning. We were supposed to be meeting at Amala's.'

'Sam!'

'I can't help it. It's hard to keep track of everything. I feel bad for missing drama, but if I do get to live with Michelle and Dave, I might have to move schools anyway, so I won't be able to do *Bugsy*. It's getting so complicated.'

'You might be okay,' says Leah. 'Emily Ashton goes to our school, and she lives on the other side of town. And truthfully I'm more worried about me and you than I am about school.'

'What do you mean?'

'I don't know.' Leah picks at a piece of cardboard, then looks up at me. 'It's nothing,' she says. 'I just worry that if you find your perfect parents and stay friends with Josh we won't get to hang out together so much.'

'We will,' I say. 'At school, like you said, and it's only temporary – Michelle and Dave won't watch me half as much as Reilly's mum and dad.'

'But we've hardly seen each other lately.' Leah's eyes water up.

I don't know what to do or what to say. It was her idea to find my perfect parents, but now it's like she wants to take them away.

'Leah,' I say. 'You'll always be my friend, but you know how much I want perfect parents.'

Leah stares at me. 'But you've been so hung up on finding them that you haven't even asked me about mine.'

Her dad. She was supposed to go to the cinema with him today. How could I be so dumb and selfish? I've been so busy juggling all my things, I totally forgot about Leah and her dad.

Leah is sitting with her head down, picking her fingers.

I sigh. 'He didn't turn up again, did he?'

Leah shakes her head. 'No. Just sent a message to Mum saying he was busy, and he'd try another time.'

'I'm sorry,' I say.

Leah looks up and wipes her tears on the back of her hand. 'Mollie said we should be used to it now. She didn't even dress up, but I put on the yellow dress that you said looked nice when I wore it to the Downs.'

'It did.'

Leah forces a smile. 'Thanks. And sorry.'

'What for?'

'For this,' she says. 'I can usually laugh things off, but sometimes it gets too much, especially when Dad does that, and Mum's out with Jug-ears all the time.'

'I thought you said he was okay.'

'Oh, he's all right. But he calls Mollie Molls, trying to be cool, and she hates it. He's a total wally. He drives a Nissan Micra.'

'Oh yeah,' I say. 'That'll make him a wally.'

Leah laughs as she wipes her eyes.

'I am sorry,' I say. 'Shall we do something this afternoon?'

'No, you're okay. You get back to Reilly's house. You don't want to upset them any more. I'm just glad we're back on track to find your perfect parents.'

'Then tomorrow,' I say. 'I'm going back to Michelle and Dave's to finish the fence, but I could meet you here in the afternoon. And we could talk more then?'

'Okay,' says Leah. 'If you're sure.'

'I am.'

'Good.' Leah smiles as she pushes herself up.

I look at her. It's great to have my best friend back on board.

'What?' she says.

'Nothing.'

'Yes, there is.'

I smile. Yes, there is. Why can't I say it? *You're my best friend*, that's all I have to say.

'Sam, you're worrying me,' says Leah. 'What is it?'

'Okay.' I take a deep breath. 'You did look nice in the yellow dress.'

'Blurgh!' Leah pretends to be sick. 'I'm never wearing it again.'

We both laugh.

CHAPTER 52

I GET CONFUSED

'Well done, Sam.' Reilly's mum pokes her head around Reilly's bedroom door. 'Not only are you back, you're actually half an hour early.'

'I know,' I say. 'I thought with the holidays running out, I'd spend more time with Reilly.' It doesn't matter which house I'm in, all I seem to do is lie.

'That's nice,' she says. 'But could I have a quick word?'

I glance up at her. Even when I've done something good, I'm still in trouble. 'But I got back—'

Reilly's mum shakes her head at me, then glances at Reilly who's crashing another plane. 'It'll just take a sec.'

What does she want?

I get up and follow her onto the landing.

'Sam,' she whispers. 'Can you keep Reilly up here for a while? Only I need to ice his birthday cake.'

'Oh.' I smile with relief. 'Yeah, sure.'

'Thanks,' she says. 'And, Sam.' She pulls me towards her office. 'You are coming, aren't you?'

For a moment I think she means Disneyland, but when I scout her desk I can only see cookery magazines and pieces of paper.

Reilly's mum leans forward to get my attention. 'You haven't forgotten, have you? Tomorrow. Reilly's birthday?'

'Oh.' I squirm. 'No, I've not forgotten, it's just . . .'

'Just what?'

'I'm supposed to be going to Lewis's,' I say, waiting for her to go mad.

'You've been there today.'

'I know,' I say. 'But I finished early, because Leah was upset about her dad so I went to see her.' I keep telling lies, but some of them are partly true.

Reilly's mum sighs.

'And I did get back early today,' I say quickly, 'and tomorrow is only for the morning. I'll make sure—'

'Okay. Okay.' Reilly's mum holds up her hands. 'But make sure you're back by two. You can help us get things ready for when his friends come around.'

'I will,' I say.

'Good. Now go and keep him entertained for an hour. I've got so much to do for his party and then Tom is going back to work the day after.'

I turn to go.

'Oh, wait, Sam!' Reilly's mum whispers urgently.

What is it now?

I huff and turn back.

'Did you want to get him something?' she asks.

'What?'

'Reilly? Do you want to get him something for his birthday?'

'I haven't got any money,' I say.

'I'll give you some.'

I wait on the landing as she goes into her office. A drawer slides open and coins rattle in a tin.

'Here.' Reilly's mum comes back out and puts a five-pound note and some coins into my hand. 'You know the sort of thing he likes.'

'Okay,' I say, putting the money in my pocket.

Reilly's mum smiles.

'Right,' she says, 'I'd better get back to this cake. If only he were interested in football. Goal posts would be so much easier to make than planes.'

I smile but as I walk back into Reilly's room, I'm trying to work out how I can do everything tomorrow and still get back here for two. Everything is getting so complicated I don't know what are lies and what is the truth. I'd forgotten all about drama today even though being in *Bugsy* is one of the main reasons I started the Perfect Parent Project. And I really don't want to upset Reilly. I just need to get to Michelle and Dave's as early as I can, so I'm back in time.

I sit down next to Reilly on the bunk.

'I landed on crack a toe,' he says.

'Krakatoa,' I say.

'Yeah,' says Reilly. 'Now all I've got to do is pick up the gold and take off.'

He presses the O and the right thrust button. The TV speakers rumble as his plane gathers speed down the runway. Reilly leans forward.

'Keep pressing the thrust,' I say. 'Keep pressing it.'

White lines and buildings blur as the plane goes faster. Reilly's pressing the buttons so fast his tongue pokes out with concentration.

'What now, Sam?' he says. 'What do I do?'

'Press the top left,' I say.

The plane's engine starts to die.

'No, that one.' I reach across, but it's too late. Reilly's plane has ditched at the end of the runway, the gold bullion lying on the ground.

'I pressed the wrong one, didn't I?'

I smile. 'Yes.'

'But I can do it again.'

'Yeah. Do it again.'

I lean back against the wall.

Reilly doesn't know I've got plans. All I've got to do is ask Josh for a sleepover and if that goes well, I could be gone after the weekend. But I feel bad thinking about leaving Reilly when I'm sitting next to him.

I'm sorry I want to go, Reilly. I will miss your arghs when your plane crashes. I'll miss your smile when it finally takes off. I'll miss your taekwondo kicks and I'll miss you jumping round in your Sharkasaurus *pyjamas. I'm sorry I told Michelle and Dave it's you that's the foster-kid and not me. But at least I found out that they think looking after foster-kids is a good thing. I'll only have a few hours with them tomorrow, but that might be long enough to find out if they would consider adopting me.*

How do you tell someone you like them? How do you tell someone you like them so much that you would like to live with them? How do you tell someone you want to be with them so much that when you go to bed at night you can't wait to see them in the morning? It's a hundred times harder than asking for a sleepover. You can't just turn up on the doorstep with your suitcase and bags, and say, 'Hi, I've come to stay for a while, only I hope that while turns into for ever.'

CHAPTER 53

I'M A FUNNY ONE

I'm back at the rainbow houses and Dave just shouted across the garden to Josh and Michelle that he's pretty sure I just painted the same panel four times. Michelle laughed and said Dave should consider himself lucky to be with me because Josh was getting more blue paint on himself than the fence. That's when Josh turned around holding up his hands like the Hulk. I laughed but I didn't really feel like it, because Dave says he thinks with the four of us painting we could be done by lunchtime. That's why I've painted the same panel four times. That's why I've been wishing Michelle and Dave lived on The Clift, because the fences there go on for ever. I'd be painting them for a month, not two days. And now one of those has gone, I feel like I'm counting every second that ticks away.

'What's up, Sam?' Dave says quietly. 'You seem . . . I don't know . . . a little preoccupied. If you're tired, you can go home if you like, or just have a rest for a bit.'

‘No,’ I say, trying to shake the troubles out of my head. ‘It’s okay. I’ll be all right.’

I look around the garden. I have to find something else to do just so I can come back next weekend.

‘Oi.’ Dave nudges my arm. ‘You’re doing it again!’

‘Oh, sorry,’ I say, moving the brush down the fence. ‘I was just thinking, can we do the shed too?’

‘Ha!’ Dave laughs. ‘The amount I’m paying you two, I’m going to be broke by the time we finish.’

‘And we could ask your neighbour if he wants his done too. It looks like his fence is falling down compared to yours.’

Dave drops his brush in the paint pot. ‘You’re going to have us painting the whole street at this rate.’

I grin. I don’t tell him that was the plan.

‘But seriously,’ says Dave, giving me a look I’ve not seen before, ‘what’s up, mate? Anyone would think you don’t want to be at home.’

‘It’s not that,’ I say, looking across at Josh and Michelle. ‘I just like it here.’

‘And we like having you here.’ He picks his brush up again. ‘But surely you want to spend time with your mum and dad?’

‘Not really.’ I shrug. ‘I live with them all the time.’

Dave laughs. ‘Well, I guess we can all think that about our families sometimes.’

I don’t answer. We were painting the fence but now Dave’s talking about parents again. It’s like he knows something is up, but if he does, why am I still here? I try to think of something to say to change the subject but it’s like Dave knows it’s a sensitive topic because he says, 'Sam, all I know is that parents try to look out for their kids, and maybe I was lucky because mine were pretty great. I didn't want to leave.'

'So why did you leave home when you were eighteen?'

'Blimey.' Dave looks shocked that I remembered. 'Do you actually listen to everything I say?'

'Yeah. But why did you? If I had the perfect parents I'd never want to leave.'

'Oh,' Dave chuckles. 'I never said they were perfect. They used to complain about the state of my bedroom and the smell of my trainers, but they were pretty good. But I had the fire brigade, then I met Michelle.'

'What's that?' Michelle looks across when she hears her name.

'Nothing,' says Dave. 'Just telling Sam how wonderful you are.'

'Umm.' Michelle grins. 'Don't believe that for a minute.'

Dave laughs then says, 'Sam here reckons we should paint the shed after this.'

'But it doesn't have to be today,' I jump in. 'I can always come back next week.'

Michelle laughs. 'You won't want to come back after Dave's burnt all the burgers on the barbecue.'

'Once,' says Dave. 'I burnt them once!'

'Are we having a barbecue?' asks Josh.

'Yes,' says Dave. 'But I've got to go to the garage and get some coals.'

'Cool. Can Sam stay?'

'Course,' says Dave. 'If he wants.'

‘Yeah,’ I say. ‘Please.’ *Yes!* I clench my fist by my side. It’s not a sleepover but it is at least two more hours with them.

Dave smiles. ‘That’s sorted then. Now let’s get on with this.’ I grin and start painting again. Today is going much better than yesterday. It’s like Michelle and Dave have run out of questions so I’ve not had to tell any lies. I watch Dave move his brush side to side on the fence. I don’t know if I love him, or Michelle, but I do know that I like them lots, and sometimes when we’re talking, I already feel as if I’m part of the family. And they must like me too, mustn’t they, otherwise they wouldn’t let me stay so long? I just wish I knew *how much* they like me. Do they like me enough to want me to live with them? It would be great to know now, so I don’t just turn up one day with all my clothes in a suitcase, like Paddington.

Hey, Dave, I say in my head. *I love being with you and Michelle, and I know we’ve only met four times, but do you think I could move in with you and have my own bedroom, with a proper bed that doesn’t creak every time someone moves on the bunk above?* I wish I could say that, but how can I ask when I’ve not even had a sleepover? I’d love to do that at the weekend. I’d love to wake up and have breakfast with them in the morning. I wonder if Michelle wears a dressing gown. I wonder if Dave wears pyjamas. I don’t know what Reilly’s mum and dad wear. Their bedroom door is always closed, and they’re already dressed and busy working when I get up. Are all parents like that?

Dave crouches down and scrapes the earth away so he can paint the plank of wood at the bottom of the fence. I dip my brush into my tin. I could ask him now. *Can I come for a sleepover? If yes, can I come and stay for ever?*

I crouch down beside Dave. I could say it now.

He looks across at me and smiles. 'Just got to clear the earth. So it doesn't get clogged in the brush.'

'Yeah,' I say. I dig my left hand into the dirt and make a small trench.

Now, Sam, ask now.

'Dave . . .' I say cautiously.

'Yes, Sam.'

'Can I ask you a question?'

'Course,' Dave grunts as he digs more earth. 'You can ask me anything.'

'Okay.' I take a breath.

'What is it, Sam?'

'I was . . . I was wondering if . . . I wondered . . .'

Go on, Sam, you can.

'I was wondering . . .'

'What is it, mate?' Dave gives me a quizzical look.

'I was thinking . . . Can I come with you to the garage to get the coals?'

'Is that it?' Dave chuckles.

'Yeah.' I let out a deep breath.

Dave shakes his head and smiles. 'You're a funny one, Sam,' he says, ruffling my hair.

I smile. Yes, I'm a funny one.

The sleepover question is going around and around in my mind, all the time me and Josh are in the park playing Frisbee. But that's not the only thing – my head won't stop tingling ever since Dave ruffled my hair.

It was just a hand on my head, I tell myself – it was only there for two seconds, and then it was gone. But if it's gone, why does it still feel as if it's there? It's like when I burnt my hand on the Bunsen burner at school. Except this feeling is nicer. I thought of messaging Leah, but she might think I'm weird, and anyway, I'm meeting her later. But that tingling was still there while Dave filled up with petrol and got the coal. And it's there while I watch him talking to my perfect gran outside his house.

'Sam,' Josh shouts as the Frisbee whizzes past my ear. 'Come on.'

I bend down and pick it up.

Josh runs over to me. 'What's up? You've not caught one for ages.'

'Nothing,' I say. 'I was just thinking.'

I watch as Dave points across at me and Josh. I wonder what he's saying about us . . . *That's Sam over there, me and Michelle are thinking of adopting him.* Or, *That's Sam, Josh's new friend who says he lives down the road.*

Out of the corner of my eye, I see Josh looking at me.

'Sam, what is it?' he asks.

'Oh, nothing. I was just wondering, do you think we could have a sleepover tonight?'

'I don't know,' says Josh. 'I'd have to ask Auntie Michelle and Uncle Dave. I've never had a sleepover at theirs. If they say no, maybe we could have one at yours instead.'

'N-no,' my voice cracks in panic. 'I mean . . . no, I don't think that's a good idea.'

'Why not?' says Josh. 'I've stayed at loads of my other friends' houses. I don't eat lots or fart.'

I laugh nervously. 'No, it's not that,' I say. 'It's my mum.'

‘What’s wrong with her?’

‘Oh, nothing. It’s just she doesn’t like people in the house. She doesn’t even have her own friends round.’

‘Okay, no worries,’ says Josh. He gives me a strange look, like he thinks what I just said was weird. ‘I’ll go and ask Uncle Dave now.’

‘No,’ I say. ‘Not now.’ I run after him in panic. ‘It’ll be horrible if he says no. Maybe ask when we’re having the barbecue. I’ll go to the loo or something, and you ask while I’m gone.’

Josh shakes his head. ‘Sometimes you’re weird. It’s only a sleepover – it’s not like you’re moving in. Anyway, Uncle Dave looks like he needs rescuing from Mrs Shepherd.’

‘But she’s nice,’ I say. ‘I’d like her for a gran.’

‘Ha,’ Josh laughs. ‘You must be desperate if you want a gran who knows everybody’s business. Uncle Dave says we don’t need a neighbourhood watch when she’s around. Anyway, what’s wrong with the grans you’ve got?’

‘Nothing,’ I say, looking at Mrs Shepherd who’s now pointing to the bench at the top of the park. ‘I just don’t see them much.’

‘Why not?’

‘Oh, they live miles away.’

‘What? Like Cornwall.’

‘No, Australia.’

‘Australia?’

Why did I say that?

‘Is that where you come from? You don’t have an Australian accent.’

‘No,’ I say. ‘My mum and dad came over here before I was born. But that’s why I miss grandparents so much.’

‘Right,’ says Josh like he doesn’t believe me.

‘It’s true.’

‘Yeah. Anyway, I’m going to rescue Uncle Dave, otherwise we’ll never start the barbecue.’

He runs across the grass. Why did I say my grandparents live in Australia? I could have said Cornwall or Weston-Super-Mare – loads of old people live there, and it’s not like Josh would come and visit them anyway. The trouble with talking about families is that people always want to know more about mine. I don’t know who my grandparents are, or where they live. It would have been easy to tell him they were dead, but that would be a horrible thing to say if they were still alive. I’d like to think I have real grandparents but maybe they don’t even know I exist.

Josh stops in front of Dave and Mrs Shepherd. She smiles and holds her hand out a metre from the ground, then up to Josh’s head, like she’s saying, *Last year you were this tall, now you are this tall. Can you believe how much he’s grown?* I smile. Josh said I must be desperate but I’d love for Mrs Shepherd to be my gran. I’d like her to smile and tell me how much I’ve grown. We could even make notches on the door.

My phone buzzes in my pocket.

Sam, don’t forget, be back by 2.

Reilly’s mum is like having an alarm clock buzzing in the middle of my head.

Okay, I type. I will.

I DIDN'T KNOW

I didn't know the wind would blow the barbecue out.

I didn't know Dave would run out of lighters.

I didn't know he would have to go back to the garage.

I didn't know that when he came back and finally lit the barbecue it would take ages for the coals to get hot.

I didn't know that when Michelle and Dave have a drink, they are twice as funny.

I didn't know that Dave would let Josh plug his Xbox One into the new TV and let us play Super Mario.

I didn't know that time goes twice as fast when you're having fun.

I didn't know it would feel so good when they said okay to Josh asking if I could come for a sleepover at the weekend.

That's when I felt so happy that I wanted to do a fist pump and shout, 'Yes!'

That's when they said it was getting late, and maybe I should ride my bike back before it got dark.

That's when I put my hand in my pocket for my phone and found some coins and a five-pound note.

CHAPTER 55

OH, REILLY ☹

Oh, Reilly. I'm so sorry I missed your party.

I'm so sorry I didn't help blow up your balloons.

I'm so sorry I didn't dance around the room playing musical statues.

I'm so sorry I didn't see you blow out the seven candles on your aeroplane cake.

I'm so sorry four of your friends didn't turn up.

'I'm sorry, I'm sorry.' That's what I said to Reilly's mum and dad.

'It ... was ... his ... birthday,' said his mum, slowly but loudly. 'Was it really too much to ask for you to come back?'

'I had another puncture.' I was already in trouble, but I still couldn't stop another lie coming out.

'Sam.' That was Reilly's dad. 'Couldn't you have at least phoned? That's what we gave it to you for, and it was getting dark.'

'That's not the point.' That was Reilly's mum, looking like she was going to cry. 'It was his birthday.'

I tried to say sorry again, but no words came out.

'It's like you just don't care.' That was Reilly's mum again. 'You know how much he wanted you there. Even after everyone was gone, he was waiting for you on the stairs.'

'I forgot where I was,' I said loudly. 'I lost track of time.'

'So it wasn't a puncture.' That was both of them catching me out.

That's when I shouted, 'I had to go to the shop!'

'The shop?' said Reilly's mum.

'Yes. That's what made me late – I had to get—'

'No.' Reilly's mum waved me away. 'I've heard enough.'

'But you don't understand,' I said.

'What don't we understand?' That was Reilly's dad.

'We understand that you *chose* to miss Reilly's birthday.' That was Reilly's mum.

'I didn't choose,' I said. 'I just forgot.'

'You seem to forget a lot of things.'

That's when I snap, 'Okay, okay. I get it. I missed Reilly's birthday, but it's all your fault. Why do you need to know where I am all the time? You don't do that with Reilly. He can go to his friends for tea and sleepovers. He doesn't have to call you every half an hour.'

'That's different,' said Reilly's mum.

'Why? Because you're his real parents? Well, I'm glad you're not mine.'

'Sam! That's very, very unfair.' Reilly's mum had tears in her eyes.

That's when I stormed upstairs, came into Reilly's room, saw him with his head tucked under his duvet.

I'm sorry, Reilly, I say to myself, as I lie on the bunk. *I am sorry*, but I think he's so upset that I need to say it out loud.

'Reilly . . .' I whisper.

I wait for the bed to creak, for his jellyfish head to appear over the side. But Reilly doesn't move.

'Reilly,' I say. 'I'm really sorry.'

I reach up and poke his mattress gently through the slats.

'Reilly,' I say more urgently. 'I'm sorry.'

I close my eyes. My heart thuds in my chest and my throat begins to ache. I would never have missed Reilly's birthday on purpose. I was just having so much fun with Michelle, Dave and Josh that I forgot.

My phone buzzes in my pocket.

Where were you?

Argh! No! I facepalm. I've got so much going on that not only did I miss Reilly's party, I forgot to meet Leah too.

I'm so sorry, I type. I totally forgot.

I waited at Eric for ages.

I feel bad.

You should. The PPP was supposed to be fun. I didn't think you'd just drop everything else.

It wasn't supposed to be fun, I type. It's a BIG DEAL to me.

Other people have BIG DEALS too.

I hate to think of Leah being upset in her bedroom. I didn't mean to hurt her. I didn't mean to hurt anyone.

Leah, I type. I'm really sorry. I am, but you don't understand.

Leah, please. Tell me what's wrong.

Fine. Jug-ears dumped Mum last night, and she's been crying ever since.

Is that why you're upset?

Leah?

No. He didn't turn up again. My dad.

Argh! I'm sorry.

I'm going now.

No, don't. Leah, I messed up bad.

I sniff, wiping tears from my eyes. I want to tell her I'm sorry again. I messed up big time with her dad.

Leah

Leah

I stare at my screen, waiting for the ticks on my last three messages to turn green. But Leah has already gone.

My day started off so brilliantly, but now it's all gone wrong.

The bunks creak. Reilly's upside-down head appears.

'Hi, Sam,' he says quietly.

'Hi, Reilly.' I try to smile. 'I'm sorry about your birthday.'

'It's okay if you forgot,' he says. 'Mum and Dad got me a remote-control truck, and my friend Marlo got me a Lego Batman. See!' He holds a tiny Batman over the side of his bed.

I smile.

'I didn't forget, Reilly,' I say. I lean over the bed and reach into my rucksack. 'I got you this on my way home.'

Reilly's face lights up. 'What is it?'

'Open it and see.' I hand him a paper bag.

'It feels like slime.' Reilly grins. 'Is it slime?'

'No, Reilly, it's not slime.'

Reilly flips back onto his bed. The bag rustles.

'Yes!' he says. 'You got me a jellyfish!' Reilly's head is back over the side of his bed waving a squidgy green jellyfish. 'Sam, you got me a jellyfish, just like me.'

'Yes.' I smile. 'Just like you.'

Reilly looks at his jellyfish, then back at me.

'I don't want you to go, Sam,' he says.

'I'm not,' I say. 'It'll be all right.'

'No.' Reilly shakes his head. 'I heard Mum say they were going to move you.'

'What?' I sit up so quickly I bang my head on the bunk.

'Yeah,' he says. 'They were arguing in the kitchen. Mum said something about moving you, but then they closed the door so I couldn't hear.'

I stand up in the room. My head swims in panic. I knew it. I knew it.

'Are you sure, Reilly?' I say. 'Are you sure that's what she said?'

'Yes.' Reilly nods. 'Mum said she wants it sorted before Dad goes back to work.'

I knew it. Reilly's mum and dad are just like everyone else. They are getting rid of me. I was right about the photograph. It's so Reilly can remember me, and they're doing it now. Reilly's dad has come back to tell me, before they all jump on a plane and go to Disneyland without me. But I'm not going to let them get rid of me. It's always people getting rid of me. I'm going to get rid of them first.

I pick up my bag and open my drawer, stuffing some pants and socks inside. Then I get my coat from the hanger behind the door.

'What are you doing, Sam?' Reilly gives me a worried look.

'It's okay, Reilly,' I whisper. 'Everything will be okay, but I need to go.'

'No!' Reilly kneels on his bed. 'You can't! You can't.' His face screws up like he's going to cry. 'Please, Sam. Don't go.'

I step up onto my bunk and hold out my arm.

'I'll see you again, Reilly,' I say. 'Promise.'

'No!' Reilly wraps his arms around my neck. 'Don't go, Sam, please don't go.'

I pull myself away from him. I don't want to leave Reilly, but I have to get out of here. I don't want to wait for Rock Star Steve to come in the morning; I don't want to say goodbye to people who don't want me any more. I don't want to go into another stranger's home and start all over again.

'I'm sorry, Reilly.' I walk towards the door. I don't want to look back. I don't want to see him cry.

'Mum!' he shouts. 'Sam's leaving!'

I open the door and run down the stairs.

'What's going on?'

Reilly's mum comes out of the lounge.

I twist the lock and fling the front door open.

'Sam,' shouts Reilly's dad, 'where are you going?'

I pick my bike up off the grass and see Reilly's mum and dad in the doorway.

'You're getting rid of me! I hate you!' I yell so loudly my throat hurts. 'I hate you. And you hate me too.'

Reilly's dad steps towards me. 'No, Sam, of course we don't.'

'You must do!' I shout. 'Otherwise you'd take me to Disneyland.'

'What?'

I run out of the gate with my bike. I have to get away from here, but my legs feel as if they're running on the same spot like a cat in a cartoon.

'Sam. Sam!' Reilly's dad's footsteps thud on the pavement behind me. I jump on my bike and start pedalling, faster and faster. My heart pounds, and I'm shaking so much with anger that I can hardly breathe.

'Sam!' Reilly's dad's voice echoes in the dark.

'No!' I shout. 'No! I'm going where someone wants me!'

I'm leaving, I think to myself. *I'm running away again, only this time I've got a place to go.*

CHAPTER 56

HELP ME

Dave's giant TV lights up the front garden like a cinema screen.

I'm standing at the door, wiping tears on my sleeve. They stopped while I was cycling along the cycle path, while I thought about what I was going to say to them, turning up so late in the dark . . . *Hi, I'm back! You know you said I could have a sleepover at the weekend, well, do you mind if I stay tonight and never leave?* But now I'm outside the door, the tears have come back. Finding the perfect parents was supposed to make me happy, not make me cry. I wipe them away again. I can't let Michelle and Dave see me upset. I want them to want me because they like me, not because they feel sorry for me.

I swallow. All I have to do is raise my hand and lift the knocker and it will all be over. All I have to do is—

A hallway light flicks on, lighting up the coloured glass above the number thirty-six.

I didn't touch the knocker. I'm sure I didn't. I step back. The latch clicks and the door opens.

'Sam!' Dave looks at me, startled. 'It's you. Chelle said she thought she saw someone go by the window.'

'Y-y-yes,' I stammer.

'What is it, mate?' He looks at my bag. 'I thought we said the sleepover was at the weekend.'

'It's . . . It's . . . It's not for the sleepover,' I say.

'Then what is it, mate?'

'It's . . . It's . . .'

'Who is it, Dave?' Michelle calls out.

'It's Sam.' Dave looks at me like he knows I've been crying. 'Mate, you'd better come in.' He steps aside and I walk into the hall. 'Why don't you go and sit in the lounge.'

'Hi, Sam.'

I glance up to see Josh standing at the top of the stairs, but I'm too upset to reply. I turn into the lounge. Michelle is sitting on the sofa.

'Hey, you,' she says, smiling. 'What brings you here?'

I stare at a paused picture of a man helping a woman make a clay pot on the TV.

'Sam?'

I can hear Michelle, but my body is numb.

'Not now, Josh.' Dave is talking to Josh on the stairs. 'I think Sam needs to talk,' he says.

'Do you, Sam?' Michelle shuffles along the sofa.

'Put your bag down,' she says. 'Come and sit here.'

I put my bag on the floor and sit down beside her. Dave perches on the arm of a chair.

'What is it, Sam?' he says. 'Have you had an argument with your mum and dad?'

I stare at the TV. My body is numb and my tongue is too.

'It's okay, my love.' Michelle wraps her arm around my shoulder. 'We all have them. I packed my bag once too, but I got halfway down the street and realized I hadn't put in any knickers.'

I smile.

'Hey, that's better,' says Dave, ruffling my hair. 'Do you want to talk about it?'

'I don't know.' I stare at the floor, but I can sense Michelle and Dave looking at each other.

'I'll get us a drink,' says Dave. 'Juice okay, Sam?'

I nod.

'It'll be all right, Sam,' says Michelle. 'But do you think we should call Mum and Dad and let them know where you are?'

'Don't know.' I shrug. 'Don't think they care.'

'I'm sure they do,' she says quietly. 'No matter how much you might not think so right now. Sometimes everything can get blown up, and the smallest things turn from mice to elephants in our minds.'

'Elephants,' says Dave, handing me a drink. 'I think you're confusing him even more than he already is.'

I hold the glass. Dave sits back on the arm of the chair.

'So what shall we do, love,' says Michelle. 'Call someone?'

'No,' I say. 'Can we just sit here? Just sit here and watch TV?'

Dave and Michelle glance at each other. Michelle nods like they've just communicated in a secret language.

'Sam,' says Dave. 'We've got something to ask you.'

Will you come and live with us? Can we adopt you?

I take a sip of my drink.

'Michelle and I have been talking. And . . .'

'And we've been thinking,' Michelle takes over. 'That you've been around here quite a lot.'

'Yeah.' I nod. 'Because I like it here.'

'I know, my love. I know you do.' She reaches out and holds my hand. 'But we know something's not right. Mrs Shepherd told Dave she saw you hanging around outside the house before you'd even met Josh.'

'I wasn't on my own,' I say. 'I was with Leah, my friend, but she hates Frisbee so I was just waiting for someone to play it with.'

Michelle smiles and rubs my hand. 'Sam, it's not just that, it's some of the things you told us, like living at number ninety-six when . . .'

'But I told you why that was.'

Dave and Michelle look at each other like they are communicating in code again.

Dave leans forward and reaches into his back pocket.

'Sam,' he says. 'Mrs Shepherd gave me this earlier on.'

He pulls a piece of paper out and starts to unfold it.

I stare at the paper.

Wanted

Two adults (or one) prepared to look after
and love an 11-year-old boy. And he promises to
do the same for them.

No dogs.

Or cats.

Or gerbils ...

My heart thuds like a drum.

'I'm ... I'm ... I'm ...'

Michelle leans towards me.

'Sam,' she says softly. 'Is this you?'

CHAPTER 57

I'M SORRY

'I'm sorry.'

'Sam.' Michelle sits down next to me. 'You've got to stop saying that. It's fine. Just tell us what's going on.'

I stare down at the rug.

Out of the corner of my eye I see Dave sitting forward, his hands clasped together. 'Don't worry,' he says. 'You can tell us everything.'

I open my mouth and try to talk, but after wanting something for so long I don't know where to start.

'Aren't you happy at home?' asks Michelle.

'No,' I mumble. 'Not really.'

'Is it your mum or dad, or are you just not happy in yourself? Maybe at school . . . or . . . I don't know . . .'

The red rug goes blurry. I blink, but all that does is squash my tears and make them come out. I can't keep it in any longer. I have to tell them otherwise my heart might explode.

I lift my head. Josh is standing in the doorway. He smiles at me nervously, like he's not sure if he should be here or not.

I take a deep breath.

'It's not school,' I say. 'It's . . . It's . . . It's at home, but it's not my mum and dad. They're not my mum and dad. They're Reilly's.'

'But I thought you said Reilly was a foster-child,' says Dave.

'I know.' I swallow. 'I lied. The foster-child isn't Reilly. It's me.'

Dave and Michelle look at each other and for once it seems neither of them know what to say.

'Is that why you wouldn't let Josh have a sleepover at yours?' says Dave. 'Because he would find out?'

'Yes,' I say. 'But I was going to tell you. I was going to tell you all, but I just wanted to be certain first.'

'Certain of what, Sam?' asks Dave. 'What did you want to be certain of?'

'That I'd found my perfect parents.'

'Your perfect parents?' says Michelle, looking confused. 'How do you mean, Sam?'

'It's what I've always wanted,' I say, looking at the floor. 'That's why I did the Perfect Parent Project. I'm fed up with being passed around like a football. I just want to find someone, or two people, who love me as much as I love them.'

'Mate.' Dave leans forward. 'We can see you are upset, but you're not making much sense.'

Michelle wraps her arm around my shoulders. 'Sam,' she says gently. 'Did you think it was us? That we could be your perfect parents?'

I nod.

'Wow, Sam,' she says. 'I don't know what to say. That's . . . That's very sweet.'

She looks at Dave. Normally he would crack a joke, but suddenly the room feels like a frozen lake, until Michelle says quietly, 'Sam, do you want to tell us about it all?'

They want me to tell them my life story, but even if I had my folder with me, I wouldn't know where to start. But they're waiting, and if I want them to be my perfect parents I have to explain everything – all of my plan, all of my lies – or they'll never trust me.

'My mum gave me away when I was little. I was too young to remember much about her. Since then I've been in nine different houses, with eleven different foster-parents. But none of them wanted to keep me, not for ever anyway.' I look around the room to check that no one is bored, but Josh and Dave are looking right at me, and Michelle is crouching forward like she's waiting to see what happens next on one of her TV shows.

'I was at school with my friend Leah, and we were talking about me wanting to be in *Bugsy Malone*, but I hadn't put my name down on the list because I get moved from schools all the time.' I look up. Dave and Michelle nod like they want me to continue. 'We decided that instead of waiting for my perfect parents to adopt me, I should try to adopt them. So I made a poster.'

'This one?' Dave nods at the poster on the table.

'Yes,' I say. 'And we put them through the doors of the posh houses at The Clift with the huge gardens and indoor swimming pools. Then I went back to wash cars to see if I could get to speak to people, but it didn't work. I came here too, which was when I saw you, Josh, through the window.' I look at Josh. 'You were opening your Xbox on your birthday. And I thought ...'

'You thought, *What a great way to get an Xbox!*'

'Dave!' Michelle punches Dave on the arm.

'What?' says Dave with a smile. 'I'd probably do the same!'

'But it wasn't that,' I say. 'I just thought you looked like a proper family, like one in the movies.'

I wait for Dave to say something funny, but he just looks at Michelle and I can't tell what they are thinking.

Michelle rubs my arm again. 'It was really brave to tell us all that,' she says. 'Are you okay now?'

'Yes.' I sigh with relief. 'I think so.'

I lie back on the sofa. My secret is out. All my lies have flown through the window. I feel relieved but also like crying at the same time. It's as if I've been locked in a room without windows or lights, and now I've found the door. I'm still scared of the outside, but at least Michelle and Dave are here to help me. *They're brilliant*, I think to myself. *I would love them as my perfect parents*. And now I've told them, all I've got to find out is whether they want me.

CHAPTER 58

THE DECISION

'I would have been your friend, anyway,' says Josh as he revs his car with the controller.

I smile.

'And you know,' he goes on, 'I kind of get it. It's not quite the same, but sometimes at night, when I worry about something bad happening to my parents, I think, *I'll be okay. I can always go and live with Auntie Michelle and Uncle Dave . . .*' Josh looks at his controller, then at me. 'Not that I want my parents to die of course. Just saying that Auntie Michelle and Uncle Dave are pretty cool. And they did get me this Xbox like you said.'

'I know,' I say, embarrassed. 'I wish I hadn't said that.'

'It's okay.' Josh flies his car off a ramp. 'Uncle Dave thought it was hilarious.' The car lands and smashes through a wall. 'Sure you don't want to go two-player?' Josh glances at me.

'No,' I say. 'I'll just watch for a bit.'

I lean back against a cushion on Josh's bed as he weaves his car between bollards and traffic. Normally I like having the sound up loud because it makes it more exciting. Now I'm wishing Josh would have it on mute so I can hear Michelle and Dave talking in the kitchen.

They've been down there for nearly half an hour. I've been to the toilet twice to try to listen, but all I heard was my name and Michelle saying, 'It's a shame,' and Dave replying, 'Who do you think we should talk to?' Then they stopped, like they sensed I was up here listening. I wish I knew what they were saying, but then I don't want to know if it's bad news. It's like when I bashed my mouth falling off my bike and I had to wait for ages, wondering if the dentist could save two of my teeth or would have to take them out.

'Argh!' Josh's car flies off a ramp and lands in a river. 'Twenty-three thousand, six hundred and thirty,' he says, reading out his score.

The TV goes quiet. I hear a click and a knocking sound, like Michelle and Dave are making coffee downstairs.

'What do you think they're saying?' I ask.

'Don't know.' Josh shrugs. 'But they always know what to do.' He presses X. A new game starts to load.

'Sam.' My stomach flips at Dave's voice. 'Come down here, mate.'

Me and Josh look at each other. Dave's voice is clearer, like he's walked out of the kitchen and into the hall. Josh hits the pause button.

'Sam.' Dave's voice grows louder like he's climbing the stairs.

Part of me wants to stay, in case it's good news. The other part wants to run away from the bad.

‘Sam, do you want to come down a sec?’ Dave says from the door.

‘Yeah,’ I say, pushing myself off Josh’s bed. Josh puts the controller down.

Dave steps aside, and I walk out onto the landing. My legs are shaking so much that I’m scared I’ll fall down the stairs.

‘Just go on down, mate,’ Dave says quietly.

Quiet means it’s serious. Quiet usually means bad news.

My stomach flips again.

I turn into the lounge and see Michelle sitting on the sofa. She smiles at me. I know that smile, but that doesn’t stop me taking a step, then another.

Michelle taps her hand on the seat beside her.

‘Come and sit here, Sam,’ she whispers like we are in church. Then she smiles again. The smile I’ve seen a hundred times before.

The living room door clicks closed behind me.

My stomach ties in knots as I sit down next to Michelle.

‘Sam.’ She holds my hand. ‘I . . . we . . .’ She glances up at Dave and swallows hard, then turns back to me.

Please don’t smile, I think to myself. *Please. I know that smile. Please don’t.*

It’s a Sam-we-think-you’re-lovely smile.

It’s a Sam-you’re-a-good-boy smile.

It’s a—

‘Sam, we love having you around.’

I knew it. It’s a Sam-we-love-having-you-around-but-you-can’t-stay smile.

Michelle sighs. ‘We really do, and we both still want you to come over. But ...' She glances at Dave, as if telling him it's his turn to take over.

And my heart sinks because Dave swallows hard like a bee is stuck in his throat. And I know what's coming next. 'It's just ... well, Sam. It's not possible for you to come and live with us permanently.'

'But you have Josh here,' I say desperately. 'What's the difference?'

'We do,' says Dave. 'And we love Josh, but we don't want him to live with us all the time. Otherwise we'd have had kids of our own.'

'Oh,' I say, looking at the ground.

'But, Sam,' says Michelle, 'you can still come here, whenever Josh comes.'

'But ... But ...'

Michelle glances at her watch.

I stop.

What have they done?

Dave looks out of the window as car lights flash by.

They've called the police! That's what took them so long when they were downstairs talking.

I stand up.

'Please let me stay,' says a voice. 'Please. I won't lie again. I'll be good – I won't ever run away.'

'I'm sorry, Sam,' says Michelle. 'It's not that simple.'

'Why not?' My voice cracks. 'Maybe we have a trial, just for a few days. That could work, couldn't it? And if you don't like me, we can decide then. And we don't even have to go to Disneyland.'

'It's not a question of liking you. It really isn't.'

I look at them both. I'm losing. I'm losing. Everything I thought I loved is being taken away.

'We're sorry, Sam.' That's Dave.

'Please . . . Please . . .' That's someone crying.

I screw up my eyes.

The someone crying is me.

'Sam, love . . .' Michelle stands up in front of me and holds out her arms.

I want her to hug me, but only if it's going to be for ever.

Another car's lights flash by.

I step back towards the doorway.

'You've called the police,' I say. 'I know you have. You're just like everyone else!'

Michelle and Dave look at each other then back at me.

'Sam,' says Dave, 'you need to calm down.'

'No! You don't know what you've done. You're all the same. You're just like everyone else – you pretend to like me and then get rid of me.'

'Sam,' says Michelle. 'Please come and sit down.'

'No,' I say. 'I don't want to sit down.'

'Then let us drive you home.'

'No!' I pull away from her. 'You don't understand – that's the point, there is no home!'

I turn and run into the hall.

'Sam!'

I hear two voices shout, but I'm already out of the front door, heading for the gate. I start running – the cars are shadows, the street lamps are blurred. I wipe my tears on my arm, but in seconds my eyes have filled and everything goes blurry again.

'I hate you!' I shout. 'I hate you. You're all the same.'

I run around the corner, down the street where I pretended to live. How can I have been so stupid? Why did I think anything would be different? Adults are all the same – they tell me everything will be okay but then let me down again and again. This isn't my street.

I don't belong here.

I don't belong anywhere.

All I do is live in houses that I can never call home.

ERIC

'I hate you! I hate you!' I say out loud even though it's so dark that only the stars are here to listen. 'I hate you! I hate you!' I say again.

I've been in Eric for what feels like hours, trying to calm down, but my chest is still aching like all the cardboard boxes have fallen on top of me, and an elephant is sitting on top of them. I liked Michelle and Dave, they were my perfect parents, but I didn't realize how much I wanted them until the hope was taken away.

'I hate you! I hate you!' I shout, but the more I say it, the more I realize it's not just Michelle and Dave I hate, it's everyone – it's Brad and Angie, Ralph and Jean, Chris and Helen, Jasmine, Ryan and Kim, Reilly's mum and dad – everyone who ever said they liked me then let me go. Looking for perfect parents was pointless. They don't exist, even if for a moment I thought Michelle and Dave were the ones. All I wanted was to live with them. I wouldn't have cared if they had five dogs and a hundred gerbils. I didn't mind that they don't have a big drive or space for a basketball hoop in their titchy garden. I didn't care about Disneyland – Thorpe Park would have been fine, or even the bowling alley and Nando's. I didn't care. I just wanted to be with them, to say goodnight to them when I went to bed and to have been sure that the same parents would still be there when I woke up in the morning.

I look up at the stars but as soon as I do, they start to turn blurry.

I wipe my tears on my sweatshirt.

I want to run now, but the streets are too scary and too dark.

I pull cardboard over me and curl up in a ball underneath.

'I hate you,' I whisper. 'I hate everyone.'

But the trouble with hating everyone is that, when I run away, I've got nowhere to go.

CHAPTER 60

TORCHLIGHTS

I don't remember falling asleep. But I remember my dream.

There was a kite in the sky, zigzagging across the sun.

And there was a dog chasing its shadow across the sand.

And there were children playing in the sea. Mums and dads holding their hands, as they jumped over the waves.

And a boy on the beach with a towel wrapped around him, shivering as he watched everybody.

That boy was me.

I wish the sun was out now. I wish I had a towel to keep me warm, but all I have is pieces of cardboard and the moon.

I wrap my arms around my knees, trying to stop myself shaking. I look at my phone. Seventeen missed calls – two from Leah, two from Rock Star Steve, nine from Reilly's mum, four from a number I don't recognize. Six voicemails. The last one was left at five past ten. I don't need to play them to know they are all asking where I am, that it's time I went back. I can't stop thinking about Michelle and Dave, and the sad looks on their faces when they said I couldn't stay. But I'm so tired and cold that I'm not angry with them any more. I just want to go somewhere warm and sleep. Even Reilly's. He'll be asleep on his bunk now, wearing his *Sharkasaurus* pyjamas, or the new ones his grandparents gave him. Or maybe he's awake, holding up his hand, pretending it's a plane in the dark. I hope he's not worrying about me. I hug my legs tighter. The agency will never let me go back to Reilly's house, not after this. But I don't want to just disappear and leave him. I know how it feels like to wake up and find everyone has gone. Maybe I'll go back first thing, when it's light, sneak into his room and whisper, 'Hey, Reilly! Hey, Reilly!' And he'll roll over and wipe the sleep out of his eyes, and he'll smile and say, 'Hey, Sam! Where have you been?' And I'll smile and say, 'I'm sorry, Reilly, but I'm not staying, I have to . . .'

I swallow hard as tears trickle down my cheeks. I don't want to leave Reilly, but I can't stay where no one wants me.

I roll over on my side and sink down into the cardboard. *I'll sneak back and see you, Reilly. I will. Or maybe when I'm older, I'll come back and meet you outside your school.*

'Down here – are you sure?'

I open my eyes. Blue lights flash around the buildings. Voices and footsteps echo along the alley.

'In there?'

The footsteps grow louder.

Torchlights flash against the walls.

'Sam! Sam!'

A man's voice. I don't know who it is, only that they are looking for me.

The cans rattle.

I sink down further into the cardboard. I don't want to stay here, but I don't want to be found.

'Are you sure?'

The ladder rattles.

'Sam!'

My heart thuds hard. The voice grows louder, like the man is now peering over the top of Eric.

How did they know where to find me?

I peek through a gap in the cardboard and see a silhouetted figure as the torchlight flashes around the inside of Eric.

'Are you sure it's this one? Only … only it seems to be full of cardboard. Sam, are you in there? It's okay, son. No one is mad with you. We just want to know that you're safe.'

It's either people from the agency or the police. Probably both.

I crouch down further.

'Sam, if you're in there, please come out. We can talk about it, then get you safely home.' I don't need to see his snakeskin shoes to know that's Rock Star Steve talking to me from out in the alley.

Cardboard crumples, like it does whenever I first climb in.

'Sam.' The torchlight stops, pointing right at me. 'Sam,' the voice sighs with relief. 'Come on out – I can see you now.'

I stay still.

The man gently lifts my cardboard roof away.

I squint in the torchlight.

'It's okay, I've found him.' The man shines the torch beam away from my eyes, lighting up the inside of Eric. I see a police officer's face and uniform. 'Come on, son,' he says, holding out his hand. 'Out you come now.'

I reach out and he pulls me up.

'You okay?' he says quietly.

I want to answer, say that I am, but I'm scared if I open my mouth I'll cry.

'Come on. Let's go.'

I pick my way across the cardboard. Another police officer is at the top of the ladder.

'Nice and easy, Sam,' she says softly. 'Do you need me to help you up?'

'No,' I say. She backs away. I reach for the rope, climb up the side of Eric and look over the top. Two more police officers are standing in the alley and in between them is Reilly's mum and dad and Rock Star Steve.

Someone says something, but I'm too cold and too tired to hear.

I flip my leg over the side of Eric.

'Take it easy.' The police officer stands behind me as I step down the ladder.

When I reach the bottom, I glance up at Reilly's mum and dad, waiting for them to say how mad they are that I ran away, for keeping them up all night.

Reilly's mum steps towards me.

'Sam,' she says. 'Where have you been? We've been worried sick.'

I stand still. She closes the gap between us and hugs me. All I ever wanted was a proper hug like this, but my body is so numb and cold I can't feel anything.

I feel like crying, but I don't want her to see I'm upset. I don't want anyone to see me upset.

Reilly's mum lets go of me. Suddenly I feel alone in the dark, even though I'm surrounded by faces lit up by the flashing blue lights.

'How . . . How . . .' I try to speak, but no words come out.

'It was me, Sam.' Leah steps out of the shadow of the wall. 'I'm sorry. But I had to tell them.'

For a moment I'm mad that she's told them all about Eric, but then I see the worried look on Leah's face, and the wet on her cheeks where she's been crying. She walks towards me, then runs, wrapping her arms tight around me.

'I'm sorry,' she says. 'I shouldn't have built your hopes up. I thought the Perfect Parent Project would be fun.'

A lump builds in my throat. I swallow but it comes straight back again. 'It was,' I say. 'You were only trying to help, but Michelle and Dave were just like all the others. They didn't want me either.' I hug Leah so tight I don't want to let go.

'Come on, Sam,' Rock Star Steve says softly. 'Let's get you home.'

I shake my head.

He still doesn't understand.

There is no home.

CHAPTER 61

TONIGHT, I DREAM OF DISNEYLAND

The red light glows bright on Reilly's TV.

No, Reilly, I don't want the last piece of your Easter egg.

I don't want you to sneak downstairs and get me a biscuit.

I don't want you to tell me about taekwondo.

I don't want you to give me a hug.

I don't want you to promise that I can go first on the Xbox all week.

I don't want you to say we can swap bunks because I've always wanted the top one.

I just want to be quiet and left alone, but Reilly's head is hanging upside down for the tenth time since I got back.

'Did you really live in a bin, Sam?'

'Yes.'

'Cool. My friend Reece has got a tree house and my cousin Emma has a pretend shop in her shed. But none of them have got a bin. What colour is it?'

'Yellow.'

'How big is it? Could I fit in it too?'

'Yes.'

'Will you take me there?'

'Reilly, please.' I roll over and face the wall. 'I just want to be quiet.'

'Okay. See you in the morning.' Reilly flips back onto his bed. 'Night, Sam.'

'Goodnight, Reilly.' My voice cracks with tears. I think that he's finally gone, but then I hear him breathing through the gap between his mattress and the wall.

'Sam,' he whispers. 'Can you hear me?'

'Yes, Reilly.'

'I'm glad you're home.'

'Thanks, Reilly,' I say. I wish I could say I was glad too, but I'm not.

How did I get it so wrong? I thought Michelle and Dave actually liked me. They made me laugh; they put their arms around me and ruffled my hair. I thought they liked me so much they would adopt me and let me live in their home.

I was so stupid. I'm so stupid. I bang my fist on my pillow, but feel like whacking the wall. Maybe I didn't love them. Maybe the warm feeling in my chest in Wagamama was just the heat from the food. And the tingle on my head when Dave ruffled my hair was just an itchy scalp.

So stupid.

So stupid.

I screw my eyes up tight but that doesn't stop my tears from squeezing out. Michelle's and Dave's words repeat in my head.

Sam, we love having you around.

We both still want you to come over.

You can still come here, whenever Josh comes.

But I don't want to just visit. That would be like having no money and staring at a giant Toblerone in a shop. I could look, but not touch.

In the car, Rock Star Steve said I'll still be here tomorrow. He'll have an emergency morning meeting with social services on Saturday and then he'll come and see me. I don't have to be there to know what they'll be saying. It'll be like a PEP meeting without me – 'Sam does this, Sam does that. Sam's confused. Sam doesn't know what he wants. Let's try to help. He's gone too far this time. How can we help him?' I shrug in my bed, like they just asked me, 'What do you want, Sam? What were you even thinking? Let's write some things down. Let's tick a few boxes. What happens next?'

Rock Star Steve told me not to worry, but that doesn't stop a million bees buzzing in my stomach. I know what happens next – new people, new house, new school, new plan.

I had a plan.

But the plan didn't work.

I screw my eyes tighter, trying to block everything out, replacing them with happy things, things that I love – Astro Orbiter, Buzz Lightyear Astro Blasters, Big Thunder Mountain Railroad, Space Mountain, Splash Mountain. Smiling faces. Happy faces. Happy faces I wish were mine.

Tonight I try to dream of Disneyland.

CHAPTER 62

THE SILENT TREATMENT

The silent treatment starts when I sit at the dining table and every bite of a cornflake sounds like an earthquake.

The silent treatment means I can hear Reilly upstairs shouting at his TV screen every time his plane crashes.

The silent treatment means I watch through the window while Reilly's dad cuts the grass.

The silent treatment means Reilly's mum smiles at me when I lift my feet so she can vacuum under my chair.

The silent treatment means everyone makes themselves busy, busy, busy, like nothing ever happened.

The silent treatment used to make me think I'd got away with it. *I'm okay! Everyone's forgotten. Hooray! Yippee!*

But it really means that nobody talks while we're cutting our meat and roast potatoes.

The silent treatment is when Reilly waves his green jellyfish across the table going, 'Look what Sam got me. Look what Sam got me.' And his mum and dad smile but don't say anything.

The silent treatment means I hear every thud of my feet on the stairs when I head up to Reilly's room.

The silent treatment means Reilly only whispering when he says, 'Sam, please help me get my plane to pick up the gold.'

The silent treatment means I can hear the hoot of the water pump while Reilly's mum helps him take a shower.

The silent treatment means I get into bed and my stomach turns over like it's full of snakes.

The silent treatment means I try to sleep but can't – not on my back, on my side, facing the wall, facing the room, not upside down or curled up in a ball.

Because the silent treatment only means one thing.

Rock Star Steve will come and take me away tomorrow.

CHAPTER 63

GOODBYE, REILLY

'Sam, one of the rotor blades has fallen off. Will you help me fix it? Sam?'

'Yeah, Reilly,' I sigh. 'In a minute.'

The rain is trickling down the glass. I've packed all my stuff and now I'm looking out of the window, waiting for Rock Star Steve's car to come along the street. This is the last time I will stand here. This is the last time I'll be with Reilly. People always say they will keep in touch, that I can visit, just like Michelle and Dave did, but they never do. It's like they forget me as soon as I walk out of the door. I hope Reilly will be different, but he's too young to meet me on his own. He'd have to ask his mum or dad, and there's no way they will take him, not after they were so angry about having to call the police again.

My heart thuds as a car turns into the street. It's a red Peugeot 305. I breathe with relief.

It's funny, I've wanted to get out of here for the last four months, and now I don't want to go. Maybe Leah's right – it's like sometimes I don't know what I want.

'Sam. It's broken off again.'

I turn away from the window and see Reilly sitting on the top bunk, holding his helicopter in the air. 'It's this one,' he says.

I smile and walk over to him.

'Let me see.' I take the helicopter and the loose blade. 'You've lost the black cap that's supposed to be on the top. See, there.'

Reilly leans over. He smells of the bubblegum shampoo he uses. He smells of Reilly.

'Oh yeah,' he says, then looks around his duvet. 'Is this it?'

'Yeah. That's it.' I put the rotor blade over the pin, then snap the black cap on top. 'See?'

Reilly grins as I knock the rotor blades with my finger and make them spin around.

'Thanks, Sam,' he says.

I smile at him.

I want to hug you, Reilly, I think to myself. *I want to hug you, but if I do, I'm scared I'm going to cry.*

Reilly looks at my packed bag, then wraps his arms around my neck.

'I don't want you to go, Sam,' he says.

I put my arms around him.

I don't want to go either.

I don't see Rock Star Steve's car pull up outside.

I don't see him walk up the path.

I don't hear him ring the bell.

I don't hear him talking to Reilly's mum and dad.

I don't hear snakeskin shoes on the stairs.

I just hear him say, 'Come on, Sam, let's go.'

And I look at Reilly, and he says, 'Goodbye, Sam.'

And I say, 'Bye, Reilly, you'll get to level four soon,' and then I pick up my bag.

And then Rock Star Steve says, 'No, Sam, you won't be needing that.'

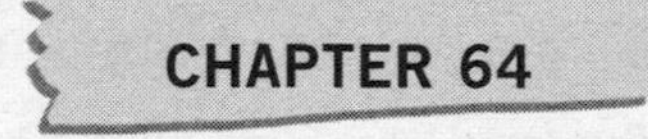

CHAPTER 64

THE PLACE I USED TO PLAY

'Sam, this has to be a two-way thing. There's no point in me talking, suggesting things, if you don't reply . . . Sam?' Rock Star Steve stops walking when we reach his golf ball. 'Come on,' he says. 'I thought us playing pitch and putt would make a change from sitting in the car or Pizza Hut.'

'It is,' I say. 'But it feels weird.'

'Because you're here with me?'

'No,' I say. 'Because I thought you'd call an emergency PEP meeting.'

Rock Star Steve stands over his ball, then looks up at me. 'No,' he says. 'I think this is a much better idea.'

'Yeah,' I say. 'It is, but you do look a bit strange playing golf in those shoes.'

'Ah, but that's where you're wrong,' says Rock Star Steve. 'Snakes were made for grass.'

'If they were alive!'

Rock Star Steve laughs. 'That's true, Sam. Very true. But at least I got a bit of a smile out of you.'

I smile properly and I don't think I've done that since I was at Michelle and Dave's two days ago.

Rock Star Steve swings his club and chips his ball onto the green.

'Good shot, Rock Star Steve,' he says, picking up his putter.

I look at him.

'What?' He grins. 'You don't think I know that's what you call me?'

'No,' I say. 'I didn't.'

'See, Sam,' he says, as we walk towards my ball. 'I know a lot more than you think, and the more I know, the more I can help.'

As I stand over my ball, I can't help smiling, cos Rock Star Steve has known what I call him all along. I swing my club back. Rock Star Steve has told me that if I relax it will help make the ball go in the air. My club comes down and the ball pops up onto the green. As we walk to where the ball landed, I sense Rock Star Steve looking at me, like he has done for the first six holes. He hasn't said anything about leaving Reilly's house, and he's said nothing about where I'm going next. I look down towards the main road. There must be another person from the authorities here somewhere. It could be the man walking along the path with his newspaper. Or the woman walking across the grass. Or it might be the people waiting to hit their shots off the fifth tee.

'There's no one else here,' says Rock Star Steve. 'I've seen you looking. It's just you and me. But I know you're not stupid. You know why we're here.'

'Yes,' I say. 'To talk about what happened on Thursday.'

'Yes, but not just Thursday. Everything, Sam. I know you've been having a hard time recently.'

Rock Star Steve sits down on the bank beside the green. I sit beside him and we look across the golf course, at the cars and buses as they snake along the road into town. I can see the football ground's floodlights, and the river, and the tower blocks. And in the distance, I think I can see the square surrounded by the rainbow houses. I stare at them, imagining Michelle and Dave inside one of them, remembering Mrs Shepherd walking her dog through the park. If only she hadn't read my poster; if only I'd never made it in the first place. Then I might have had longer to convince Michelle and Dave to have me, even just a week, or a month.

'Sam,' says Rock Star Steve. 'It's only natural you want to belong somewhere and have people love you as much as you love them.'

I keep staring at the houses.

'That's what I put on my poster,' I say, turning to him. 'That's all I wanted. I didn't need a big house with a swimming pool or to go to Disneyland.'

Rock Star Steve smiles. 'I know,' he says quietly. 'But it's okay to have dreams. Everyone can have those. That's all you were trying to do with your project – make your dreams come true.'

'Yeah,' I say. 'I was.'

I told Rock Star Steve all about the Perfect Parent Project on the second tee. I even showed him a copy of the poster. I thought he would say I'd done the wrong thing, but all he did was smile, then chuckle about the no dogs and gerbils. It feels such a long time ago now, when me and Leah went to The Clift and posted them. The interviews on the

Downs with Leah wearing her yellow dress and me feeling nervous in my *Bugsy* suit. My heart was full of hope of finding my perfect parents then, but now it feels emptier than it did before we started.

Rock Star Steve leans forward. 'Listen, Sam,' he says. 'You know we chatted a bit about maybe seeing some of the places where you grew up?'

'Yeah.'

'Well, how about we do that now?'

'What, before we go to another foster home?'

'No.' Rock Star Steve shakes his head. 'You don't know everything, Sam.'

I look across at him. 'Well, I know we haven't come here just to play golf.'

'You know me.' Rock Star Steve smiles.

'Yeah,' I say. 'You're Rock Star Steve with the snakeskin shoes.'

'Ha, yeah, and you're Sam – little c, big C – McCann.'

I smile. 'How do you know I call myself that?'

'You've only said it a thousand times. Come on.' Rock Star Steve stands up. 'Let's take the clubs back, and then we'll go, if you're ready. Doing your life story folder didn't seem to help you, but perhaps there's something down there that will.' He nods towards four tower blocks, down by the river.

'Is that them?' I say. 'The tower blocks I remember?' I stare at the buildings, so far away they look like blocks of Reilly's Lego. Part of me is excited; a bigger part of me is scared about what I will find there. It's like putting my hand in a dark box and not knowing if something will bite.

Rock Star Steve looks at me, like he can see the confusion on my face. 'You can do it, Sam,' he says. 'You're a brave lad, after everything you've gone through.'

I'm still not sure, and I think Rock Star Steve notices because he takes my clubs and says, 'Come on. We'll hand these in and go.'

There's a slide; there's a climbing frame; there's a roundabout and a concrete tunnel that two children are running through.

It's just a park.

It's like any park.

But this is my park.

The park where I grew up.

I spin around, trying to take it all in again – concrete tunnel, roundabout, children on the climbing frame. I shake my head slowly.

I want to remember, I want to . . .

Red kite . . . tower blocks stretching into the sky . . . red kite . . . me walking backwards . . . red kite . . . I screw my eyes up tight, but that's where the memory ends.

Try again, Sam, I think. *Try again.*

And I do, but it's like someone has erased that bit from my brain.

'It's okay,' says Rock Star Steve. 'It's going to feel strange. Like when I go back to visit my parents. Everything feels smaller – the house, my old bedroom, even my parents seem to have shrunk.'

'But it's my park,' I say, disappointed, 'and I don't remember anything. I thought I'd find something. But it feels like I was never here.'

'Just take your time,' says Rock Star Steve.

I hear the roar of an engine. I look up between the tower blocks and see a plane and its white vapour trails cutting across the blue sky. Nothing, I remember noth—

Tower blocks. Red kite.

Tower blocks. Red kite.

Me walking backwards.

I keep looking at the sky.

Another step. Then another.

'Careful, Sammy.' My mum's voice. 'Sammy, look where you're going.'

Tower blocks, red kite.

'Sammy!

There's a shadow behind me, and I just know it's my mum. I squeeze my eyes tighter. I want to see her face, her smile, but that's where the memory ends.

'Sam . . . You'd better stop there, mate.'

I shake myself out of my thoughts and see Rock Star Steve standing behind me on a path below the wall.

I take a deep breath, looking back across the park – concrete tunnel, swings, slide, children spinning on the roundabout.

Rock Star Steve steps up next to me. 'What did you remember, Sam?' he asks.

I think of telling him I saw Mum's shadow, but like my mum, the shadow has already gone.

'I just saw a kitc,' I say.

'That's all?'

'Yes,' I sigh. 'That's all.'

Rock Star Steve puts his arm across my shoulder. 'It's okay, Sam. We can keep trying.'

'It's like doing a puzzle,' I say. 'But there are too many pieces missing, and the pieces I do have don't mean anything. It just makes me want to smash the puzzle up and start a new one.'

'I know it's frustrating, Sam. But it's important we know where we come from, why we act and look as we do. Like I know I get my appalling dress sense from my mum, and my good looks from my dad.'

'Yeah, right.' I smile.

Rock Star Steve smiles too, then says, 'But that's not what makes you you.'

'A foster-kid,' I say.

'No,' says Rock Star Steve. 'A foster-kid might be *what* you are, but that's not *who* you are. They aren't the same thing.'

'I don't understand,' I say.

Rock Star Steve steps to the side and lets a woman pushing a baby in a pushchair go by.

'It's like . . . I'm a foster-care worker,' he continues, 'but that's not who I am inside. It's what's inside us that counts. It's what's in there, but most importantly it's what's in there.' Rock Star Steve points first at my head, then my heart. 'You're a good kid, Sam. Don't you ever think that you're not. And you have so much to give. I've seen how much you love Reilly.'

I smile. 'Yeah, I do.'

'You've got so many good things inside you, you've just got to learn to let them out. I know that must scare you, but you can't pretend to be anyone different – you have to be who you are. You shouldn't worry about telling people you're a foster-kid.'

I turn and look at Rock Star Steve. He's said lots of things to help me, but it's time he told me where I'm going.

'What happens now?' I say. 'I know you said I don't have to leave yet, but Reilly's mum said they were going to move me.'

'No,' says Rock Star Steve, looking confused. 'They're not going to move you.'

'They are. Reilly told me. He heard them say that.'

'No, Sam.' Rock Star Steve shakes his head. 'You must have got the wrong end of the stick. I told you before. Tom and Sarah are lovely people, and they care about you. You should have seen how worried they were the other night. They must have called every number in their phone book, and Tom was knocking on every door in the street.'

'So they aren't going to get rid of me?'

'No, mate. I don't know how many times I need to tell you. You've got to try to trust people and stop looking to run away. You might not have many memories of growing up, but you've got to trust people to help you make new memories of your own.'

'But I did trust someone,' I say. 'I trusted Michelle and Dave.'

'Yeah,' says Rock Star Steve. 'But maybe you were looking in the wrong place. Maybe the people you should trust are a little closer to home.'

'Reilly's mum and dad?'

'Yes, and Reilly too. I'm sure you've already got good memories with him.'

I smile to myself as I think about Reilly hanging over his bed like a jellyfish, jabbing the buttons on his Xbox One controller. In my mind I see his tomato-sauce grin and him laughing when his dad took us for a ride in his pretend helicopter. I remember thinking his dad was cool. And I remember the hug Reilly's mum gave me when they found me in Eric. It wasn't a fake hug. It wasn't a foster-parent hug. She hugged me so hard I could feel her fingers on my back when she let go.

I sigh. I'm tired of running. I'm tired of not being able to trust people. I don't know if I ever will, but I want to try.

'Can we go back now?' I say.

'You sure?' says Rock Star Steve.

'Yeah,' I nod. 'I'm sure.'

CHAPTER 65

I GOT IT WRONG

'It's okay to get upset, Sam.' That was Reilly's mum. 'I get upset too, and it's even harder if you keep it all in your head.'

'You have to talk about things, Sam.' That was Reilly's dad.

'So why did you give me the silent treatment?' That was me sitting between them on the sofa.

'The silent treatment?' Reilly's mum and dad looked at each other.

'Yeah,' I said. 'You didn't talk to me all of yesterday, not even when I helped you load the dishwasher. You were mad with me all day.'

Reilly's mum took a deep breath, like the next thing was important. 'Sam,' she said, 'we weren't mad with you, we were mad with each other. We felt as if we'd let you down, that we weren't good foster-parents. We were trying to work things out. The silent treatment wasn't about you, it was about us.'

'But Reilly said you were going to move me,' I said.

'No!' They both shook their heads.

'Sam,' said Reilly's dad, 'that's not what Bug heard.'

'But he told me he overheard you talking. He heard you say move.'

'Well, he may have heard the word "move", but that wasn't about you.' That's when he looked at Reilly's mum, then back at me. 'We were thinking of moving. All of us. So I'm closer to work and Sarah doesn't have to spend so much time here on her own. But we decided not to. We don't want to unsettle you and Reilly. And besides, we would make those kind of decisions as a family.'

'Oh.' That was me. 'So, me and Reilly got it wrong?'

'Sam.' Reilly's mum put her hand on mine. 'I think we all got it wrong.'

They both smiled. Reilly's dad stood up, said he was going to check on Reilly, because he was up in his room on his own.

Reilly's mum looked at me.

'Sam,' she said, quietly. 'I know we've had some difficult times, but you need to know how much we think of you, and how much we want you to be a part of this family. All this has been very new to me, to all of us. I might have a *Foster-Parent Handbook* that tells me what to do and what not to do, but that didn't prepare me. It didn't help me understand how I was feeling, and it didn't help me understand what you were going through either. What I do know is that Tom and I think loads of you, and Reilly adores you. I love it when I hear you laughing and messing around with him.' Reilly's mum gulped back tears. 'Sometimes I'm down here laughing as much as you.'

I smiled when she said Reilly's name.

She held my hand. 'All that time you thought I was nagging you, it wasn't that I didn't want you to go out, it's just that I wanted you here, safe with us. I want for us to do things together, make new memories.'

That's when my eyes filled with tears. I looked at the carpet, at the blank TV, at the pictures of Reilly on the wall above the fireplace even though it was blurred.

I wiped my eyes on my sleeve.

'I don't have memories,' I said. 'I don't have any family. I don't have anyone who wants me.'

'You do have family.' She smiled at me. 'You've got Reilly, his dad and me. And you've got this house and you've got your room.'

She looked like she meant everything she was saying, but I still couldn't believe her. After talking to Rock Star Steve, I knew finding the right parent was about trusting them, and caring about them. That trust was far more important than living in a big house with a huge swimming pool. But I still couldn't forget about one thing – the thing that had been in my head ever since I went into Reilly's mum's office that night. I wanted to ask her. I needed an answer, but every time I went to speak, no words came out.

'Sam?' Reilly's mum wiped a tear away from my cheek. 'Is there something else you want to say?'

I nodded.

'Then just say it, my love. We have to be honest with each other, and talk things through.'

'Okay,' I said. I looked up at her.

Say it, Sam. Say it.

'Okay.' I took a deep breath. Here it goes. Here I go. 'If you all like and care about me so much,' my words rush out, 'if I'm part of the family . . . why aren't you taking me to Disneyland?'

'What?' asked Reilly's mum, surprised.

'Disneyland,' I said. 'You're all going – I saw the brochure in your room, and your names on a piece of paper with ticks against yours and a cross against mine.'

'Oh, Sam.' Reilly's mum smiled. I waited for her to say that they needed time alone as a family, that sometimes a break from each other can be a good thing, but she kept smiling. 'That's not what the cross meant. It meant we don't have a passport for you yet. I wanted to keep it as a surprise – that's another reason I wanted you to go to the photo booth with Reilly.'

'Wait. I'm confused,' I said. 'I thought the photo was for my wall.'

'It was,' said Reilly's mum, 'but then I was going to get one of you on your own, so I could send it off with the passport form.'

'Oh!' I suddenly felt stupid.

Reilly's mum ruffled my hair. 'Did you really think we would go without you?'

'Yes,' I said, 'I really did. I thought you and Reilly's dad were going to send me to a respite home in Weston-Super-Mare or somewhere.'

Reilly's mum smiled. 'Well, I think that would be very unfair. And, Sam . . .' She paused. 'I've been thinking, how would you feel about calling us Sarah and Tom? Reilly's mum and dad is quite a mouthful.'

'I don't know,' I said. 'It feels a bit weird.'

'Just try it,' she said.

'Okay . . . Sarah.'

We both laughed, then Sarah suddenly put her finger up to her lips, as Reilly came jumping down the stairs. 'Not a word,' she whispered. 'He hasn't got a clue.'

'Reilly, wait,' his dad shouted, but he was too late because Reilly had already bounced into the room in his taekwondo gown with a 'Hiiiii-ya!'

'Look, Sam. I got my first belt,' he said.

'It's cool, Reilly,' I said.

'And I learnt a new move.' He threw his left arm in the air and kicked with his left foot. He spun round and fell over on the rug. 'Hang on,' he said. 'I can do better ones than that.'

Sarah smiled.

Tom smiled.

I smiled. I didn't know what I was feeling but all the lovely things Reilly's mum just said had made my heart swell like a balloon. They really did like me – they really wanted me. I'd got everything wrong. *This is what it feels like to have a family*, I thought. I wanted to tell them that, but most of all I was so mega-excited that I wanted to jump up in the middle of the room and shout, 'Hey, Reilly, we're going to Disneyland!'

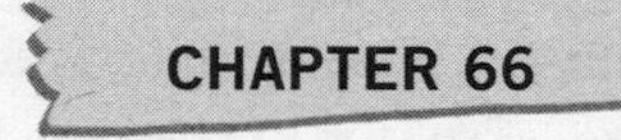

CHAPTER 66

MY BEST FRIEND

'Don't delete it, Sam!' Leah reaches across the school dining table. 'You can't delete all of them. Just because they aren't perfect.'

'I wasn't going to,' I say, turning back to the photo of 'THE WINNING TEAM! ☺' from bowling on my phone. 'I was just looking.' For a while I was angry with Michelle and Dave, but seeing the way they're smiling back at me in this photo, I can't be upset with them any more. They didn't know I had selected them as my perfect parents. They just thought I was a good friend for their nephew to hang out with during the holidays. It wasn't their fault I had bigger plans. It doesn't mean they're bad people. They told me that we can still meet up, if I like, but that I might need a little time to myself first. I'd love to see them again – in fact, Josh has been messaging ever since because he got a game called Demon Zombies for his Xbox and said I should get it too, so we can play online. He also said he'd let me know when he's going to his uncle and auntie's again, so maybe I can go and play

Frisbee. I scroll through the photos on my phone – one of me in the back of the car with Josh, the photo of me and Josh sucking worms in Wagamama. I smile. I'd like to get Demon Zombies, and I will meet him, but I think Michelle and Dave are right; I do need a little time.

'See,' says Leah. 'Wasn't all bad, was it?'

I look up. 'No. It wasn't.'

Leah smiles. 'Might not have been successful, but it was the most fun I've ever had doing a project – remember when we got the suit, and when you panicked washing that guy's car?'

'I was scared,' I say. 'I thought I'd blown my cover.'

'Oh, wait,' says Leah, putting her sandwich down, 'this was the best one.' She holds her hand up to her ear like she's talking on a phone. 'Hi, Mum, can I go to ten pin bowling?'

I can't help but laugh.

'Uh, I was like, *What?*' Leah looks sideways at her imaginary phone. 'Especially when you said, "Love you, Mum!"'

'Hey, you made me say that! And Josh was looking right at me. My face was burning.'

'I was wetting myself,' Leah giggles. 'Love you, Mum.'

We burst out laughing.

Two girls from Year Nine glance at us with a weird look as they sit down at the other end of our table. I look back at my phone. I've just been laughing but that doesn't stop me feeling a bit sad inside. Leah takes a bite of her sandwich and looks across at me.

'It's okay,' she says. 'You don't have to say anything.'

I pick up my carton of orange juice. I don't have to say anything and I can't say anything because suddenly I feel a lump in my throat.

I sip from my drink.

Leah takes another bite of her sandwich.

I swallow hard. 'I did like them though,' I say quietly.

'I know, Sam,' says Leah. And I think she does know. 'Does it make you wish we'd never started the project?'

'No. We might not have found my perfect parents, but I did find out a lot of things – like who I am, and that I need to trust people, and be honest. I also realized that I love Reilly, and that his mum and dad are actually really nice.'

'I think they are,' says Leah. 'You should have seen how upset Sarah was when you ran away. She was crying in the car when we were driving to Eric. She thought someone had taken you.'

'I know. I told you all the things she said to me yesterday. I think she actually does care.'

'And them taking you to Disneyland must help!'

'Oh yeah, that helps loads.' I smile as I look across the dining hall. Lewis is sitting at a table with some of his friends. Leah glances over her shoulder.

'You should go and talk to him, Sam,' she says.

'I know. But I can't tell him the truth about why I missed the *Bugsy* practices. I don't think he'd understand. From all the pictures of him and his brother in his house, I think he already has the perfect family . . . Although his house isn't massive and they don't have a BMW M5 . . .'

'Maybe that's what we really found out,' says Leah, 'that people can't tick everything on your list, or anybody's list. Sometimes we have to take the good things and forget about the bad. And maybe perfect parents don't exist. Maybe parents are like everyone else – they have their faults but that doesn't make them bad people. When parents annoy us – asking where we're going, where we were, why we're late – it's only because they care. '

'Blimey,' I say. 'You sound like Mrs Sorrell.'

'It's true though.' Leah looks around the canteen. 'We might think other people have perfect parents but sometimes it's easy for people to look happy on the outside.' She nods across to a table by the window. 'Like everyone thinks Louisa Harwood is happy, but I know that she doesn't get on with her mum, and Salim is always complaining that his dad pushes him too hard to get in the football team. And then there's me of course. I love my family, even my dad, but they are far from perfect.'

'I know,' I say. 'And I'm sorry about your dad not turning up. And I'm sorry I forgot to meet you too.'

'Sam, it's okay.' Leah leans across the table. 'You've apologized a hundred times, and besides, I've not told you the latest news.'

'What?'

'Turns out Jug-ears isn't so bad after all. He made up with Mum, and bought her flowers and me and Mollie two Easter eggs, although Mollie said he only did that because they were half price.'

The dinner bell rings. Everyone around us picks up their plates and heads to the waste bins. Me and Leah do the same.

'Catch up later?' she says as we walk.

'Yeah,' I say. 'But I've got drama first.'

'Okay.' Leah scowls. 'Just don't ever forget about me again . . . or else!'

'I won't. And . . . and . . .' I stop walking.

'And what?'

I check around the canteen to make sure that no one is listening.

'Sam, you're freaking me out,' says Leah.

'I just wanted to say thanks. And . . .'

You can say it now, Sam. You have to trust people.

I take a deep breath.

'I just wanted to say, you are my best friend.'

Leah grins. 'Thanks, Sam, you're mine too. For a moment I thought you were going to give me a hug!'

'Nooo!' I shake my head. 'Wouldn't do that.'

'It'd be tragic,' says Leah.

'Yeah,' I say. 'Tragic.'

CHAPTER 67

NOT ACTING OUT

'It's okay, Sam. We forgive you for not turning up,' says Lewis. 'Just means I get to splurge you . . . at least ten times!' He pretends to shoot me with a splurge gun.

Amala and Darrius laugh. I go to apologize again but Mr Powell cuts in.

'So,' he says. 'Let's do some hot-seating to warm up. We can do it in *Bugsy Malone* characters. See what you learned over the holidays. Who's first up?'

'I'll go,' says Lewis.

He steps up onto the stage, and we gather in a semicircle around him.

'Okay, ready?' Mr Powell asks.

'Yes.' Lewis nods.

We all fire questions.

'What's your name?'

'Bugsy.'

'How old are you?'

'Twelve.'

'Why are you called Bugsy?'

'It's a nickname, but I don't like it because it actually means crazy.'

'Don't forget the four 'w's,' says Mr Powell, 'who, when, why, what.'

'What do you do?'

'I'm a gangster.'

'When?'

'Nineteen twenty-nine.' Lewis suddenly switches to an American accent. 'In a flashy world of underground crime, hoodlums and dance girls.'

We all laugh.

'Excellent, Lewis,' says Mr Powell. 'Who's next . . . Sam? Hurry, let's not lose momentum.'

I step up onto the stage. My heart thuds as eighteen eyes look at me. Here goes.

I take a deep breath like I'm diving deep underwater.

'Who are you?'

'Sam.'

'Fat Sam?' says Amala.

'No,' I say. 'Just Sam – little c, big C – McCann.'

'How old are you?'

'Eleven.'

'What do you do?'

'Go to school?'

Everyone giggles.

'Sam,' says Amala. 'We're supposed to be in character.'

'It's okay,' says Mr Powell, staring at me. 'Let's see where this goes. Four 'w's.'

'What's your favourite subject?'

'Drama.'

'What do your mum and dad do?'

'Don't have any.'

'You don't have any?'

'No.'

'What happened to them?'

I shrug.

'You can't shrug,' says Darrius. 'You have to say something. Did they die?'

'Don't know.'

'So who do you live with?'

'Foster-parents.'

Everyone goes quiet.

'Sam,' says Lewis. 'I'm confused. Which parts of this are true?'

'All of it,' I say. I look at Lewis, wondering if he remembers what I said about having a real brother and a mum who didn't want to meet anybody. He nods at me, as if to say, 'Go on.'

I smile.

'I'm a foster-kid,' I say, relieved. 'But that's not who I am. I'm just Sam.'

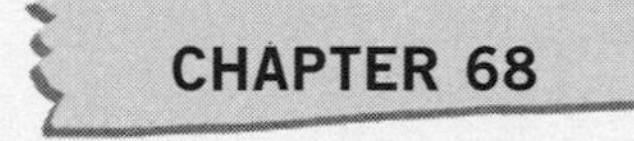

PHOTO BOOTH

'Are you ready?' That was Sarah again.

'No, our faces aren't in the middle of the screen.' That was me.

'Wind the seat up,' she said. 'So it's higher.'

'Okay. Get off, Reilly.' That was me again.

'I'll stand up, you spin me.' That was Reilly.

'You'll fall off.'

'I won't.'

I spin the seat, turning Reilly as the seat winds up. He starts singing a tune, like he's playing a xylophone. 'Ding. Ding. Ding.'

'Ha-ha-ha.'

'Ha-ha-ha.'

That was both of us laughing because he looks like a fairy spinning in a jewellery box.

'Have you done it?' That was Reilly's mum again.

'Yes.'

'Yes.'

Me and Reilly are still giggling, our bums sliding as we both try to fit on the seat.

'Ready?'

'Ready!'

'Nothing's happening.'

'Have you put the money in, Sam?'

'Ha-ha. No, I forgot.'

I put four coins in the slot.

The countdown clock on the screen says, 'Get ready. 5 . . . 4 . . . 3 . . .'

'Pwah, Reilly, have you farted?'

'It wasn't me. It wasn't me!'

'2 . . . 1 . . .'

Flash! Flash!

'What? No!'

'We'll send one to Tom,' Sarah says as we wait outside for the photos to come out.

'Hi-ya!' Reilly is aiming karate kicks at me and I'm trying to grab him and tickle his belly.

'Aww, boys, what were you doing?!'

We stop and Sarah shows us the picture. Reilly's eyes are like slits, his mouth wide open, and I'm climbing off the seat, laughing with my fingers clamped over my nose.

'Let's take another,' says Sarah.

'I'm not going back in there,' I say. 'It stinks.'

Reilly laughs. I grab him again.

'But you need a sensible one, Sam.'

'No,' I say, looking at the pictures. 'I like these.'

'But you can't have Reilly on your passport!'

I laugh, then keep a serious face for the next set of photos.

And that's when we start to walk home.

And I can't stop looking at the photos of me and Reilly. Because I love them.

And that's when I go to my room.

That's when I put my first picture on my bedroom wall.

ACKNOWLEDGEMENTS

There are many parts of Sam's story where my own experience helped me write what he was going through. There are also many parts where I needed help. Huge thanks to Chrissie Reeder for answering all my questions, and clarifying points, no matter what time of day or night those questions arrived.

Big thanks to Sam McCann (a teacher at Princess Frederica Primary) for allowing me to use his name.

Massive love and gratitude to my daughter, Lois, for all the pub chats where you helped me whenever I got stuck with Sam's story, when you were so busy writing your own. Tallulah, well, it's just more love and more Nando's ♡.

I'll also add my good mate, Jon Bentley Smith, for the friendship, but also because any book of mine looks weird without his name. I'm going to add Clare Wallace here for making chats with my agent, a chat with a friend.

And finally, big thanks to my editor, Lucy Rogers (LR1). I'm sure you won't miss my awful first drafts, but I will miss your pink notes in my margins and selfless drive to make my writing and stories the best they can be over these past four years. I hope there will be no more late-night edits and twitchy eye.

And this really is the last thing: huge thanks to you the reader, the children, teachers and librarians who allow me a few precious hours of your time to read what takes me a year to write. You make it all worthwhile.

READ ALL OF STEWART FOSTER'S BRILLIANT BOOKS!

STEWART FOSTER

CHECK MATES

'Warmth, quirkiness and a light-hearted touch'
GUARDIAN on
THE BUBBLE BOY